Mo

Curse

Thaddeus Nowak

www.thaddeusnowak.com

Published by Mountain Pass Publishing, LLC.

ISBN: 978-0-9852851-0-4

First Printed: February 2012
Second Edition: February 2014

Set in Adobe Garamond Pro
Cover art by Mallory Rock
Map and castle illustration by Thaddeus Nowak

Mother's Curse

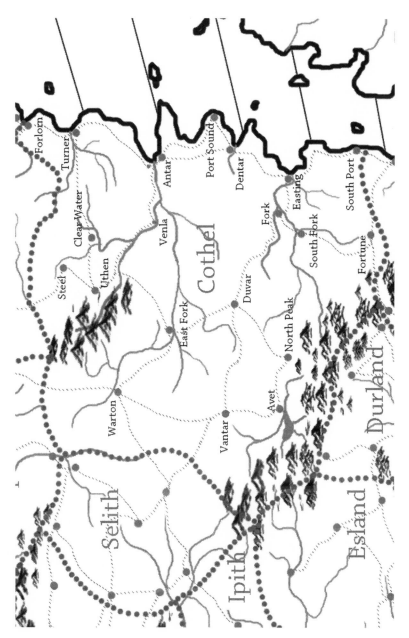

Map of Cothel and surrounding area

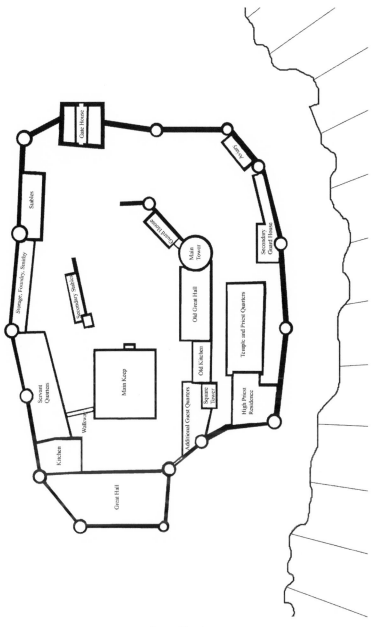

Antar Castle

Acknowledgements

I would like to thank the many people who have helped make this work possible. My wife Sherri, my best friend Chad, my brother Joe and his wife Samantha, my other brothers Dave and Dan and their wives Jenni and Linda, my parents, my reni-friends T'ger and Alysia, and the others who have inspired and offered advice. Any errors left in the work are entirely mine.

Chapter 1

Stephenie closed the cover of the old book that was on her lap and leaned against the cold stone of the crenelation behind her. It was long past being too dark to read, even for her excellent sight, yet she had been unwilling to return to her rooms. It had taken her some effort to misdirect and finally lose Jenk and Samuel, determined as they were to protect her. That had been just before the midday meal and many hours had passed since she had last seen them. She knew they were punishing her for simply trying to get a bit of time by herself. However, she had been on top of the tower since before evening meal, a common place for her to try to escape her troubles, so there was no excuse for either of them not locating her.

"Well, I'm not going to be the one to give in. They simply need to admit I outwitted them and come collect me."

After a moment, she sighed, feeling more guilt than anger. She consciously stopped biting her thumbnail and placed her hands on the book. If her brother found out they had lost her, Jenk and Samuel would be in a significant amount of trouble and despite how annoying they could be, Stephenie liked both of them. She knew they had enough to worry about without having her add more to their burdens. *It's just I can't always have them staring over my shoulder.*

Glancing down the side of the tower, she could see the peaked roof of the old great hall below her. A faint glimmer of metal reflected where hail had chipped away at the thick green patina of the copper ornamentation decorating the roof's ridge. In the darkness, not much of the old slate roof forty feet below her could be discerned. The roof simply blended into the night, but she knew that if someone brought light into the decaying hall, dozens of small glowing points would be visible like stars in the night sky.

Frowning at the lack of maintenance, she looked away, not wanting to think about just how deteriorated things were becoming. Instead, she glanced over her left shoulder and out to the sea. A layer of rolling clouds obscured the stars and moons, but she could see hints of the waves rolling toward the cliff a couple of hundred yards to the east. To the north, lights flickered throughout Antar city, showing an unusual amount of activity for recent weeks. She watched for a few minutes as some of the points of light gradually moved toward the cliffs and switchbacks leading to the few ships anchored in the deep harbor. The distance, the droning wind, and the waves crashing upon the steep cliffs below the castle covered the din of angry people arguing over position and rights to board the ships. Earlier in the day, she overheard a couple of young guards talking about the need for every available soldier to be at the docks tonight to prevent a riot and to ensure that supplies were unloaded and brought to the castle before people tried to board.

Even though it was too far away to see the details, she could tell by the angry movement of the lights that the docks were undoubtedly a scene of chaos and violence. No person of wealth wanted to remain in Antar and they were paying a fortune to be given passage on the two ships that arrived late in the day. The trouble was, there were too many who wanted to leave and most of those did not have the ransom prices the ships would be charging.

Stephenie fought back the tears that were building behind her eyes and looked down at the great hall that she favored far more than the other halls built in the last two hundred years. The old building had far more character and charm. The newer buildings had been larger and grander, gilded on almost every surface, but they seemed far colder and less personal than the drafty great hall that was part of the oldest section of the castle.

"If Josh or father were here the roof would have been fixed." Biting her upper lip and shutting her eyes against the pain of loss coursing though her veins, she wished again they had taken her with them. Left behind, she was a prisoner of her mother. Only Jenk,

Samuel, and Doug treated her with respect, if not stiflingly overprotective. She didn't belong here in the castle.

A laugh broke the quiet of the night, drawing Stephenie's attention to the outer wall and the silhouette of a pair of soldiers. A muffled sound indicated someone probably had said something to chastise the inappropriate noise, but a moment later the laughter came again.

Stephenie closed her eyes and took a deep breath to refrain from cursing. The soldiers were green, hardly having had any training. Many might even have been conscripted in the last week or two. Her mother had ordered a shifting of the soldiers and those who had worked hard and managed to attain positions in the castle had been unceremoniously sent out into the city and surrounding country side, and the new recruits given the normally respected positions in the castle. Her personal guards were the only ones she knew who had not been shuffled out of their normal roles.

The troops from her mother's homeland were now in charge of the castle defenses as well as the city. The change had angered and alienated all those she had at one time called friend and the result was a city in chaos.

Stephenie opened her eyes and looked west into the dark country side. Joshua and her father were out there somewhere, but she had no idea where they were or what was happening. Although she had written to them several times, neither had responded in the last twenty days.

Turning away from their silence, she looked down the side of the tower at the great hall, leaning out further over the edge. The wind picked up, blowing her long red hair into her face. She normally kept it braided, but Joshua always liked it loose. She leaned out a little further, testing to see how far over the edge she could lean before she fell.

Breathing deeply, she looked again at the sharp ornamentation on top of the ridge. At one time, they were beautiful copper dragons and horses. She tried to imagine what it would feel like to fall on top of them, the metal beasts tearing and cutting her flesh. *Perhaps they would cut me in two. Maybe a point would lodge in my skull.* She knew the roof would not withstand the impact of her body falling the forty feet and wondered what it would feel like to burst through the time-worn rafters. She relished the thought of the fractured slate ripping through her body, leaving chunks of skin and entrails hanging in the hole she would create. *If I do it right, I'd land on the old high table.* She grinned at the thought of a servant coming in to check on the noise and seeing what was left of her. She would not call out from the pain, she would not give them the satisfaction. Her mother deserved to take on her curse.

The salty breeze picked up again and pushed her just a little further and she could feel herself tipping. Turning away she regained her balance and avoided a messy demise. She swore just under her breath. *Though it would serve Josh and father right for ignoring me, I won't punish Jenk and Samuel.*

She looked to the small structure on the south of the tower roof that held the door and spiral stairs coming up to the roof. "Where are they?" She demanded, jumping to her feet, no longer content to wait. She took her book and went to the other stairs on the north side, which were used to go down.

The stairwell was dark and the stone steps old and worn, but she had navigated the narrow stairwell for the last ten years, ever since her father had spited her mother and allowed her to move into the old tower. She passed the top level, which was an old weapon storage room that was no longer used. The old tower was near the center of the castle complex and no longer useful for protecting the outer walls.

At the next level down, she began to sense someone was in her room. She had always been able to feel when someone was near, even if they were separated by stone walls and a floor in this case. It was something she had kept secret her whole life. Only her mother knew she was unnatural and her mother would tell no one. Her mother knew she was born that way and if it was discovered, everyone would know her mother must have committed some act against the gods. It was the only reason a daughter would be born a cursed witch.

Stephenie paused on the landing before descending the stairs to the level of her rooms. She closed her eyes and tried to determine who might have invaded her privacy, but after several moments gave up the effort. *I might be cursed with Elrin's taint, but I could hardly learn any spells in this place.* Sighing, she continued down more quietly, not that she had made much noise before that, but she hoped to catch the intruder by surprise.

On her floor, which was the fifth one from the ground, there was a large landing, where the narrow spiral staircase she was using, led to a larger set of stairs that followed the outer wall. The southern staircase going up to the roof exited on the floor above her. The larger stairs had permitted furniture and equipment to be carried up to her floor, which was about fifty feet in diameter. Aside from her parents, the tower had given Stephenie a bigger set of rooms than anyone else in the castle.

Drawing her dagger, Stephenie carefully pushed open her door, which sent the metal hinges creaking. At that moment, she regretted never oiling them. Her reasoning had always been that she did not want someone sneaking into her room; she never expected the need to do it herself.

Giving up on stealth, she slid to the side, keeping the door between her and the majority of the room. "Who's there?"

"Your Highness, it is Doug."

Stephenie pushed the door all the way open. She could see the shadow of her third bodyguard standing near her bed. "What are you doing in the dark? And more importantly, how dare you enter my room? These are off limits. Josh will hear about this."

Doug raised his hands. "Please your Highness, keep your voice low and do not light a lamp. I have been sick with fear for what might have happened."

Stephenie could sense the fear on Doug. Her ability to sense people's feelings was minimal, just strong emotions generally. The level of fear he emitted made her very nervous. Keeping her voice low, she asked the question that had been nagging her most of the evening. "Where have Jenk and Samuel been hiding?" She came into the room and shut the door behind her. She did not think Doug, Jenk, or Samuel would ever try to take advantage of her and the three of them had many opportunities over the last three years. However, she felt very territorial about her rooms.

"My Lady, that is the problem. I have not been able to find them anywhere. I went looking for them when I came back from visiting my parents. One of those damn Kyntian soldiers said they had left the castle earlier. He claimed they were carrying a couple of bags between them and when he asked, they told him to mind his own business."

"They abandoned me?" Stephenie clenched her fists, irritated at having felt concern about their not being able to keep up with her when they had really deserted her.

"My Lady, that is what someone wants us to believe. I know Jenk and Samuel. They would never abandon you. They are loyal to Prince Josh and your father. Even if your mother, the Queen," he added with some distaste, "ordered them directly, they would refuse, as would I." Doug moved carefully away from her bed and groped around for a chair.

While her room was dark, enough light came in through the narrow windows that she could easily see the shapes of the furniture in her room. She did not know if her night vision was just better than everyone else or if it was related to her being a witch. However, she had always been able to function well in very low light and it was not something she could ever ask anyone, not unless she was ready to burn. After Doug sat in the chair near her desk, she moved to the bed and sat facing the large man.

"You see my Lady, the three of us have been saving part of our pay. There is a loose stone in the barrack near my bunk. We have a fair savings established so perhaps when the war is won and things go back to normal, the three of us might one day be able to buy a public house and retire. If they were going to do something dishonest and abandon you, they wouldn't leave all that money. They would have at least taken their share even if they left mine."

"And the money isn't gone?"

"We are the only three that know about it. So I think something has happened to them. I was afraid something had happened to you as well and was torn between waiting here for you or searching. I had hoped that you had gone on one of your little rants and decided to hide."

"My little rants." Stephenie took a deep breath. She could hear Doug's reproach, but considering what he was saying, he might be justified. "I just wanted a little time on my own. The three of you know I would never leave the castle, not since the last time. What could have happened to them?"

Stephenie noticed Doug nod his head, then perhaps thinking she would not be able to see him, he spoke. "Yes. We had your promise and I for one would not have thought you'd have left the castle. The only thing I can think of is that some of your mother's soldiers took them when they were looking for you or perhaps one of them lied and said you were seen leaving the castle. They might have gone looking for you. If that happened, then they could be anywhere.

"The thing is, I asked around quietly and no one I would trust to tell me the truth saw anything. Then I got a real bad feeling and snuck off through some of the old passages and came here. To be honest, I would have gone out looking for you if you had not turned up soon. Perhaps in the dungeon. I fear they took Jenk and Samuel there."

Stephenie felt her arms tremble. Somehow she needed to get word to Joshua and her father. "You can stay here tonight. In the morning we'll send a message to Josh."

Doug stood up. "I don't want to risk it. You are just turned seventeen and all we would need is someone to come up with your breakfast and find me here. They would assume the worst and then they'd force me away. I'm just one person. I can't watch you all the time; I have to sleep. I know some people whom we can trust, some of the old castle guards. I want to bring in at least eight of them. I can use Prince Josh's name and the authority he gave us to pull them in and assign them as your guards."

"I've got some things we can use to pay them if needed."

Doug smiled. "Thanks. I don't think that will be a big issue, these men would do what was needed even if they were not paid right away. They would do it for Prince Josh."

"Okay. In the morning, we'll go out into the city and find them."

"Ma'am, no, I fear I need to do this now. I can't protect you alone in the city. Lock and bar the door. Don't open it until I get back. I will sneak out without your mother's soldiers knowing and be back before morning." He stood up and moved to the door.

"Doug."

"Yes?"

"I'm sorry for causing so much trouble."

"My Lady, you wouldn't be Prince Josh's little sister we've all grown to curse about if you didn't." He sighed, "none of us ever thought you to be too much trouble. Just frustrating sometimes. I'll be back. Lock and bar the door." Without saying anything else, he left the room.

Stephenie felt him quickly descend the stairs and when he was out of her range, she turned the lock and then picked up the heavy wooden bar and placed it into the iron brackets. She wondered for a moment that none of her guards ever commented on her using the bar. It was heavy, even for them, but she had always been strong and quick. It had made her excellent at sword combat. A moment of concern froze her in place, *could they suspect I'm a witch?* The fear faded quickly as she realized Doug would not have come to warn her about the others being missing if they had. Instead, they would have turned her over to the priests to burn.

She looked about her room. It held very little resemblance to the rooms her four older sisters had when they lived in the castle; little ornamentation and few frills typical of a princess decorated her walls. The circular floor had been divided down the middle with a wall that separated the area into two nearly equal halves. The outer room here, with her bed and desk was mostly utilitarian. The stone walls of the tower were covered in thick, but not overly decorated tapestries. A fire place on the west side provided warmth when needed, but that was something else she did not often need, for she was seldom cold.

The back room held clothing, both the dresses her mother required and the more masculine clothing her father had permitted, probably in an effort to spite her mother. It had never been a secret her mother did not care for her youngest daughter, only the reasons remained between them. Inexplicably, that hate caused her older brother and father to indulge her and instead of doing all the traditional things a princess was required to do and be, she became Joshua's honorary younger brother.

"Except they would not take me with them to the war." Putting aside her anger at them, she focused on her more immediate concerns for safety. She did have all her belongings on this floor and someone would have an easier time ripping up the floor in the room above her than hacking through the reinforced door, but her supplies were limited. She checked the back room and found a jug of water left over from her breakfast, enough for perhaps a couple of days if she drank only a little. Food was more of a problem. Most of the meals that were brought to her would not keep, so there were no useful leftovers and she had not thought to maintain a supply of soldier's rations.

For equipment, she was, if anything, oversupplied. Joshua had taught her to use various weapons and although she favored the rapier and long dagger her father had given her, she would not hesitate to take one of the many swords, bows, spears, or staves that were neatly stored in her back room. Her skill and commitment had won over the guards, who soon learned on the practice field, that if they went easy on her, she would leave them as bruised and sore as if the weapon master had it in for them.

Quickly and without additional light, she assembled a collection of throwing knives, leather armor, clothing, and a handful of spare coins she had amassed. Stuffing the extra clothing, fire kit, whet stone, money, and miscellaneous gear into a small leather backpack, she put her gear just inside the door of her back room where it could be quickly retrieved, but would not be obvious to casual inspection.

Working by feel, she sat down and braided her long hair and tied off the ends. She changed out of her more comfortable breaches and blouse and into the leather reinforced pants and armor she used for training.

When she was done, she slumped back in her chair. There was nothing for her to do now but wait for Doug and to worry about Jenk and Samuel.

Chapter 2

Stephenie awoke. The morning light still held its dim golden hue while waiting for the sun to crest the horizon. She shifted her head, trying to work out the kinks that had built up overnight. Rubbing her eyes, she rolled out of bed, still dressed in her leather armor and boots. She wasn't sure when she had fallen asleep, but she did remember breaking down and crying for fear of what might have happened to Samuel and Jenk.

She retrieved the jug of water and drank only a small amount. She peeked out of the window on the west side of the tower, remaining far enough away from the glass that most people would not be able to see her looking out. The inner court yard was filled with wagons, as it had been for the last couple of weeks. A few servants were milling about; carrying supplies and hurrying on errands. She noticed a couple of soldiers on the western curtain wall, but nothing that looked unusual.

It was far too early to expect her breakfast, but she had hoped Doug would have returned before morning. There were places to sneak in and out of the castle if you knew what you were doing. The old castle guards knew of them, but that information had not been passed on to her uncle's men that now served her mother. It was a risk to leave the castle's weak spots unprotected, but the ousted soldiers had little time or inclination to pass on their knowledge and Stephenie had not wanted to give up her potential escape options.

But even with these weak spots, sneaking in during the light of day would be difficult at best. She balled up her fists and paced about her room. Doug could always come in through the front gate, *but if mother is behind this, she'd bar them entry or make them disappear as well.*

After another circuit around her rooms, she sat down on her bed. If her mother had taken her guards, there were two possibilities Stephenie could fathom, *they had been forced from the castle or been locked up in the dungeon.* She closed her eyes, unable to figure out what purpose taking her guards would serve and so unable to decide what was more likely.

"There is no chance of me getting into the dungeon unseen." Stephenie knew most of the secret and back passages around and through the castle, but the dungeon was, for good reason, devoid of secret entrances. Her mother's soldiers now controlled that dark and unpleasant part of the castle under the main keep and would bar her access. "Especially if they had something to hide."

Stephenie moved to her desk and quickly wrote a letter to Joshua, explaining that her guards had gone missing and she either needed to come to him or he needed to send word to some trusted soldiers to come to her aid. She admonished him briefly for not writing to her, then wished him and father her love. She sanded the ink and while waiting for it to dry, lit a candle so she could seal the letter.

Once the letter was complete, she pulled off the leather jerkin and put on one of her dresses. It would cover her leather clad and booted legs while not being overly restrictive. The boned bodice tied in the front so she did not need a lady in waiting, yet the ties were hidden for propriety by a sash that tied to her left side with a small bow. It was an outdated fashion and looked rather silly, but it was a compromise she made to get her way.

With her father and brother gone, her mother refused to allow her into the main keep in anything other than a dress. Fortunately, she had a number of dresses that fit her disobedient and rebellious nature.

She pulled up her skirt and tied a long dagger to her left thigh and two throwing knives on her right thigh. Standing in front of the silver mirror, she adjusted the ends of the bow on the dress to mostly cover the dagger she had attached to a belt around her waist. Not being allowed to carry a sword was another requirement and something she had not yet been able to manage a way to conceal.

She grabbed a large leather shoulder bag couriers used and placed it over her shoulder, further concealing the dagger. Putting her letter into the bag, she closed her eyes and tried to reach out with her witchcraft to see if anyone else was in the tower with her. Sensing no one, she removed the bar, unlocked the door, and carefully slid into the circular stairs that rounded the outer wall of the tower. She quietly descended, trying to minimize the sounds of her hard soled boots. She felt no one else on any other part of the tower as she passed by the lower floors. When she drew near the ground floor, she could sense to the northwest a few men in the guards barracks, but the old doorway between the tower and the barracks had been sealed long ago.

At the ground floor, she turned off through the large oak door into the old great hall. Again, she sensed no one nearby and quickly moved around the old tables and past the many fire places to the outer door at the far end of the hall. At the outer door, she paused again, opening her mind to see if anyone might be waiting for her, but so far, it remained free of people.

She opened the door and looked immediately ahead and to her left. A large square building, that was just about as long as the old great hall and more than twice as wide, stood in ugly contrast to the delicate stone work of the old castle. Built more than two hundred years ago, the new keep was not very new. However, the tightly dressed stone had weathered well and was still a much lighter tan than the old gray stone of the original castle, which was many hundreds of years older in construction.

Standing four stories high, the new keep was a massive block of unadorned stone; an imposing figure that dominated the center of the southern third of the castle grounds. It sat apart from the outer walls, save for a second story walkway that allowed the servants access to the keep from their quarters. The building was designed to hold out should the outer wall fail. That was the theory at least. Stephenie knew of the tunnels that burrowed through the bluffs under the castle, linking many of the buildings and providing secret access to many of the rooms inside the main keep. The massive stone walls provided the means necessary to hide passages and openings. If invaders ever did breach the outer wall, it would be far too easy to gain entrance to any building.

Not seeing any guards waiting for her, Stephenie descended the old steps, turned left, and headed past the old kitchens. Ahead of her was the new great hall, which made up part of the southern curtain wall. Four guard towers protruded above the chimneys and peaked roof, providing arrow cover.

The new hall was an after thought to the design of the castle. It was added by one of her ancestors about one hundred and fifty years ago. He wanted extra space, and despite the expense and reduction of protection, placed the new hall in the only location available at the time, attached to the outside of what had been the southern curtain wall. Being detached from the main keep, it required guests to walk outside and around the back to gain access to the hall. It's massive size and gilded interior was diminished by the less than spectacular approach.

Moving quickly, but without obvious haste, Stephenie rounded the back of the keep and headed to the larger of two kitchens in the castle. This one sat between the new hall and the two story high servant quarters, which unlike the hall, was attached to the inside of the western curtain wall. This kitchen was supposed to serve both the royal family and guests in the keep as well as the hall when it was used.

The new kitchen smelled of baking bread and roasting boar. The morning meal for the servants would have already been served and cleaned away. However, the meal for herself and the other nobles in the castle would not be served for a while yet.

She walked through the large door that was opened to the chill morning air, releasing the heat coming from the fire pits and ovens. A servant, startled by Stephenie's presence, bowed and gave a hasty apology that Stephenie accepted so she would not offend the young girl.

"Where is Cook Raven?"

"Your Highness, Cook Raven is in the back kitchen. Please allow me to fetch her."

Stephenie smiled at the scullion maid and shook her head. "Please, carry on with your tasks, I will find her. Thank you."

"Yes Ma'am." Bowing away, the young girl retreated from the kitchen on her errand.

Picking the route through the kitchen that required the least number of people to bow to her, Stephenie managed to reach the back kitchen with only four groups of people offering to fetch Cook Raven for her. However, Cook Raven had caught wind of her approach before she reached the smaller room near the outer wall where sweets and cakes were often dressed and readied for presentation.

"Your Highness."

"Hi Raven, I need to ask you a question." Stephenie kept her voice low even though she sensed no one close enough to overhear her.

"Of course Ma'am. I am at your disposal."

Seeing a bit of ginger root on a tray, Stephenie's hungry stomach growled just enough to be heard.

"Please, Ma'am, help yourself."

"Thank you." Stephenie grabbed a couple of pieces and quickly ate the first. Once she had swallowed enough to avoid chewing while talking, she drew Raven out of view in case the older cook reacted in such a way as to draw attention. "Can you tell me if they have new prisoners in the dungeon?"

As expected, Raven's face showed a great deal of surprise from the question and then a frightened countenance filled her face before she schooled her expression. "Ma'am, I would not be made aware of any dealings that take place in the dungeon. My skin crawls to think of that place, though I have never myself set foot in there." She drew the mark of Felis across her left arm. "Ma'am, what cause would you have to ask me of such thing?"

Stephenie kept her expression neutral. "Raven, how many meals were you asked to prepare for the prisoners this morning?"

Cook Raven's face cleared with a bit of understanding. "Ah, the same as the last three weeks, twenty five." She swallowed and then glanced past Stephenie to confirm they were alone, continued more quietly. "Ma'am, what is your concern? Do you fear for someone?"

Stephenie shook her head, fear filling her heart despite her calm demeanor. "Raven, please forget that I ever asked you the question. I am not popular at the moment. Instead, let me take this tray and a few other sweets and you can claim I hounded you about getting more than my fair share."

"Ma'am?"

Stephenie shook her head, picked up the tray and grabbed some random candies from the shelves and added them to the sweet meats. Once she had more than she could eat, she nodded her head to Cook Raven and left through the kitchen proper, grabbing a couple of loaves of bread and a partial round of hard cheese, still wrapped in cheese cloth. Outside the kitchen, she put the bread and cheese in the satchel while munching on the candies. It felt wrong to eat sweets when Samuel, Jenk, and Doug might be dead or at least being starved, but she could not toss aside the food while someone from the kitchen might notice.

Walking under the stone walkway that bridged the servant quarters to the second floor of the main keep, she passed a group of three soldiers that gave her their normal disapproving look before continuing on without comment. Her mother insisted that if she wanted to act as a common soldier and play with weapons, she no longer deserved to be given any special attention from the soldiers. It had actually caused the native soldiers to bow and scrape more than they had done, owing in no small part to the fact that Stephenie had proven herself more than capable with any weapon she had trained to use and had always treated the soldiers with the respect they had deserved.

From her mother's soldiers, sent from Kynto by her uncle, King Willard, the lack of respect was palatable and clearly intended as an insult. Stephenie did not let their cold disdain draw her into conflict with them. That would only feed their sense of righteousness. The Kynto soldiers, while they might act better than everyone else, were not fundamentally better than her father's soldiers. She would never underestimate them, for they were no easy force to overcome, but they did not intimidate her. What grated on her more was that her mother would do such a petty thing.

The morning was still quite young, but she knew that Seneschal Renild would be awake and working. Her mother had not replaced him for the same reason she had not replaced the lower servants, there was no one from her Uncle's men here who could actually "replace" him. Seneschal Renild was not the oldest man in the castle, her father's Keeper of the Wardrobe was at least a decade older. However, Seneschal Renild's family had served that post for generations and it seemed all that breeding and heritage had culminated into a man who was exceedingly skilled at organizing and managing the castle's daily needs. Stephenie's grandfather, before he died, often declared that the man was able to get twice the work out of the laziest person while making the person feel good about the work.

While Stephenie did not have any basis for comparison, she knew that the servants respected and trusted the old Seneschal and that respect and trust were a powerful force. What was more, Stephenie liked the old man, despite the fact that he sometimes looked at her with a longing that was absurd for a man of his age. She knew he would never act on such a thought with any girl her age and so she was silently pleased with the implied compliment.

She rounded the northwest corner of the new keep and looked over to the collection of supply wagons, stacked high with crates. They had been sitting in the courtyard for more time than seemed appropriate. Her Uncle's troops were supposed to escort the food, blankets, and other goods her father needed to continue fighting. For the goods to languish here for nearly two weeks seemed unacceptable. Doug had told her the Kyntian soldiers had given some excuse that it would be better to wait for additional supplies and troops to arrive instead of making multiple trips to the front. Stephenie's problem with this logic was that while it might be more efficient to make a single trip, if the supplies were needed now, running out would not be just an inconvenience, but could easily mean the deaths of many hundreds or thousands of men and that could mean losing the war.

She pushed down her anger, there was nothing she could do about the supplies at the moment; the fate of Doug, Jenk, and Samuel was where she needed to focus. She felt her eyes watering and the thought of how cruelly she had treated Jenk and Samuel by managing to escape their protection. They had only her best interest at heart. *Please don't let them be dead.*

She wiped away the tears that had formed and steeled herself to be calm. Giving into the fear and anger would not help. She turned and easily climbed the steep steps to the keep's main entrance. Her daily trips up and down the numerous steps of the large tower to her rooms had given her stamina unmatched by most people in the castle.

At the top of the stairs was a large set of double doors that met in a point ten feet above her head. She unlatched and pushed open the normal sized door set into the left of the larger doors. A guard moved out of one of the alcoves on the sides of the dark entrance chamber. "What's your name and business?" he asked in very accented Cothish.

Stephenie met the guard's eyes and resisted shuddering. Now that her father was away, she always felt the sensation of bugs crawling over her skin when in the keep. Entering her mother's domain drew up thoughts of stories where adventurers enter dark lairs of some horrible creature, *like a nest of giant spiders.* It was something that seemed to cling to her skin like a bad smell and she wondered if her mother had arranged to have the priests of Felis spell the keep.

"I am here to see Seneschal Renild and you know who I am."

The guard curled his lip ever so slightly and mumbled in Kyntian that she was a dumb bitch. Stephenie ignored the comment, continuing to pretend that she had never learned her mother's language. She simply waited until the guard moved to the slightly larger inner doors and knocked to signal those inside the keep someone wanted to enter.

"The dumb bitch wants to see the Seneschal again."

Stephenie frowned in spite of herself; it was one thing for the guard to mutter the slur under his breath, but another thing when they used it as a common reference to her. She schooled her expression as the smaller door inside the large inner door was unbarred and opened. The young guard inside the entrance hall looked at her with an almost apologetic expression.

"Your Highness," he said in stilted Cothish, holding the door open for her.

Stephenie bowed her head slightly and walked quickly through the door into the dimly light entrance hall. Normally dozens of lamps would illuminate the three story high hall, providing enough light that the statues, art, and tapestries could be appreciated.

However, since all that remained were bare walls and floors, there was little point to wasting the oil.

The entrance hall still contained a pair of stone staircases on either side of the room leading up to the second floor and a wide balcony that allowed those above to lord down on people entering the keep. The stone balusters were carved with intricate detail and skill. They were art in and of themselves and remained only because they were built in and could not easily be removed.

Stephenie exhaled, trying to clear her mind of the unpleasant feel of the air and the sadness for memories that almost seemed impossible to regain. She had played chase with Joshua and his friends on those stairs. She had gazed many hours at the woven images of Lord Devon riding a dragon to battle. She had rolled down the carpeted steps, in a rather painful and not so thought out dare. Now a guard stood with a detached menace at the foot of each staircase.

Having no intention of seeing anyone in the royal household, she pushed aside the building sense of loss, ignored the less than attentive guards, and headed under the balcony into the open hallway that led through the heart of the keep on the first floor. In the dim light, she could see the reinforced door at the far end of the hall and wished again for a way to get past the three guards that would be standing on the other side. It was the only access into the dungeon, and like the front doors and the stair wells, it was guarded constantly.

She stopped halfway down the hall, at the third and last door on her left. She knocked and when she heard the clerk inside give her permission to enter, she pushed open the door.

Inside, the room was almost twice as long as it was wide. Several desks were scattered about and many shelves and cabinets lined the walls. Stacks of parchment, books, and papers filled most open spaces. Despite the amount of documents, the room appeared neat and organized. There were two doors on the long walls near the back of the room, one on either side. Stephenie knew the back wall was hollow and contained a secret passage that she had used occasionally to move about the keep unnoticed. There was no entrance to that passage on this floor, but it was a convenient secret that few shared.

Only one clerk was in the room, a young man named Cedric who tended to work more hours than the other five clerks who used this office. It took him a moment to look up from his hurried writing in the ledger before him. When he did, he immediately rose to his feet and gave Stephenie a gracious bow. "Your highness. How may I serve you?"

Stephenie was too anxious to smile. "I need to see the Seneschal."

"Of course." Cedric eyed the tray of confections still in her hand and began to turn toward the door on the right hand wall.

"Please, help yourself," she said holding out the tray. Cedric hesitated a moment, but then chose a small piece of candy. He did not eat it immediately, but resumed his movement to the door. Stephenie followed, winding through the desks and cabinets. Cedric knocked on the door, went in to announce her, and then held the door for her. He retreated quickly once she was in the office that was about half as large as the outer one. This room held a single desk and as many neatly organized book laden shelves as the outer office. A door behind the desk led to a storage room, which in turn led to yet another room in the always maddening maze that was the keep.

Seneschal Renild was standing and came around his desk to meet her. "Your Highness. What may I do for you?"

"Seneschal," Stephenie said, pain and fear leaking into her voice. Seeing his concerned expression, she schooled her emotions as best she could. "I need to have a letter sent to my brother most urgently." Setting down the tray of candy on a nearby stack of papers, she fished the letter she had written out of her satchel.

"Ma'am?"

The odd expression on the Seneschal's old face caught her off guard. "What?"

"Well, I thought you had lost faith in me and had one of your guards find someone else to send your letters." Seeing her confused expression, Renild continued. "I had heard an off hand comment that your man Doug was seen carrying a letter out of the castle the evening before last."

Stephenie's mind raced. "He went to help his parents. They had sent word that they needed his assistance dealing with some trouble.

The letter was one he received. Why would I lose trust in you? Of all the people left in the castle, you are the one I would trust the most."

"Oh. My apologies Ma'am."

Stephenie realized she was sensing a great deal of anxiety from the old Seneschal. "What is going on?"

The gray haired man glanced about the room uncomfortably. "Ma'am. I love his Majesty and my country, but I am left out of many things since the war has started and he left."

Stephenie's eyes narrowed. "What is going on?" she repeated.

"Ma'am. I have a wife and children and grandchildren."

Closing her eyes, she pushed down the anger at her naivety. *How could I have not simply assumed?* She chided herself for not realizing her mother would exert control on everyone she could. She opened her eyes and looked into the remorseful and frightened eyes of a man who now appeared as old as he was. "Here," she said holding out the letter for him to take.

"Ma'am?"

Stephenie shook her head and turned away. "If I came and you didn't have a letter from me, she might think I got the truth from you."

"Though you may not know it, His Majesty and his Highness Prince Joshua still think about you."

Stephenie paused in her step, forcing back tears that were threatening to burst forth. "Thank you." She took another step and then turned back to the Seneschal. "You don't know what happened to Doug, Jenk, and Samuel do you?"

"Has something happened?"

The startled look on his lined face let Stephenie know he was telling the truth. "They have all disappeared." Without another word, she turned back to the door and left quickly. She nodded to Cedric's appreciative comment about the candy, but avoided his gaze.

Once she was back in the central hall, she closed the door to the clerk's office and sank back against it. She could sense the guards on the other side of the door to the dungeon and the guards in the entrance hall. At the moment, no one was able to see her and she wanted nothing more than to fall into despair. She never really had a doubt that her mother was behind the disappearance of the last people she considered friends. *But that the cause might be that she thought I was sending a letter without her knowledge.*

Wiping away the tears that had worked their way through her hardened exterior facade, she looked again at the dungeon door. She could not be certain how many guards were stationed down there. In her father's care, the dungeon always had at least ten men on duty. But her mother was even more paranoid and could potentially have twice that number. Additionally, while she had stole away a few times to see the dungeon, it was one place her father and brother had never truly given her freedom to roam. Which meant she was far less familiar with the layout and would not know where her guards might be held.

Anger burning away the tears in her eyes, she turned and took off down the hall. The guards on the stairs noticed her hostile posture and woke to attention at her approach.

"Floor above prohibited."

"Out of my way, I am a member of this family and can go where I want."

The guard, perhaps sensing the danger radiating from her eyes leaned back, but did not completely give way. "You, no weapon up stairs," he said, pointing at her dagger, clearly visible with her satchel having bounced off her hip in her haste.

Fueled by a need to confront her mother that had been building for the last couple of weeks, she drew her dagger, flipped the blade around, and jabbed the pommel into the soldier's gut. She pushed past the startled young man and hurried up the stairs, ignoring the empty walls and missing statues. At the top, she turned left toward the stairs leading to the third level, but slowed to a stop as she noticed Regina coming down those stairs.

Her older sister's face, framed in long brown hair, darkened when their eyes met. "What are you doing here, you spoiled little chit?"

Stephenie glared into Regina's brown eyes as her sister continued to descend the stairs. Regina was slightly shorter and considerably heavier, so Stephenie was not surprised when she remained on the second to last step to maintain the illusion of advantage.

"You are dressed as a common pig in some hideous monstrosity. What is your purpose in being here?"

Stephenie forcefully swallowed an angry retort. Of her three older sisters, Regina was the one she disliked the most. Three years older, Regina was three times as cruel as anyone else in her family except for her mother.

"Well? You daft as well as disgraceful in every possible manner?"

"I am here to see mother."

"At this hour? You should go back to playing soldier in your stupid tower. You can leave mother alone, she has more important things to do than listen to your whiny little complaints."

Stephenie's jaw tightened. "Why are you here again? Too frightened to remain with your husband, or did he finally toss the cow out of his house?"

Regina rushed down the last couple of steps and swung her hand to slap Stephenie across the face, but Stephenie easily caught her sister's wrist and having straightened, was now a head taller.

"Father and Josh have taught me. I'm no stupid little girl. I could help them instead of wasting time here."

Regina pulled her arm free and turned slightly away. "Father should not be fighting this war. He should be getting Islet back. They will kill her if he persists. Mother tried to get him to listen to reason, but the bull-headed idiot is going to get our sister killed."

"Islet was taken by the Senzar. You think they would free her if we stopped fighting? What if they demanded we hand you over in her place, you think we should do that as well?"

"We'd sure hand you over."

"If father was to stop fighting, the other countries would not be able to continue the fight and the invaders would get whatever it is they are after and once they do, they'll come after us. They won't free her, no matter what we do."

"You don't know that! She was a better younger sister than you ever were. It should have been you that was captured or better yet, killed as Kara was. Islet behaved. She was a proper lady and princess."

Stephenie watched Regina's eyes roll over her with contempt. She forced herself to relax. *Arguing with a fool only makes me one.* Without another word, she turned back to the stairs and walked past her sister.

"Bitch," Regina sneered.

At the top of the stairs, their argument had already drawn the attention of two of her mother's guards. They were both grinning and looking rather pleased. "My mother," Stephenie demanded as if they were three years old. Their eyes drew together with a slightly greater than normal amount of contempt. However, one of the soldiers turned and led the way to her mother's private chambers.

Outside the gilded doors stood four more guards, one of which opened the door a crack and slid inside at her approach. Everyone stood in a stony silence until the guard returned.

"She will see you."

Stephenie said nothing and walked past the guard that was holding the door open with just barely enough room for her to pass. The discipline Joshua had instilled in her kept her from shouldering the guard on her way past, but just barely. She needed to conserve her energy and focus for her real enemy and avoid being drawn into petty issues that were only done with the intent to intimidate her.

Her mother's outer office was nothing more than a waiting area. A single lamp did a poor job of illuminating the tiled floor. A couple of uncomfortable chairs sat against the stone wall and next to the fireplace that was never lit. The intent was to make anyone who actually came here to call on her mother as uncomfortable as possible.

Stephenie ignored the outer chamber and went through another set of doors into her mother's actual office. This room was larger and unlike most of the other rooms in the castle, had not been stripped bare of its furnishing. A thick carpet covered most of the floor. The fireplace on the left wall was blazing and filled the room with a comfortable radiance. Pictures of her mother's family and scenes from Kynto covered the walls. A large oak desk was near the far wall. Statues and other works of art were scattered about the room. Above the fire place were four portraits of brown haired ladies, her mother, Regina, Kara, and Islet. Her father, Joshua, and herself did not rate portraits in her mother's study.

"Mother," Stephenie said calmly as she curtsied in the middle of the room.

Her mother said nothing, her schooled expression could have been used to listen to the chambermaid discussing the folding of blankets. However, Stephenie could sense the waves of anger and some anxiety coming from her mother. Forcing herself to be calm, she tried to open herself further to see if there was anyone else within hearing distance. She felt the distant presence of the guards outside the outer chamber behind her, but her greater concern was for the secret passage concealed in the wall directly behind her mother. Fortunately, it was empty as always, and Stephenie was fairly certain her mother still did not know about the passage.

"What is it you want?"

"Mother," Stephenie forced a differential tone as she straightened and approached the front of the large desk. "Something has happened to Doug, Samuel, and Jenk. I do not know where they have gone." Her mother's face held firm its cool impassiveness, but Stephenie sensed a changing of emotions in her mother.

"Are these men your lovers that you refer to them so casually? Of course your honor is long since destroyed, so really it makes no difference."

Forcing herself to remain calm, Stephenie replied just as coldly. "You know full well I have not been with anyone. They are my personal guards. If you were to make such accusations of ladies who now are escorted and protected by soldiers, no woman in this household would—"

"No woman of this house carries on as though she was a boy playing at war. But perhaps you are right. I should probably worry more that you'd draw a woman to your bed than a man."

"Father and Joshua do not treat me like this."

"Only because you are worthless and unneeded. We had daughters enough for the important kingdoms, all of which were nicely married and settled. The King allows your absurd behavior because there is no one to marry you off to. You should have died in your cradle."

Stephenie forced a laugh and shook her head. "Now, now mother. Would you really wish such a thing? What was it you did again? The gods don't curse the daughter unless the mother does something very bad. We both know I was born this way, so it was something you did."

Her mother rose to her feet. "You evil beast. Out of my sight."

"What are you going to do about it? You kill me and the curse falls on you. I know that's the only thing that's kept me alive so far."

"Do not flatter yourself so. Plenty can be done to you without killing you." Her mother calmed, straightened out her dress, and resumed her seat. "So for what purpose do you waste my time?"

"We both hate each other and would rather not have to deal with one another. So let's fix the problem. Send me to father and you won't have me around and that will mean I am out of your hair and sight." Her mother smiled and Stephenie knew the answer she would hear.

"Dear girl. Your father left you here to protect you. Fighting two countries away against an army of heathen Elrin worshipers is no place for someone like you. You might switch sides."

"How dare you!"

"I dare what I please! I am the Queen and I control your life. You will obey me!" The Queen pushed her shoulders back and calmed her face. "Now the issue of your guards, we—"

"What did you do to them?"

"Me?" The queen shook her head. "I did nothing to them. I heard from the captain of the watch that they were all seen at various times leaving the castle. It seems they must have become fed up with your inconsiderate behavior, which would get them into trouble. If you cared so much for them, then perhaps you should have treated them better."

"They—"

"Enough. I am sick of listening to you complain. Since we don't want any fatal harm to come to you, I have already arranged to have guards, that are a bit more loyal and not so disrespectful as to abandon their posts, watch over you."

"I don't want your mindless idiots. I'll have some of the old guards come back from the city." Stephenie shifted to the right and instinctively waved her left hand before her as the inkwell left her mother's hand. The crystal container and loose ink shifted right in its flight and just missed her head. She heard the crystal thud into the thick carpet and roll before coming to a stop.

Her mother was again on her feet. "You will show your Uncle's soldiers respect!" Taking a breath, the Queen continued more calmly.

"You are to be locked into your precious tower and will remain there! Now get out."

Stephenie could feel the hate and anger radiating from her mother. Feeling stupid and realizing too late her mistake in confronting her mother, Stephenie turned around and left the room. She felt too sick to even be silently happy that her mother's precious carpet now had a large black stain.

In the outer chamber, she felt the group of soldiers just on the other side of the door had grown to at least ten. It was certain the order for her confinement had been given when the others had been taken. If she had thought it through earlier, she knew she should have tried to leave the castle when Doug had not returned by the morning. Now all she could do for them was hope that they were not dead and that once her father returned, they would be freed. The trouble was, her mother's behavior was so far beyond excusable that Stephenie could not see how her mother would be able to remain Queen when her father did return.

Chapter 3

Sergeant Henton tugged at the lead rope again. The horse was tired, but not as tired and irritated as he was. Ahead of him stood Antar Castle. Its thirty foot high walls on a mountain of stone and bedrock lorded over Antar city. The road up to the gate house was long and steep, a precaution against attack, but annoyingly long and pointless to a man who had not slept for a day and a half. He could understand why the others had required he deal with the problem, but it did not make him enjoy it.

"Sarge, they going to give us some rack time after all this?"

Sergeant Henton turned to private Ramous and motioned with his head for the young man to move closer. When the blond boy came close enough, Henton handed him the lead rope. "Don't ask stupid questions."

Pulling ahead of the wagon, Henton wished once again that he was back on The Scarlet and at sea instead of being relegated to being a land-bound grunt. As a marine, he had led his squad against pirates and other ships. The area of coverage was smaller and something he could visualize. While fighting on land was not more physically challenging, the tactics were different and he did not like being outside of his element. He had protested that his men would be slaughtered if required to fight in a standard shield wall formation, but the King did have need of skilled fighters and had the right to order all the troops off the ships.

He glanced once at the port. He could hardly believe two weeks had passed since he felt the rolling deck beneath his feet. He could see there was a single ship in the harbor, but anything sea worthy had gone elsewhere, taking only the people who could afford the ransom prices.

"Sarge."

At Corporal Will's voice, Henton looked back toward the massive gate house. A group of five soldiers were walking in their direction and he could see several men watching from behind crenelations on the walls. "Greetings," he called out, raising his left hand to the Kyntian soldiers and quietly signaled the wagon to stop with a quick gesture of his right. "I was ordered to bring a couple of prisoners to the castle."

The five soldiers stopped a dozen feet away and briefly talked amongst themselves in Kyntian. Despite his Queen coming from Kynto, Henton had never thought there would be a need for him to learn the language of a country so far to the north and bordering the Endless Sea, not the Sea of Tet, which he had sailed. *I guess that is just something else I was wrong about.*

"Prisoners are kept at the garrison. The castle is not the place for common criminals," a guard finally said in Cothish.

Henton eyed the Corporal who had spoken. The man had big arms under his tunic, but his neck seemed a little flabby and he could see the straining material around his waist. The man's bulk was at least somewhat from fat. He had already subconsciously evaluated the men as they had approached and the Corporal's condition fit his opinion.

"Look, I took my orders from the Captain of the Garrison and based on who we have, I happen to agree these men should probably be dealt with by your Captain of the Watch." Henton hoped Ramous would keep his mouth shut about having been up all night, that would only ensure they waited hours before these men summoned anyone.

"And why would you think that?"

"Well, that is something that should probably be discussed between me and your captain."

The Corporal smiled. "He's busy, why don't you wait here."

Henton, nodded his head. He was tired of the severe issue of dissension between the forces. On board ship, he dealt with people from many different nationalities who had different skills and they all got along. The Kyntians did not seem to want to even try. "Not a problem. Will and Zac, get up in that wagon and dump our cargo. They're rapists and murderers, so let's cut off their balls and if they die at the castle gates from blood loss, well, not my problem."

"Wait, you can't leave men on the ground out here."

Henton ignored the soldier behind him and nodded his head to Corporal Will and Private Zac to continue. Private Ramous had not been one of his marines, but someone who had recently been conscripted and handed to him. So he kept his focus on the blond, hoping he would not break.

"I said stop!"

Will and Zac had their daggers out and the tearing of cloth could be heard as they sliced down the pants of the three men in the back of the small flatbed wagon.

"Fetch the Captain to deal with these men!"

Henton glanced once at his Corporal, who calmly returned his dagger to it's sheath. Henton slowly turned around to face the five Kyntian soldiers and stood with his arms crossed and waited. After a very short period of time Henton saw the gate lift and a tall, trim man in a Captain's uniform moving toward them in a quick, but not hasty manner. Henton came to attention and saluted the officer.

"What is the meaning of this Sergeant? You will be lucky to not end up in the dungeon yourself. Prisoners are kept in Antar, not the castle."

"Captain." Henton responded crisply, still in salute as the Captain had not saluted in return. "Captain Charles ordered me to deliver these men to the castle. They were caught overnight in the progress of raping and killing people on outlying farms. We had been tracking them for several days and caught a break."

"And why should I care?"

"Well, there were eleven men in the group, three were local undesirables who managed to avoid being conscripted for one reason or another. Those three are being held at the garrison. The band was involved with many murders. We caught them enjoying themselves after murdering the three men of a family and a ten year old girl, who was strangled while being raped. The mother and three other girls, between twelve and sixteen, were what they considered to be their reward."

"And why bring the other men here?"

"Of the other eight men, five of which died in the fighting to free the family, those that lived claimed they were under your protection, as they are Kyntian soldiers. They seem to have kept the locals around solely for the purpose of being able to know which families to attack."

The Captain returned Henton's salute and moved around to the back of the wagon to look at the three men who were bound so tightly that their hands and bare feet had turned slightly blue. A look of disgust passed over the Captain's face before he turned back to Sergeant Henton. "Sergeant, bring the prisoners into the castle. I will need you to make a report. Can you write?"

"Yes sir."

"Then come with me."

Henton signaled Corporal Will to take lead of the wagon as he followed a step behind the Captain, who was again walking briskly. He heard the wagon start to move forward and peripherally noted the five gate guards spread out to make room.

Henton looked up as he passed the outer gate of the massive gate house. There was a second set of gates on the far side of the structure. Above him and to the sides were massive blocks of stone with murder holes and arrow loops. A force trying to come through the main entrance would find it a bloody battle.

As he neared the end of the gate house, a view inside the curtain wall was possible. Henton had never been in this castle and had only been inside one other castle while working guard duty for an ambassador. He felt the scale of the castle complex weigh on him.

Directly between Henton and the keep, as well as between the tower and the outer walls to the east, were countless wagons loaded with supplies. They appeared to be ready to be deployed, presumably to the front lines and he felt a sudden concern that his next assignment would likely be escorting a supply caravan. He had seen how many soldiers were left in Antar and heard rumors about the castle staffing and knew they would have to deplete the numbers significantly to protect this many wagons.

Henton turned at the sound of a man calling out something in Kyntian, which he was fairly certain was "Captain." The Captain had stopped and was now waiting for a man approaching from the west. They started talking in Kyntian and while he could not understand what was said, Henton always felt it was rude to simply stand and watch a conversation, so he turned back to looking at the wagons.

He had quickly added up a count of thirty wagons just to his south and had started counting the rows and columns to the east when he saw movement. He looked away from where the movement had been in order to try and catch it again with his peripheral vision.

It came again quickly and Henton homed in on a cloaked person ducking between the wagons. Henton took a step away from the Captain and the movement, feigning interest in the tower. The person among the wagons moved again, ducking under another wagon. Henton noticed the shape of a sword and a pack or bag on the person's back.

Turning to move into the field of wagons himself, Henton headed into a different row and behind the person. He tried to approach as quietly as possible, using just the toes of his hard soled boots. He lost sight of the person, but based on their prior direction and pattern of watching and then moving, he knew he would be gaining on them and should be able to catch them just as they reached the edge of the wagons.

He reached the last wagon and stopped. Peeking around the wagon, Henton noticed the person squatting by a wheel a dozen feet away. Suddenly the person's hooded face turned slightly in his direction and then took off at a dead run toward the outer wall and one of the towers. Henton exploded into a sprint and only because of his longer strides was he able to close the gap.

The cloaked figure suddenly skidded to a stop and turned with the intent to draw a sword. Henton did not slow, instead, he dropped low and kicked out his left foot, hitting the foot of his attacker, knocking them both to the ground. The sword scattered away and Henton used his momentum to roll on top of his opponent.

A strong fist met his chin, but having been caught in more than one bar fight, Henton easily shook off the blow. Unable to get a good hold on the squirming man below him, Henton slammed his forehead into the person's face and could feel the impact of the man's head hitting the flagstones of the courtyard.

Having knocked the fight out of the smaller man, Henton rolled him onto his stomach and twisted the man's arm behind his back.

"Get off of me!"

Henton paused slightly, the person was too large to be a small boy, but the voice was not that of a man. He heard booted feet approaching behind him. The person below him shifted and he took a foot to his back. He struggled to maintain his grip on the person's arm, but the person rolled over and with surprising strength, kicked up, rising slightly into the air. Henton only just maintained his grip. Looking into the hooded face, he could see a pair of green eyes burning with hatred and anger. Blood was running from the girl's nose and mouth.

She seemed about to try one last attempt to get free, but with the other soldiers and the Captain surrounding her, she simply ceased resiting.

"Well, if it isn't the Princess. Your Highness, whatever are you doing out here."

Henton froze when he heard "Princess." It would be one thing to tackle a scullery maid stealing, but something else entirely to assault a member of the royal family. Before he could start thinking of what punishment he might receive, the Captain smiled and patted his shoulder.

"Sergeant. I must thank you. What is your name?"

"Henton sir."

"Well, this one has been nothing but trouble. You have done me a service today."

Henton accepted his hand up and rose off the Princess who was holding her nose to try to stop the bleeding. The soldiers standing around her had expressions ranging from smug pleasure to an obvious eagerness to inflict a little pain of their own.

"You men, return her to her room and find out who was watching her and how she got out. I expect the information before I have a chance to finish a cup of coffee." He turned back to Henton, "please follow me."

*   *   *   *   *

Henton had been escorted into the keep and was sitting in the Captain's outer office with a clerk that had a scar running from his chin up to his right ear. Henton had been asked to fill out a report on his three prisoners, but since he could only write Cothish, that clerk had been assigned to slowly record the report. Trying not to yawn too much, Henton gave up on the idea that the report would be complete. Either Kyntian words were much shorter than Cothish was, or the clerk was only recording the highlights. In his mind, it really did not matter, since a full report was already recorded at the garrison. Now he was simply waiting on the Captain to dismiss him and allow him to return to his men and hopefully get some sleep. Eventually, the Captain summoned him into the inner office.

"Sergeant Henton. I understand you were on a ship up until two weeks ago."

"That is correct sir. The Scarlet."

"That would explain why I am able to find a competent man in Antar."

Henton ignored the insult of his fellow men.

"Well, we have a slight problem with the Princess. She is a spoiled child with delusions of grandeur. She wants to run off to find her daddy, which would be terrible for morale and hard for his Majesty to focus on the war if he is worried about his daughter."

"Was that what she was doing? Trying to go to the front?"

"Yes, I am afraid it was. She does have some skill at fighting, I won't lie about that, but she is nothing but trouble. She drove off her personal guards two days ago and it seems she convinced the ones I had assigned to protect her to allow her out of her room to bathe. Well, she overcame the two men, likely by surprise. They claim she tried to lure them by showing flesh, but I doubt that was the case. As I said, she does have some skill."

Thinking back to the brief struggle earlier, Henton nodded. "I would agree with that assessment."

"Good. She is trouble and has an irrational hatred of those from Kynto. Since you have proven able to at least stop her in a fight, I am putting you in charge of her confinement. It is for her own good."

"Captain, I am honored, but—"

"I have already sent dispatches to your Captain Charles. Consider it a promotion and your pay will increase to that of personal guard."

"Captain, I really must refuse. I have men—"

"Sergeant, orders are not refused. I don't know what you are used to on a ship, but on land, your Captain's command is followed."

"Yes sir. I understand, but I am worried about my—"

"Your men will be assigned as needed by Captain Charles." The Captain rose to his feet and Henton did the same. "I had thought you would be a bit more appreciative. Let me warn you that intentionally failing to keep her under control will result in punishment, not a return to your prior assignment."

"Yes sir."

The Captain eyed him one more time. "Report to the barracks next to the old tower. Lieutenant Gothi will be able to provide you with a place to sleep and introduce you to the men who will be under your command. They should be very motivated, since if they fail a second time, I will be less than pleased. Your new command starts at first light. Dismissed."

Chapter 4

Stephenie held her ribs and slowly dropped into the chair at her desk as the morning light brightened her room. She looked at the scattered mess that was her pens, ink, and blank paper. Any letter or scrap of paper with something written on it had been removed.

She glanced at the scattered drawers of her dresser, noting that all of her clothing had been pulled out, searched, and tossed against the circular wall of the tower. Having never hidden anything in her clothing drawers, she did not allow the indignity to bother her. The removal of all her weapons, armor, and training clothing, which had been paraded out of her room by her mother's soldiers in a spectacle to taunt her, did hurt.

She glanced into the silver mirror and saw her swollen nose and the dark rings forming around her eyes. They went along with the bruised arms, legs, and ribs the soldiers had left her as a small token of appreciation. There had been fifteen men, all intent on getting in at least a couple of solid blows. She had numbly received the beating, as she had the robbery of her possessions, without a sound or attempt to do more than shield her face and head. Her lack of response took the energy out of most of the blows. However, there were a couple who seemed to relish her apparent submission and they had been the ones to blacken her face and try to crack her ribs.

She opened her mouth slightly to examine her split lip and the cut in her cheek left from her teeth. The lip had healed overnight, but the gouge in her mouth ached and burned. She sighed, and for the first time in her life, considered praying to Elrin. She had never embraced the demon god in thought or action before, knowing her curse was the result of her mother's doing, not her own. However, with her current situation, she would need to be strong.

She looked away from the mirror and closed her eyes. *I will not embrace that demon.* She took a deep breath and wondered at how quickly her lip and face were healing. She knew it was her witchcraft, it was the only explanation. Somehow, it was protecting her even without her calling on it. The blows she had taken should have broken a rib or two as well as her nose and perhaps her jaw. She had seen in training how easily someone could get hurt and something broken. The soldiers had not pulled their blows, but something had absorbed some of the energy. It left her bruised and sore, but not broken.

Slowly she stood and went into her back room. It was nearly empty, as this was where she had stored most of her possessions that had true meaning for her. The swords her father had given her, the dagger she won from Joshua in a bet. Her messenger satchel with her stolen food. It was all gone. They had even taken her washbowl and clean water.

Carefully, she approached the book shelf that had rested against the center dividing wall. Her collection of books was long gone and the bookshelf, left ajar, had been moved to check for something she might have hidden behind or under it. She slowly knelt down and checked the floor boards that had been concealed under the bookcase and smiled. They had not found the back door out of her room.

She closed her eyes and opened her senses, trying to feel for people within her range. She sensed two men who had been outside her door since she had been locked in her room. There was also a third person, likely a man, coming up the stairs to her room. But there was no one she could sense in the store room above or below her room. She had worried they might have placed some guards directly below her bedroom, which would have made her escape plan more difficult.

When the new man reached her oak door, she heard a knock. "Princess. I am going to enter if you are presentable."

She rose to her feet, returned to her bed chamber, and stopped in the middle of the room next to her bed. She heard the man try the latch and attempt to push open the door. The heavy bar did not move in its tight fitting bracket.

"Princess. Please remove the bar from the door and let me in. I want to talk with you."

She shifted her weight and continued to stare at the door.

"Private, please go find a wood axe. That is an order!"

Stephenie furrowed her brows. The voice of the man talking was deep, but held no Kyntian accent. Instead the man sounded distinctly like someone from northern Cothel.

"Your Highness, I am not in a good mood this morning and I will have a conversation with you, face to face. You have until the soldier returns with the axe to open this door, otherwise I will break it down."

"Rot out there in the hall for all I care. It'll take you the better part of the day to break the door down. What do I care?"

Stephenie heard the man laugh slightly and then recognized the voice as the man who had tackled her and prevented her escape. "You damn bastard! Rot! Hit the door all you want. I hope it splinters and puts out your eyes."

"Your Highness, I think it would be wise if you open the door and let me in. We have some ground rules to discuss and if I have to waste a day breaking down the door, you can be assured that I will not put another one in its place. Which means these guards out here will be watching you as you try to sleep, eat, and change your clothes. So if you want any ounce of privacy, you will remove that bar and open the door. Once the axe is here, you lose the door, period. I will give no quarter at that time."

Stephenie balled her fists and tried to clench her jaw, but it hurt. She glanced in the mirror and walked to the door. Her chance to escape would be severely hindered if she did not have a door. She lifted the heavy bar from the brackets and braced herself for the door to be thrust open; however, it remained closed. She set the bar against the wall and opened the door.

The stairwell was lit by a lamp just outside her door. The man who had prevented her escape yesterday was standing before her; a serious look plastered across his unshaven face. His neatly cropped brown hair spoke of someone who is normally fastidious. She sized the man up as being a good eight inches taller than her and much stronger. His broad shoulders and well-muscled neck proudly held his tanned face. She could see a little shock in his brown eyes, but he kept his face carefully schooled.

"If you would be kind enough to let me in, we can have a private conversation."

Seeing no other course of action at the moment, she decided to bide her time and turned away from the door and retired to her chair. She did not feel the man follow.

"Am I to assume silence is an open invitation? That is a very dangerous way to handle men, they might assume liberties that they should not."

Stephenie sat down and turned to face the man. "Please, by all means, come in. I'd offer you a cup of tea or a biscuit, but alas, I seem to have misplaced most of my things."

The man entered, shutting the door behind him. He glanced around for a second chair and simply sat down on the bed facing her. Stephenie felt a wave of irritation rise up in her.

"Let's get to the point. My name is Sergeant Henton. You can call me Sarge or Sergeant Henton. Due to your recent attempt to cause problems by running away to the front, where a princess, no matter how skilled, would only be a distraction for His Majesty and His Highness, Prince Joshua, I have been pulled off my duty of protecting and guiding the soldiers under my care. I do not relish or appreciate being made a babysitter for a spoiled girl who should act with a greater deal of maturity. If any of my men should die because of this ridiculous duty of sitting around to make sure you stay where you belong, I will consider you directly responsible, princess or not.

"I do not know how long I will be forced into this pointless duty, since we can both assume I am simply here to insult the Kyntian troops. So let's get things clear. You behave yourself, do exactly what you are told and hopefully these soldiers will grant me my request to go back to doing something important, like protecting this country. Once that happens, you have my permission to do as you please, but I would hope that you'd have enough sense not to simply run off to the front, which would likely just result in a group of people being pulled off other tasks to hunt you down and bring you back. Again, endangering soldiers and citizens needlessly." The sergeant rose to his feet. "Do I make myself clear? Do I have your word about your best behavior?"

Stephenie glared at the imposing man, but was not intimidated. "You know nothing of me. You think me a simpleton. Fine, you have my word."

The sergeant matched her gaze, a hint of a reappraisal echoing in his eyes. "Who beat you? I didn't leave you like that. Has someone come to check your injuries?"

"What do you care?"

"A soldier never beats a prisoner, especially not a woman."

"Sergeant, you are a pawn. You are caught in the middle between me and my mother. You want to ruin your career, go ahead and pursue the issue of my beating. You'll get nowhere and you'll find there will be no one to look in on me. You see, I'm in no risk of dying, just a bit too beaten to offer any resistance."

"So you are not requesting aid then?"

Stephenie snorted. "Please, you have me cowed and obedient. What more can you want?"

The sergeant appraised her a moment more. "I doubt that. But please, understand I need you to remain here until they tire of punishing their own by putting a simple Cothel sergeant in charge of them. Once I am gone, you can misbehave as you please, but if you cause trouble for me, they will not send me back to my men. They are still young. They were marines on a ship until two weeks ago; they are not used to fighting in formations on land. We both want this over as quickly as possible."

"When am I to be fed? And what about water to clean the cuts and bruises?"

"I will check into that and have something brought up. I will leave you with the bar and your door, provided you open it any and every time I knock. If the soldiers beat you like this, I do not think it would be wise to trust them with an open door at night."

"Fine."

"By your leave, Princess." The sergeant bowed his head and left, closing the door behind him.

Stephenie immediately returned the heavy bar to the brackets. The sergeant was not what she had expected. His frank mannerism, honest appraisal of his reason for being here, and seemingly sincere concern for his men made Stephenie pause in her planning. He was definitely a highly competent man and she found her malice for him evaporate. *But I cannot let my mother destroy this country. What is she up to? What is she afraid I have tried to say to father or Josh?*

She moved back to her bed and lay down, feeling quite tired and drawn. Despite Henton's plea, she had no choice but to escape. It was her duty to her country, to her brother, and to her father. Someone had to find out what her mother was planning and put a stop to it.

Stephenie awoke slowly, the knocking at her door took a while to penetrate the peaceful sound of the rain softly hitting the tower. She rolled over and upon hearing Sergeant Henton's voice, slid out of her bed.

"I thought we had an agreement Your Highness. Have you decided to change your mind?"

Stephenie bit back an angry retort and lifted the heavy bar free. When the door again remained closed, she set the bar down and pulled the door open. In the hall, the sergeant stood; a pair of her mother's soldiers stood against the far wall with smirks across their face.

"I happened to be asleep," Stephenie said, turning away from the open door and walking slowly to her chair. She felt the sergeant enter behind her and heard the door close before she reached her chair.

"I apologize for waking you. However, I was thinking you might like some food and water. Besides, if you sleep all day, you won't feel like sleeping at night."

Stephenie tried to rub the sleep from her face, but was feeling very dehydrated. She noticed Henton had brought in a chair, as well as a plate of bread and meat and a jug of water. Taking two pieces for himself, he handed her the plate with the remaining four. After placing the jug on her desk, he returned to his chair and took a bite of his food.

Stephenie glanced at the pitcher and the empty mug that was on her desk. The bread was crustless and appeared soft; the meat was strips of beef. She put the plate on the desk and turned back to Henton, who had already finished his first one.

"Judging from your face, I suspect your mouth is bound to be a bit sore, so I asked to have the food not be too rough."

"That is much appreciated."

"But still, you are not eating. Well, you have my word the food is clean and safe. I would not poison you." He started eating his second one.

Stephenie found she could sense little from the sergeant. Not that she was ever able to sense much from most people, but he seemed to be much more of an enigma than most. She watched him finish the second helping of bread and meat, then incline his head toward the pitcher of water.

"Do you mind?"

Stephenie shrugged, but did not turn away. After a moment, the sergeant rose nimble from his chair and walked over to her desk. She watched him pour the water into her empty mug.

"If you are not going to eat any of these, mind if I take another one?"

"Help yourself."

He drank half the mug of water, then poured some more. "Look, I promise, I will be straight with you. I will not poison or drug you. Pick any of the remaining ones and I will eat it. Otherwise, I'll simply eat the rest of them and you won't get anything to eat."

Stephenie tried to ignore the hunger she felt, but she craved both the food and water. Frowning, she took a stack of bread and meat from the pile and picked up the mug from her desk. Putting the food on her lap, she used her skirt to wipe the lip of the mug before drinking the cold water.

Henton grinned, put the plate down, but took one more for himself before he returned to his chair. "I don't know much about you. The soldiers here say you are a dumb bitch who thinks she is better than everyone else and would rather play soldier than act respectably. Based on how they treated you, I'm not inclined to accept their assessment without personal observation."

Stephenie set down the mug and took a small bite of the food. She did not particularly like the soft bread, but she agreed with Henton that a hard, chewy crust would have made the cuts inside her mouth burn. She swallowed the bite and took another drink before responding. "Believe what you want. My friends respect me."

Henton smiled. "Well, I can hardly take your assessment as an unbiased one either. The problem is, no one here trusts me beyond the task of keeping you safely in your rooms. So everyone is going to tell me what they think I want to hear. The trouble is I want the truth."

Stephenie took another bite and tried to focus on Henton; she silently cursed Elrin when nothing more came to her. "I told you, this is between me and my mother. I am sorry you are in the middle, but there really is nothing I can do about it."

"I really need to get back to my men. Is there nothing you can do to apologize? Something to settle the rift?"

Stephenie shook her head and rose from her chair. She was certain the sergeant could play dumb very effectively. It was a skill she knew how to utilize as well, but just did not have the energy to play games at the moment. She watched the rain hitting the northern window and moved closer so she could look out at Antar city. She wiped away some moisture that had condensed on the inside of the glass.

Immediately, she turned back to the sergeant. "More of my uncle's soldiers?"

"They arrived mid-morning. Those of rank have come into the castle, the rest are setting up a camp to the north and west of the castle. Even here in the castle, I heard there was a fair amount of grumbling about having to set up tents in the rain." He shook his head, but did not rise from his chair. "On ship, we fight rain or sun, night or day."

She turned back to the window and watched the activity. Counting the number of tents, she estimated somewhere between one hundred and fifty to two hundred new soldiers. Moving from the north window into her back room and to the north east window, she noticed a large contingent of horses being corralled near the stables and the chapel.

Stephenie returned to her outer room and the north window. "So they are finally going to take the supplies to my father." She frowned as she watched the soldiers work on assembling a much larger tent. "They look like they are digging in for a long stay."

Stephenie felt rather than heard Henton rise from his chair and cross the room. His quiet and subtle steps worried her, as it required her to again reappraise the man as an even more dangerous adversary. When he arrived at the window, she stepped aside for him. She noted a slight frown at what he saw.

"They are indeed setting up a rather large tent. But I don't know much about troop movements on land. My career has been on ships and we have cabins to sleep in."

"You were on a ship?" she asked, vaguely remembering he had mentioned it earlier.

"I had assumed it was obvious."

Stephenie narrowed her eyes.

He chuckled. "Well, I've kept you for a bit. Perhaps I will stop by a little later." He bowed his head slightly, "Your Highness," he said as he turned and left the room, taking the pitcher and plate, but leaving the mug and the food on her desk.

Stephenie was not sure if she should be angry or pleased. He was gone from her room, but the moment she had let some interest in his background slip out, he simply left the room.

Sighing, she returned the bar to the door and paused to listen to the guards who remained on the other side. One of them had said something the other felt was funny, but she had not been able to hear what it was. After a few moments, they both agreed that "working for a hard ass wanker" was better than setting up tents in the rain.

Eventually, she gave up listening to silence and returned to the food. She had decided that it was probably not drugged, but she would not simply assume her next meal would be safe. As she ate, she contemplated what the rain and soldiers would do to her escape plans.

She still hurt from the beating and mixing in a cold rain might be more than her body would tolerate. The soldiers could be a problem if they were attentive, but if not, they could provide additional cover to her escape. However, if the supplies would be leaving soon, so would the new soldiers and a number of ones already at the castle for the purpose of protecting the wagons. That would mean a better chance to get out unnoticed.

Knowing she would not try to escape that evening, she settled down in her bed and closed her eyes.

It was well after dark when she heard Henton knock and ask to come into her room. This time she was ready for him, having woken to the sense of his approach on the stairs. There had been two guard changes since she had eaten, one just a couple of hours after the first. She had listened to the guards complain about how Henton was insisting on random guard changes, some of which were to be quiet and others noisy. She respected the attempt, since there was no way for Henton to know that she would sense the change regardless of how quiet they were. However, it irritated her to not be underestimated. She worried that there might be additional guards in the tower that were out of her range to sense.

"Your Highness, I have dinner. Seems the cooks were a little busy trying to feed some extra soldiers and it took a little longer to get yours ready."

"It's the middle of the night. At this point, you might as well have waited until morning."

He shrugged, but waited until she invited him in before crossing the threshold. He placed the plate and a new pitcher of water on her desk. After pouring a mug of water and taking a drink, he offered her the plate. "Do you want me to eat any specific one first?"

Stephenie took the plate and handed four pieces of bread and meat to the sergeant. With eight piles on the plate, it gave her even odds to avoid a drugged one. Henton took the food and sat down in his chair to begin eating.

"Are you planning to have all your meals with me?"

"Yes Ma'am, I do believe it is better to eat with company than to eat alone. Besides, there is scarcely little for me to do. My sole task is to keep you protected, there are only so many orders a grunt like me can give before running out of things to do. So what better way to make sure you don't get hurt than to sit and eat a meal and chat."

"You presume that I care to chat. You do not fear upsetting your betters?"

He chuckled. It was a sound that Stephenie could not quite force herself to be irritated at. There was something non-assuming about the laugh that lacked any obvious insult. "I take it you don't consider me your better," she said without much spirit.

"Ma'am, it has been told to me that you trained with your brother and other soldiers and fancied yourself a soldier. No one has said you were given any specific rank. These soldiers of your uncle, they seem a bit too eager to say everyone humored you in that. I sense a wariness when it comes to dealing with you. The Captain of the Watch says you are skilled and capturing you was no easy task. You put up a lot of fight, even after I had you on the ground." He rubbed his chin, "not to mention you have a solid punch that many sailors would be proud to boast.

"So that means I respect the fact that you are not a spoiled lady who needs someone to clothe and feed you. But I know nothing of your character. You hold up your end of our agreement, don't cause me trouble, let me get back to protecting my men, and that will speak volumes on your character to me."

Stephenie felt a twinge of guilt, knowing full well that she was only biding her time. Sergeant or no sergeant, she was going to leave as soon as it was appropriate. "How old are you?" She asked to change the subject.

The sergeant chuckled again. "My lady, I'm more than half way past twenty to thirty and you are what, seventeen if I do my math correctly. I know this because I was fifteen when my father decided to offer me up to the navy. My oldest brother, he was obligated to turn over for a year of service in the army. However, I was the third boy and a second spare, so he decided he'd get the nice tax break for having me serve in the navy." He grinned, "the two year contract for an additional son is a very good deal.

"It was the year the king had thrown that large party for your fifth birthday. There was a girl I had been courting a bit and I wanted to make it official during our nation's celebration. The only problem, a week before the celebration, I found out about what my father had done when the navy came to collect me."

"I'm sorry."

Henton shook his head. "It was my father's doing, not yours. Besides, the girl turned out to be not that good of a catch. It seemed she liked to wander about and frequented the beds of quite a few men after she was married. And I got one over on my father. Instead of returning after my two years of service, I stayed on as a marine sergeant. He lost the tax break at that point as well as my help in his shop.

"But the most important part is I was happy providing a service to my country and protecting and training other young men who needed my help."

"And you resent me because you put your nose in where it wasn't wanted or needed and now neither of us are where we want to be."

Henton opened his mouth to respond and then grinned. "When you say it like that, it almost sounds like I have myself to blame for being here."

"You could have let me be. You didn't have to stop me. What were you doing in the castle anyway?"

"Well, first, I do my duty, I don't look away and so yes, that means my life has been filled with more annoyance than I want. But to answer the other question, I was delivering rapists and murderers. I was protecting families on their farms from people who deserve to hang. I was protecting my men from getting killed due to someone without sense ordering them to do something they shouldn't. So yes, I do resent being stuck here babysitting you."

Stephenie began to sense an underlying frustration and anger from Henton that was mirrored in his eyes and voice. She did not know if she could trust him and suspected that there was a chance anything she said would be reported to her mother. However, without Doug, Jenk, and Samuel to talk with, she felt her mind bottled and confined. "I am trying to do what is right for the people as well. There is something going on. My father and brother and many soldiers I call friends are out there somewhere fighting and they need the supplies that are sitting here languishing.

"Someone," she shook her head, "my mother, has had anything of value, not too heavy to move, packed up and stored somewhere. There is something going on and I find all my letters between my father and brother and myself are being intercepted. My guards suddenly disappear and everyone conveniently blames that on me. I tell you, they were made to disappear. So, as a warning to you, I would watch yourself. You appear to be too friendly with me or ask too many questions and you might find yourself in a pit or cage somewhere." She watched Henton's reaction, but could not read his face or sense his emotions. She took a deep breath. "Forget I said anything. You are one man in a den of vipers and if I drag you in, that will be one more person hurt because of me and I don't need to worry about what happens to you. Keep me locked up, then go back to protecting the people and your soldiers." She looked up to meet his brown eyes, "but you should really watch how much time you spend in here talking to me. I'm sure the guards report as much as they can to my mother and if she suspects you, she'll get rid of you."

"Princess, you truly are an enigma. You tell me, a person who up until two weeks ago, was a long ways away on a ship, things that would worry most men, yet, tell me I can't verify them or risk trouble. Very interesting. Is your concern to keep me out of your rooms for my benefit or yours?" He rose from his chair. "Get some sleep, I'll be back to check on you later."

Sergeant Henton came back again in the middle of that night and at random times the next day. So far, Stephenie had refused to get drawn back into a conversation with him. She sat and stared out the window at the troops who were simply sitting around in their tents. Unfortunately, this was having the opposite effect she had hoped for; instead of Henton leaving her in peace, he chose to spend more time sitting in her room.

"I can be as patient as the sea; content to sit here waiting. Somehow I don't think you ever learned that much patience."

She did not turn her head. Her mother was also waiting for something, but she could not decide what it was. She hoped a squad of soldiers would come back to look for the supplies, but even with the supplies overdue, it would take time for someone to come looking for them. *What game is she playing?*

"Are you thirsty?"

Giving up on the silent treatment, she turned to face him. "No I am not. If you must know, I would actually like to use the chamber pot, but I prefer to do that without an audience."

"Well, as a soldier, one can be in situations where that is not an option."

"Well, as everyone keeps telling me, I'm not a soldier." She glanced back out the window. "You can't tell me there isn't something wrong here." She stood up and turned back to Henton, "They should be taking the supplies to the front, not sitting on their asses!"

Henton raised his eyebrows, but remained calm. "You want me to go ask the Queen what she has planned? Yesterday you said I should stay out of it."

Stephenie turned back toward the window, leaning against it. "Please, just leave me alone. She's killing them, so just leave me alone."

She sensed Henton rise and take a step in her direction, then hesitate and turn toward the door. "I'll be back later with some dinner." She heard the door shut and sensed him descend the stairs after a moment.

She went immediately to the door and put up the bar, made the point of stomping away, and then quickly crept back to the door. She heard some snickering, then one of the men muttering in Kyntian, "of course no one wants to go to the front, everyone knows the war is pointless." They made a few comments about Henton needing to bend her over and give it to her, in order to kill two birds with one stone, then they went back to their normal quiet chatter.

She walked over to her mirror and looked at her face. It was still bruised, but the cut on her lip was healed as were the cuts in her mouth. Her ribs were still a little sore, but her arms and legs just had surface marks. *Damn witchcraft,* she thought to herself. The healing she appreciated, but it had always forced her to keep some form of wall between herself and everyone else.

She took some dark makeup and daubed a bit around her eyes. She would have to pretend to still be hurt to keep anyone from noticing how quickly she was healing. It would have to be subtle, as she suspected Henton would expect her to be proud and try to hide her injuries, not to overplay them. A few hesitant steps and a slight grimace when eating would have to be the extent of her charade. Anything more might draw suspicion.

After touching up her face, she relieved herself and then climbed into bed to get some rest.

Chapter 5

True to his word, Henton came back for a late dinner. Stephenie ate a couple of bites and pretended to drink the water, but did not want to risk this meal being the one that was drugged. Henton finished his meal in relative silence and then sat watching Stephenie.

"You find staring at me a relaxing pastime?"

He chuckled as he had done that first evening. "You are not unattractive; I suspect you know this. But that is not what I was doing. No, I thought I would give you some news. But I wanted to wait for you to finish eating. However, as a lady, you probably prefer to eat when no one is watching."

Despite herself, she leaned forward. "What news?"

"Well, nothing of real consequence. I probably should not have made it sound as important as that. No. I just wanted to tell you that as far as I know, and have heard, your father and brother continue to harass the Senzar. The fighting as I understand it is on the other side of the Grey Mountains. Over in Esland or perhaps even as far down as Durland. The Greys are too rough to put an army through, so as long as those cursed sons of Elrin don't overpower our soldiers, the invaders won't likely set foot into Cothel."

Stephenie felt a chill whenever someone referred to witches and warlocks as cursed. Not that she had any care or sympathy for the army of invaders that came out of the Endless Sea, killed one of her sisters, and took another one hostage. However, if her secret ever came to light, she would quickly be grouped with the enemy and burned. "Why sit on the supplies?"

"Well, I have not seen the reports, but the word is, they are not needed right now. So the troops are waiting until the right time to send them."

Stephenie knew the last letters she had read more than a month ago indicated supplies were running low and the countries to the northwest were having their supply shipments attacked and destroyed. However, she did not want to argue. Instead she nodded her head. "Well, that is good to know."

"There are also no reports of any mass casualties. I had a friend on The Scarlet; he was a Priest of Felis. He was sent to the front as well. We need the power of the gods to help fight against Elrin's witches and warlocks. So you are not the only one who worries."

"I never said you didn't have cause to be concerned." Stephenie stood up and looked about her room. "You know, if you could get them to give me back a couple of my books or any books for that matter, it would give me something to do other than sit and stare out the window."

"And a princess who is not bored is one who causes less trouble."

"They took absolutely everything but a couple of ugly dresses and some blank paper. Anything to read would make the time pass more pleasantly."

Henton nodded his head and rose to his feet. He picked up the tray and put the sandwiches on her desk. He noted her nearly full mug and poured in a little more water. "Well, I will leave you for a little while. I'll check in on you a little later. Ma'am."

"Sergeant."

She waited for the door to close, then quickly replaced the bar. She sensed Henton moving down the stairs and eventually out of her range. She had kept a mental accounting of everyone she could sense and knew that while the rooms above and below her had been searched the day before, no one remained in the tower above her floor. The only two people she could sense were the guards outside her door.

However, she was not planning to fight them. It would make noise and with Henton leaving the leftover food and water, she hoped it would be a few hours before he would come back, if he would come back at all this evening.

She pushed aside her concern for the sergeant, knowing that she had to worry more about her father, brother, and thousands of soldiers who might be running out of supplies. Instead she dropped quietly to the floor and started to silently stretch her arms and legs. Pulling her chest a little closer to her thigh, she found one advantage of dresses that trousers did not offer, *less resistance in the seat to bending.*

When she was done, she blew out the lamp and made enough of a point of getting ready for bed that the guards should be able to hear her. She placed her dress on her chair and climbed into bed, but did not allow herself to drift off to sleep. Instead, she waited until the guards changed shifts. With Henton in charge, she knew it could be at any time and there was no point in sitting on the floor in her back room.

After what felt like way too long, she sensed a pair of guards coming up the stairs and she used the cover of their approach to slip out of bed. Her back room had been stripped nearly bare. The bare book case and a chest of empty drawers was really all that was left. She had not bothered to return the bookcase to the wall where it normally sat, since it normally covered a section of floor she wanted to have exposed. If she had straightened it, then her method of escape might be discovered when they finally broke down the door to her room. She had no intention of returning to these rooms, but she preferred to keep secrets.

Dressed only in socks, a thin pair of knickers, and a binding around her chest, she squatted down and waited. Once she sensed the guards had settled down to a long and boring night, she carefully removed a small board in the floor. With the key board removed, three others slid loose, revealing a pair of large, round support beams and an opening between the two just big enough for her to fit through. Cut into the top of one beam was a hollow that contained a coil of rope and Stephenie's favorite night clothes. The darkly dyed breaches, blouse, gloves, and boots were a gift from Joshua for when they would play games of hide and seek in the castle.

Quietly dressing in her clothing, she removed the rope and draped it over one of the beams in a narrow channel cut for that purpose. While she could not see the floor in the totally dark room, she knew it to be about twelve feet below her. She could drop that distance with minimal chance of injury, but the noise would give her away.

Taking a deep breath, she slid her feet into the opening and slowly lowered herself down. Wrapping the two ends of the rope around one foot to lock herself in place, she grabbed the rope with her right hand as she used her left to quietly replace the boards above her head. She struggled with the last board, finding it hard to get it to drop back down into place with only one hand. Feeling the circulation being cut off in her foot, she let out a small sigh when the board eventually dropped into place. Unwinding the rope from her leg, she slowly lowered herself to the floor.

She contemplated leaving the rope in case she needed to return to her room undetected, but changed her mind. She needed to escape tonight, with or without knowing what her mother was planning. Pulling on one loose end, the rope slid quietly over the notch in the support beam to eventually drop into her arms.

Looping it into a coil, she moved to the door of this room. Unlike her own bedroom door, this one was regularly oiled so that it made no sound. At the landing to her floor, she could sense the two guards had not moved and due to the curvature of the tower, they would not be able to see her leave the storeroom.

Reaching out with her senses, she could not feel anyone else in range. Taking a deep breath, she slid the door open just far enough for her to slip out. Closing it behind her, she quietly descended the stairs. She passed the next level and started sensing people in the guard barracks, but the tower still appeared to be empty. As she neared the ground floor, she frowned. Henton appeared to have stationed people in the old great hall. She felt two men sitting near the door to the tower, but based on where they sat, someone sneaking out of the door would not notice them until it was too late.

The man is good. Changing her original plan of simply leaving through the old kitchen door at the other end of the great hall, she continued past the closed door and down into the cellar of the tower. There were two floors below the ground level, which was really elevated off the ground by a base of large stone blocks.

The first floor held a small storage room and more stairs going down. Stephenie grabbed a hooded lamp from the store room and quickly lit it. While she knew the rooms well and could see better than most in dim light, she could not see in complete darkness.

Opening the shutter a fraction, she continued down to the next level, which was carved out of the bedrock under the castle and held a number of smaller chambers. Originally, the catacombs under the tower and the great hall stored enough supplies to hold out for months in the event of a siege. Now, they held forgotten and useless things.

Moving down a side corridor to a larger room, Stephenie continued to reach out with her senses. However, it did not appear that Henton had stationed anyone down here. Which for those who were not aware, appeared to be a cold and damp dead end. However, Stephenie knew of at least three exits from the catacombs.

Now being forced to use the catacombs instead of simply slipping away, she decided it would be worthwhile to cut across the castle complex and stop by the new kitchens for some supplies and perhaps a carving knife that she could use as a weapon.

After releasing the catch, which actually took a fair amount of pressure, she gently pushed on a section of the wall which slid back easily due to a series of counter balances. Once she was in the narrow passage, she pushed the door back into place and reset the catch. This again took a good deal of effort. She understood the catch had to be tight to keep the door locked solidly in place, but wished it did not always hurt her hand so much to reset it.

The passages across the castle complex were obviously built in different phases. This initial section was squared, with an arched ceiling; however, the stone was not neatly dressed. As with the old great hall, she thought the rough stone more attractive. Other passages were lined with different types of stone and some obviously took more time to build.

She suspected this passage had at one time tied parts of the original curtain wall to the tower. However, since the original curtain wall had been mostly torn down, one branch now led into the new keep, through what was a series of rough cutbacks and steps. She considered going into the keep to try and find out what her mother was planning, but decided a quick exit would be best. *Father can send some troops back to deal with mother.*

She passed the rubble pile that she suspected to be an exit to another part of the original curtain wall and descended a set of stairs that appeared to date to at least a third period of construction. This part of the passage was at least a dozen feet below the original passage and instead of being fairly level and straight, it twisted left and right as well as up and down.

Stephenie moved quickly through the darkness, confident in her ability to sense someone well before they would notice her. Once under the servants quarters, she climbed the wooden ladder up thirty feet through a narrow opening in the ceiling. That led into a small landing and a passage that followed the eight foot thick outer curtain wall. The wall separating her from the servants quarters, by contrast, was only about one foot of stone.

She stopped before a door that opened into a small store room on the first floor. She let herself out through a concealed door and then made her way quietly to the kitchen. At this hour, no one was about, and she reached the kitchen with ease. She collected some bread, cheese, and a couple of meat pies before going into the head cook's store room to retrieve a carving knife. Rat, one of the spit dogs whined softly at her, but otherwise made little noise. She thought to take a second knife, but these did not have sheaths, so she left with only one blade. It was sharp, but it was also thin and would not withstand much combat.

Taking one last glance around, she crept out of the office and made her way to the exterior door. Pausing at the door to check for people with her senses, she gave herself a few moments before stepping out into the night.

Pulling the door closed behind her, she remained against the side of the building with her lamp shuttered. She was close to the new great hall and the southern side of the new keep. A patrol was moving north from the guard tower on the far side of the new great hall, but they had not appeared to see her and were not moving in her direction.

She glanced north and noticed a group of people at the horse stalls that had been built against a lone section of the old curtain wall. Narrowing her eyes, she tried to make out who might have arrived at this late hour. She watched someone with the hood of a cowl pulled low get escorted by four or five soldiers toward the keep. The glint of a scabbard and armor under a cloak lent credence to Stephenie's initial thought that the man did not appear to be a prisoner.

She glanced back to the far tower of the new keep and frowned. The patrol was moving slowly. Her thought had been to use the tower entrance to get to the top of the curtain wall and then drop down to the southern side of the castle complex. The ground to the south was too rough to set up much of a camp and she expected to have a fairly easy time avoiding her uncle's soldiers.

But, who's just arrived at this time? Still huddled against the wall, she glanced back to the north. The men were definitely moving to the front of the keep. With a little luck, she might be able to get up to the secret passage in her mother's office to hear what was discussed. Hesitating, she glanced back at the tower and her escape. *Even if they discover I've snuck out of my rooms, I could hide in the catacombs for several days and sneak out once they think I am long gone.* She considered her options again and though freedom begged for her attention, she turned around and went back into the kitchen.

Trusting her senses to give her enough warning, she moved quickly into the servants quarters and raced back to the secret passage. Once secure again in her world of darkness and intrigue, she ran back to the stairs leading to the new keep.

This entrance to the keep led through a series of narrow tunnels built into the walls of the keep's multiple underground levels and the massive stone base of the keep. These tunnels led to a series of ladders that took Stephenie up to the second level of the keep. Unfortunately, access to her mother's office was not available through the passages she was using. Taking a small branch from the main passage, she moved out of the stone construction into passages constructed through interior walls. In the dim light from her lamp, she could see the back of the lath and plaster wall and had to twist her body to avoid scratching her arms and shoulders on the rough materials.

She stopped in front of a small door that led into a dining hall. Sensing no one present, she placed her supplies next to the seldom used door, opened it, and slipped into a room that she had refused to use since her father and Joshua had left. She quickly left the dining hall, moved down a couple passages and into a small room currently used to store linens. A small set of shelves partially blocked the concealed door in the back of the room. Stephenie moved it just enough to open the door and slid into the passage. She would put the shelves back on her way out.

This set of passages required her to take a set of narrow stairs down to the first floor and then run past the Seneschal's offices. She could sense someone in Renild's office, likely the old man still hard at work. At the far end of the passage, another set of stairs led back up to the second floor and then to a ladder to the third floor. She took a left and rushed to the passage next to her mother's office. Sensing one man and her mother, she slowed to avoid making noise.

Carefully, she crept around a corner and to the wall behind her mother's desk. Stephenie strained to hear her mother's shrill voice as she closed upon her destination.

"It is about time they sent someone. That bitch has been causing too much trouble."

"Ma'am, you must keep your daughter under control. You don't want it getting out what she is. Plus, we need her alive to perform the sacrifice."

Stephenie's blood froze hearing Raul's voice, but was unsure if it had been the fact that he knew what she was or the mention of a sacrifice that had frightened her more.

"I'd cut out her heart and eat it now if I could."

"You must wait. If it is not done correctly, Elrin's curse will fall to you."

She had never heard of a way to break the curse, but obviously Raul and her mother had. It had been the only reason her mother had not found a way for Stephenie to suffer a fatal accident. She knew now that she must not get caught at any cost.

With her ear to the wall, she tried to hear what was said next, but it was mumbled too quietly. With slightly trembling knees, she shifted her body slightly and knelt down so she would not put too much pressure against the wall. She waited several more minutes without hearing more, but she was not sure if that was due to the fact that her blood was pounding in her ears or because they were talking quietly. Cold fear made her limbs ache. She had to reach her father and Josh.

Stephenie pushed aside her overwhelming desire to get away from her mother and took a deep breath. She took another one, feeling calmer, and put her ear back to the wall. However, she still heard nothing additional for several more minutes. Eventually, she sensed additional people approach the door to her mother's outer office. At least four people entered, but what she sensed from one of them disturbed her. He was different somehow.

"Lord Esilberen," her mother said with an insincere sweetness. "I am glad you finally arrived. Have you agreed to our terms?"

"You kept me waiting long enough. However, we have agreed. Your daughter in exchange for withholding support from—"

Instinctively, Stephenie leaned back and to the right, away from the wall just before the wood splintered and exploded into the secret passage. She had covered her face with her arms, but could feel numerous small cuts.

Even before the dust settled, she was on her feet. She tried to focus her eyes, but the light from her mother's office was blinding after spending so long in darkness. She saw her mother just a couple feet away and could tell by her body language that her mother had not expected whatever happened.

"There's a rat in your walls."

Stephenie's vision cleared some as her attention was drawn to a tall man she presumed to be Lord Esilberen. Sensing a slight chill, far more pronounced than when she was around priests using their powers, she hopped over the rubble of the destroyed wall, grabbed the lantern, and moved as quickly as possible through the dark passage. Behind her, she could hear her mother's shrill voice 'bring her alive!'

Running through the narrow passage was difficult and Stephenie scraped her shoulders on the rough lath and plaster several times before she reached a wooden ladder. She slipped the lamp handle over her wrist and hastily descended the tall ladder that would take her down to lower levels of the keep.

Hearing the sounds of armored men reaching the ladder above her, she dropped the last few feet and banged her knee against the stone wall as she landed. The pain just added to a growing list of injuries.

The secret of the passage already compromised, Stephenie stopped at the first concealed door and released the catch. Roughly pushing open the door, she barreled across and out of a small store room. She turned a corner and skidded to a stop, sensing a group of people coming up from the lower cellars of the keep. *Damn.* Quickly, she turned, backtracked to a side hallway and ran up the stairs to the ground level of the keep.

Hearing and sensing people quickly descending from the grand stair case, she charged into a guard standing sleepily next to the outer door. The young man reacted too slowly and Stephenie dropped him with a solid punch to the jaw. Without missing a step, she easily threw aside the locking bar and pushed open the heavy door. Behind her, she could hear guards shouting in Kynton to stop her.

Stephenie ran down the steps of the keep, taking them four at a time. Across the court yard and halfway to the gatehouse, Stephenie caught sight of a dozen guards. Knowing she would not make it past them, she sprinted toward the old great hall, hoping she could make it to the other catacombs. If she could get far enough ahead of the men, she could hide in one of the numerous secret passages and rooms.

Not bothering with the heavy main door, she ran to the far end and down the steps into the old side entrance. The old door stuck for a moment, but a solid kick freed the swelled wood from the jam and she ran down a short passage and then up the steps into the old kitchen.

Panting from the exertion and panic of being chased, she spared a brief curse for the person who had built the castle with so many steps. She rushed from the kitchen and was halfway across the old great hall when Henton and another man appeared out of the doorway that led to her tower and the entrance into the catacombs. The look of surprise in Henton's eyes was almost enough, but with soldiers only moments behind her, she could not take the time to explain. *And he's stronger than me,* echoed in the back of her mind.

Knowing she could not turn back, and praying to Elrin that for once her witchcraft would obey her command, she centered her frustration, pain of betrayal, and fear for what her mother was planning, drew upon those energies and released a primal scream. Not knowing for certain what she was doing, she flung her left hand before her. Feeling a surge of heat and cold flow through her, she watched with surprise as Henton and the other man were flung back through the doorway.

Feeling drained, she nearly sank to her knees, but managed to grab the edge of one of the old tables and steadied herself. After a moment, she forced herself upright. *Move.* Pushing past the exhaustion, she started to run again, passing Henton, who was laying against the round wall of the tower, moaning softly. The other man she knew to be dead, his head and neck crushed when he was thrown backwards. The realization that she had actually killed a person passed through her with a sense of detachment.

Hearing soldiers in the great hall, she ran to the right and down the wide stairs leading below ground. Stumbling on the uneven steps, she slowed enough to open the shutters on the lamp a little further before continuing at her reckless pace.

After descending two floors, she turned to the right and down a side passage that led to a number of store rooms. The rooms were empty save for the raised cedar flooring.

The sound of booted feet slapping against the stone passage drew Stephenie's attention behind her. After having expended so much energy against Henton and the other soldier, her senses had dulled and she could barely feel the man who had just entered the passage.

Panic lending her strength, Stephenie sprinted past several side rooms and then turned into the second from the last one. On the far side of the room, behind several pillars that had been erected to support the ceiling, she knew there was an old entrance into hidden passages. She had used it only once, many years ago and she hoped she could pull up enough of the cedar floor to open the door concealed beneath it before the soldier reached her.

Skidding to a stop, she dropped to the floor, tipping the oil lamp on its side. Not bothering to waste time righting the lamp, she searched for a gap between the boards in the flickering light. Finding an opening big enough to force her fingers through, she heaved up a large section of the floor that was not attached to the rest. Straining under the weight, she tossed the section aside to reveal a wooden door in the underlying stone floor. This door had a pull, but the ancient wood had swelled, forcing her to strain even more to pull the door free.

Sensing a soldier closing behind her, Stephenie released the pull, dropped low, and swung her right leg behind her. It collided with the soldier's leg, sending him tumbling to the floor instead of tackling her as had been his intent.

Cursing her mother for taking her weapons and herself for leaving her supplies in the passages, she noticed a dagger the soldier had dropped. Picking it up, she advanced on the soldier who was rolling over to regain his feet.

Jumping, Stephenie performed a leaping kick into the man's face. She landed hard, missing the edge of the wooden floor. She stumbled back onto the old door, which cracked under the impact.

Reflexes she knew were born from her witchcraft allowed her to keep her balance. Hearing more men approach, she turned, jumped off the door, reached down, and heaved it up again, this time it pulled free and she swung the door to the side. The soldier she had kicked was getting to his feet on the other side of the open door. She could see in his face he was contemplating slamming the leaning door shut to trap her. Snatching the flickering lamp from the floor, she jumped into the opening as the door was pushed shut.

She landed on the stone steps, but was knocked down by the door hitting her head. Tumbling a few feet, she slowly regained her senses and her feet. Behind her, the door was being pulled open again.

Cursing, Stephenie started down the rough stone passage that sloped deeper into the stone bluffs under the castle. She wanted to run, but exhaustion and injuries had accumulated to a point where she could not push herself beyond a labored jog.

She took several random turns in the hopes of losing the man behind her, but not being familiar with this section of the catacombs, she feared getting lost or worse, running into another group of soldiers pursuing her.

She paused when she reached a section with a wooden floor. "Where am I?" she murmured. There was a railing on the right side that partially blocked a dark opening in the stone. The left side was simply part of the stone passage. She approached carefully and tried to peer into the darkness, but nothing was visible.

She was about to turn up the lamp when she sensed a soldier approaching. She turned and his boots started slapping against the stone as he rushed her. She held out the dagger and tried to center herself. She wanted to draw upon her powers again, as she had done with Henton, but as the man closed the distance, she knew it was not going to happen. Turning, she tried to run as the man leaped at her.

Jumping to the side at the last moment, she avoided most of his force, but he put an arm around her leg and pulled her to the wooden floor with him. The sensation of hitting the floor was interrupted by cracking and tearing and a sudden feeling of weightlessness. Stephenie scratched at the rotting wooden planks as they broke apart beneath the weight of their sudden impact.

The soldier cursed as they tumbled into darkness. Stephenie refused to call out, wondering only if there would be a series of copper ornaments that would rip open her flesh before she crashed into something solid enough to kill her.

Chapter 6

It was dark and Stephenie ached all over. Her arms burned with what felt like hundreds of little cuts and scrapes. Her knees and ankles were throbbing as much as her head. She tried to look around, but there was absolutely no light. She smelled a pungent combination of urine, blood and oil.

Below her was something cold and somewhat squishy. Slowly she tried to sit up and had to toss off several pieces of wood. As memories of what happened returned, she realized she was laying on top of a dead soldier. Scrambling away from the body, she stumbled over the debris of the walkway that had given out beneath their weight.

"Hello," she called out and heard her trembling voice echo back to her. Fear of being caught was pushed away by the fear of being trapped alone in the dark forever. "Hello!" she called again much louder.

After several moments, she neither heard, saw, or sensed anything around her. Shivering from fear as much as the chill that had settled into her body, she searched with her hands in all directions to see what was around her. She felt a wall to one side, but nothing on the other sides.

"Damn it. I need light."

She sighed. Feeling disoriented, she crouched down, uncertain if perhaps she was on a ledge, and taking a step in any direction would lead to her tumbling away into more darkness. After a few moments to build her confidence, she felt further around her immediate area.

Among the remains of the rotten walkway, she felt a sticky substance. Bringing her fingers to her nose, she identified it as lamp oil. "So, no light. Thanks for nothing Elrin."

She knew the dead soldier was close by. Since she wasn't wet with urine, it was likely that the soldier had soiled himself when he died. "Unless I happened to land in a waste pit," she added ruefully.

Carefully, she searched around, hoping to find the dagger she had lost in the fall. She found the broken remains of the lamp, but not the weapon. She also realized the floor was mostly level with mortar joints. "So I won't be falling off a cliff? Unless this is just the ledge they use to push people to their deaths." Slowly she expanded her search, but did not find the dagger.

Eventually, apprehension of touching the dead man lost out to the apprehension of being alone in the dark with no weapons. After a brief moment, when she realized she had become disoriented in her prior searching, she found the body of the soldier. She found another dagger and removed it. His sword had become bent when he landed on it and she could not draw it from the scabbard. "Elrin, you really want to play with me before I die."

She found his belt pouch and after fumbling to untie it in the darkness, gave up and cut the leather straps. She tried to identify the contents by feel and aside from a number of coins, she found two keys, a locket and chain, and two pieces of wood that she could not identify by touch alone.

She contemplated taking his cloak, but the blood and urine that had seeped into it prevented her from doing so. His leather armor was too big for her and so she carefully backed away from the man.

Once away from where they fell, she could tell she was in a larger chamber by the echo of her foot falls. She contemplated waiting in the hopes that someone searching would come and she could be found, but that would only end up with her mother winning.

Biting her upper lip, Stephenie started to slowly walk in a random direction. She held her hands before her and tested every step before committing her weight. The going was very slow, but eventually she felt stone in front of her. With just a moment of exploring with her hands, she knew the surface was round and smoothly dressed. "A pillar." She circled the stone pillar and judged it to be at least three feet in diameter. Reaching up as high as possible, she could not feel the top.

"Hello," she called again, listening to the sound of her voice around her. "Wherever I am, this is a big room." She leaned her head against the stone and folded her arms around herself to keep warm. The painful tugging of her shirt on her arms drew her to find a couple of splinters of wood. They did not feel rotten, so she suspected she picked them up when the wall in her mother's office was destroyed and she had covered her face with her arms.

Sighing, she turned her back to the pillar and slid to the floor; tears sliding from her face. She had been a fool to try to find out what her mother was planning and so far she had not even had time to contemplate her discoveries. She never expected her mother's machinations to frighten her so much. "That man must have been a Senzar warlock. He wasn't a priest, that much I know." She remembered the overwhelming need to move away from the wooden wall just before it exploded inward on her. Her mother was making deals with the Senzar to undermine the war. Cothel was the primary force against them. "The damn bitch!" If the country disintegrated, her father and Joshua would be without support and they would fall against the Senzar witches and warlocks.

"That is why none of her brother's forces have gone to relieve them. She's going to take the treasury and anything valuable and use the wagons to go north, leaving Antar to rot in chaos. That has to be what is happening."

Stephenie stood up and started forward, but stopped. "Which way did I come from?" Realizing she had lost her certainty of direction when she rounded the pillar, she stepped backwards and brushed the side of the pillar with her arm. "Damn it." She took a deep breath and flexed her slightly swollen right knee. "I'm not even walking straight."

Taking another deep breath to calm herself, she considered her options. *Every room has to have walls.* "If I keep going in one direction, I will eventually find a wall and walls have doorways and passages which have to lead somewhere."

Taking a carefully measured step forward, she slowly progressed through the darkness, encountering another column after nearly fifty paces. "Either I'm not going straight or this is one huge room." Being as careful as possible to remain in a straight line, she moved around the stone pillar. After another thirty paces she encountered a wall at a sharp angle. Smiling at the hope she had been going the long way down the chamber, she kept her left hand on the wall and her right hand before her and continued forward.

After one hundred paces, she stopped. *This really is a large room.* She tried to concentrate on the sounds around her, but all she could hear was her own breathing and the hurried beating of her heart. She turned her head, searching for any glimmer of light, but found nothing but darkness. Resolved that her only other choice was to give up and die, she started counting paces again. At sixty-five she swore and turned away from the wall, holding her foot. "Damn rock. Damn soft boots."

She wiped the moisture from her eyes and reoriented herself with the wall. Then, knelt down to feel what had caused her foot so much pain. It was a broken piece of stone at least three feet wide and a foot high. She could rock it slightly, but it was far too big for her to move. Moving around the obstacle, she found some additional fragments of stone, most of which were smaller.

Finding the wall again, she carefully moved her hands over the smooth surface, not finding any breaks. "Well, it either came from further up, or was something else." She tried to console herself with the thought that it was a broken statue and not a piece of the ceiling, but the flat sides of some of the fragments make the argument weak in her mind.

More carefully, she continued forward, sliding her boots over the gravelly floor, generating a sound that carried into the large room. She paused every few steps to make sure the sound stopped with her movement and kept checking the stolen dagger tucked into her belt. After only a dozen steps, she felt the wall give way and turn ninety degrees. Carefully, she continued forward and sobbed with relief when she soon felt the other side of what was obviously a side passage.

Taking a deep breath, she started down the side passage. After just a couple of steps she could tell the amount and size of the rubble was growing. Crouching down, she fumbled with her hands to feel her way along until she reached a point where she had to start clawing on top of the debris to move forward. "Damn Elrin!" she swore as the realization the passage had collapsed grew more pronounced. Slipping to the left, her hand passed over some cloth as she kept herself from getting wedged between a couple of large stones. Examining the cloth a little further, she felt it tear to pieces in her hands as if the material was ancient. Suddenly her fingers slipped into a shallow hole. After a moment's realization, she snatched her hand away from the skull and fell backwards down the rubble. Panic filling her mind, she scrambled away from the rubble and back into the large chamber where she collapsed to the floor.

"Damn her. Damn my mother!" She sobbed with frustration, "what have I done to deserve this?" Her voice echoed through the darkness. "Why?" She put her head on the cold stone and closed her eyes. *No more. I'm done.*

She opened her eyes and for a moment was startled by the darkness around her. Realizing she was not dreaming, Stephenie slowly sat up. *How long have I been down here?* Her throat was dry and her stomach rumbled with hunger, but aside from those measures, she could not be certain. *If nothing else, I need to warn Josh and father. I have to find a way out.*

Slowly rising on cramped and sore legs, she walked in the direction she thought was the wall and rubble filled passage. She did not want to think about the body that was left half exposed in the debris from the cave-in. But the realization that no one had come to remove the body worried her. *Was that the only way out?* At the wall, she turned away from the passage and went the other direction, using her right hand as a guide.

Until she had explored every inch of the dark chamber she had to hope there were additional exits. *And it would seem I've got nothing better to do with my time.* She continued walking through the darkness and after almost six hundred paces, found a corner in the room. There was a small, circular pedestal standing four feet high in the corner, but nothing was resting on top of the stone. Adding it as another unanswered question to her growing list. Stephenie continued along the wall for two hundred paces before finding another passage. Carefully exploring the opening, she judged it to be at least fifteen feet across, a good five feet wider than the first one she found.

Without further remarks, she traced her fingers along the smooth right hand wall of the side passage. As she walked, she could feel the twists and bends in the passage as well as the general downward slope. After more than two thousand paces she slowed and then stopped. She wanted to go up, not further down into darkness. She was also worried that she had not felt any additional side passages. *Though there could have been some on the other wall and I just missed them.*

She pounded her fist against the wall. Joshua had given her trouble so many times for being brash and rushing in to something without thinking it through. But she always feared getting paralyzed with indecision if she should try to think about things too much before acting. She closed her eyes and listened to her memory of Joshua's voice chastising her for some stupid prank.

Sighing, she pulled down her pants and used the wall to balance as she squatted to relieved her bladder. *Just doing something always feels better.* Moving away from the puddle of urine, she refastened her belt and continued downward, telling herself the passage was large and smooth, so it had to go somewhere. *And if not, I can always go back up the other side and search for another exit from the pillar chamber.*

After an indeterminable amount of time, Stephenie began to notice the sound of water falling and that immediately reminded her how thirsty she was. Picking up her pace, she continued down listening to the growing sound of water.

Suddenly the stone walls and floor gave way and she stopped. Below her feet she heard the creak of wood, the sounds of water echoed around her, and the slightest of breezes moved across her face. Feeling dizzy without a visual point of reference, she crouched to her hands and knees. Reaching out to the right, she felt the round, but worn slats of a railing. Stretching to her left, she found a similar railing, but based on the sounds, the area to the right was a vast open space, while the left was closed in.

What is all this? she asked herself, uncertain if she truly wanted to know. Pressing her hands against the beams below her, she tested her weight against the ancient wood. They were damp with moisture, but felt solid. She tested a few more and found no sense of give.

Standing up slowly, she reached out for the railing and took a step forward. The wooden passage had a steeper slope than the stone passage. *Perhaps I am almost to the end.* Thinking about the promise of water, she slowly started moving forward, always keeping a firm hand on the railing.

After twenty paces, her left foot did not stop where the wooden floor should have been and the railing snapped away under her sudden weight. Reaching out into the darkness in front of her, she found no sign of the wooden passage.

Her breath was forced from her lungs a moment later when she collided with something that did not bend to her weight. She gasped for breath as she slid down what might have been an ice flow. Smashing into a sharp stone, she spun away and continued to slide over the glassy surface below her.

A moment later the little breath she had regained was forced from her lungs as she bounced off another rock and into a pile of loose rubble.

When she could breathe again, she screamed with a pain born from frustration and hate. "Damn you mother! Damn your curse! You should be Elrin's spawn, not me!" She sobbed and let tears fall. Her forearm burned with what she knew to be a deep cut and her ankle was sprained. "You made me a thrice cursed witch, but what good has it done me?" She was sprawled in the rubble with her feet over her head. Slowly she removed her hand from the bleeding cut. "So simple, I just let my blood drain." She shook her head and pressed her forearm into her stomach to stop the bleeding. *Damn you Elrin for not giving me the power I need when I need it. But you've failed to kill me. You'll have to do better than dropping me, that's failed twice.*

Slowly, she twisted herself around and sat up. Finding the dagger still at her waist, she cut off her left shirt sleeve and made two strips that she wrapped around the long cut. It was hard to do in the dark, but she was relieved she would not have to see how bad the cut was. It was throbbing and she knew it would have made her sick to look at.

She turned her head, trying to place the location of the falling water. *With my luck it will be just out of rea—* She blinked her eyes, not certain if what she saw was simply a result of the fall. However, even after several moments, the dull glow in the distance did not disappear.

Reaching the location of the dim glow was much harder than Stephenie had anticipated. Most of the rocks underfoot were wet and slippery and in the overall darkness of the chamber, she still could not see around her. Which made the orange-red glow nothing more than the thin piece of hope floating in a great nothingness. For a while she feared it would be too high to reach, because the rubble she was slowly descending led down. With her left arm unable to grasp and her right ankle swelling in her boot, she knew she would be a pitiful sight to any of her trainers. But she had to wonder how many so called men would actually press on if they were in her place.

She remembered stories she had heard of burning rock that existed in some mountains to the south and what it would mean if that was what she was pursuing. She shivered, *if so, I shouldn't be this cold.* Pushing herself forward, as she neared the glow, she found the ground surprisingly clear of debris and nicely level. Crouching down, she discovered more flat stones with tight joints. Gaining confidence, she moved closer, now seeing details highlighted in the glow. From a couple feet away, she realized she was looking at a fissure in the side of a large stone wall. Feeling the smooth surface near the opening and the loose stone at her feet, it was obvious the wall had cracked.

Rising up on her toes, she could see a long opening in what was a ten foot thick wall. The level of light on the far side was much greater than what was reflected through the opening. She looked down at her dirty and bloody hands and grinned with relief. Despite her haggard appearance, it was reassuring to actually see herself and not simply be something felt in the darkness.

She pushed and pulled herself up the broken wall until she could see more clearly through the opening. However, the narrow angle of view showed her nothing. Turning her head, she concentrated on listening for any sounds coming from the other side of the wall. She could hear running water, but after waiting several minutes, heard no other sounds.

She turned her head to the darkness of the cave behind her. There was also water somewhere in that darkness, but the prospect of searching blindly for it was less than appealing. *At least if something wants to kill me, I'll see it.* Without further delay, she pulled herself into the opening and used her right arm and left foot to move through the narrow crack. The tight, oddly shaped break in the wall was difficult to navigate, scraping and wedging limbs painfully in the uneven space. However, she managed to push past the worst section without crying out in pain. When she reached the far edge, she paused again, listening for any sounds. When nothing but the water was heard, she moved further until her head extended out of the fissure.

Stephenie gasped in spite of herself. Before her was a huge chamber with a dome easily as tall as her tower if not higher. The chamber was so wide she could not see the other side even with the dim lighting that filled the vast cavern. The most startling sight was the city built of stone that spread over a series of rolling hills. The illumination appeared to be coming from many lamps burning throughout the city. However, she could see no movement or any signs of life.

All that reading I've done in the library and never have I ever heard mention of this place. She chided herself for thinking her father's library would mention something like this, it did not even mention the catacombs. Her knowledge of them had come from what Joshua had shown her and her own private exploration.

Stephenie moved slowly across the graveled ground that separated the outer dome of the cavern and a small stone wall that surrounded the city. The four foot high wall appeared to be a single solid piece of stone, topped with small decorative finials spaced at regular intervals. If she had not ached from several injuries, she would have considered easily scaling the wall. However, the dull throbbing of her still slowly bleeding arm combined with the oppressive silence kept her from doing any more than peeking over the top of the wall.

On the other side, she noted a street lamp on a metal pole. A dim glow emanated from a glass enclosure. The light was steady and without the fluctuation that would be expected from a burning flame. She squinted, trying to get a better look at what was producing the light, but a cobbled street lay between her and the lamp, making it too far to see details.

Behind the lamp was a row of two story stone buildings, each sharing the walls of its neighbors, but yet still having slightly different characteristics, like children of the same parents. A peaked slate roof, glistening with moisture, covered the buildings, but Stephenie could see no gutters.

Stepping back from the wall, she turned to her left. A few hundred feet away, she could see what appeared to be a large door in the outer dome of the chamber opposite an arch in the four foot high wall. Behind her, the outer dome and the city wall disappeared off into dimness.

Feeling somewhat light headed from loss of blood and lack of water, Stephenie quietly drew across the gravel to the door in the outer dome. It was arched with a narrow peek that stood at least thirty-five feet high. At the base, it was twenty feet across. A thin line ran down the center, separating the highly decorative scroll work on what was likely two doors. Gold, blue, red and green colors filled the field between the raised stone, depicting a series of geometric patterns and motifs. When she grew close enough, she stepped onto the cobbled street leading from the city to the door. She ran her hand over the huge door, sensing a tingling and chill that had nothing to do with the ambient temperature of the chamber. "Witchcraft," she mumbled under her breath.

Turning around, she looked back into the city. The four foot high wall was broken by the archway that mirrored the form and size of the doors. Beyond the arch was a small circular plaza surrounded by a series of street lamps, barely a third of which produced any light. Grand buildings formed the borders of the plaza and delineated at least four streets that led into the city.

Looking down, Stephenie noted a thick coating of damp dust covering the cobblestone street in a way that was more obvious than the same coating on the gravel she had crossed. Noticing no foot prints but her own, Stephenie resolved herself to continued isolation.

Shivering from the cool air and the loss of blood that was still slowly soaking into the bandage around her arm, Stephenie stopped hesitating and walked quietly under the arch and into the city. Taking a quick look around, she dismissed the streets that followed the city wall and looked instead at the other two streets. The main one was opposite the archway and wider than the second one that went off to her left.

The buildings surrounding the plaza were all two or three stories with elaborate facades, ornamented windows, and large doors. The door of a stone building to her right stood open and appeared to be off its hinges. The dark interior appeared to contain a counter of some sort.

Unnerved from the silence, Stephenie moved to the nearest street lamp that was still glowing. The light box was at least six feet off the ground and out of her reach. However, from where she stood, the rusting and dust-covered housing appeared to contain a crystal at least the size of her thumb. Glancing around, Stephenie noticed what appeared to be an old wooden crate next to a column in front of the building with the open door.

Wanting a closer look, she went to retrieve the crate, but the old wood simply collapsed when she touched it. She stared at the pile of soft and soggy wood fiber for a few moments. *They don't plan to make this easy.* She looked back at the rusty pole and wondered if she could push it over. She shook her head, not because she thought she could not, *but I am not ready to start breaking things. Who knows what might take offense.*

Sighing, she turned back to the open doorway. The thin stone door was fractured and broken. Small bits of stone extended from the door jamb, still holding part of the door. From where she stood, she could tell the interior was deserted. A crumbling wooden counter divided the interior space, separating the entrance area from a darker area that appeared to contain desks and chairs.

Mustering the courage to ignore the prickly sensation of being watched, she entered the dark building. Masses of decayed material and wood lined one of the outer walls in what had obviously been a row of chairs. Now, inside the building, she could see the remains of at least a dozen desks, some partially standing, others collapsed into piles of rot.

Carefully picking her way over what might have once been carpeting, she moved around the counter, just looking at the various remains littering the room: odd bits of metal, a number of ink wells, molded and decayed bits of wood that once might have been small portraits of a loved one.

"It's like Josh's room, bits of everything scattered about, only worse." She wrinkled her nose at the musty smell. The remains around her were old. *Very old.*

Bending down, she tried to pick up a piece of blackened paper from the floor, only to have it crumble at her touch. Next to it, she removed a ceramic cup from the floor and had to pick off the remains of the carpet that came with it.

The inside of the cup had a dark film, as if whatever had been in there molded, evaporated, and then mostly dried out long before the desk had crumbled and sent the cup across the floor. Feeling her thirst grow at the thought of tea, Stephenie set the cup carefully on the floor and rose to her feet. She took one more turn about the room and headed outside. She did not have the nerve to enter the dark stairwells and interior doors.

"Outside again, but not," she mumbled as she looked up into the darkness above her. With the dim street lights failing to clearly illuminate the ceiling of the chamber, she could almost feel it was simply a cloudy night. *But there is also no breeze, no sounds of night, nothing but distant water running.*

With only limited hesitation, she turned onto the main street and headed deeper into the city and generally toward the sound of water. On both sides of the wide street were many stone buildings. Crumbled wooden signs, that had long since broken free of the steel supports, littered the sides of the streets. Had there been people moving about, she would have considered this to have been an upper class location in Antar city, *if Antar was made of huge pieces of solid stone and not wood.* Further down the street, she found a lamp that had fallen over. Examining the pole, it appeared to have rusted and fell over in slow motion. The glass housing around the dimly glowing crystal was still intact.

Curiosity getting the better of her, she looked over the housing and found a latch that had long ago rusted into place. Frowning, she looked up and down the street, wondering at her inborn desire to make sure she was alone in a deserted city before vandalizing a broken street light.

Carefully using the heel of her boot, she pressed on the glass until a panel snapped and fell into the housing. Bending down again, she reached in and removed the crystal. Concentrating, she could feel the slightest tingle of witchcraft from the crystal, but aside from that, it felt only like a cold piece of clear quartz.

Feeling slightly better for having a bit of light to keep with her, she continued down the street, occasionally looking through a window to see the remains of a room. After the third storefront she passed, she wondered at the reason all of the furniture and even drapes, carpets, and accessories had been left behind. Even in the desperate flight from Antar, people were still taking their belongings. They removed their drapes, even ones far less decorative then what Stephenie suspected were here. *Why would everyone desert a city and yet leave almost everything behind as if they were simply going across town to visit a friend?* She was hesitant to consider an answer. This city had been deserted and abandoned for a long time. Antar castle and city above had been there for as long as memory could recall and the original castle even before then. Had any of those above known about a city deep in the rocks under their feet, there would have been stories.

Stephenie used her stolen crystal to look into a shop that reminded her of a bakery, with a large oven in the back wall and the remains of shelves still partially attached to a side wall. The sparkle of something shiny and shaped like a pendant caught her eye. Looking closer at a mass on the floor, she paused and then stepped quickly away from the window as a shiver of fear rolled down her spine.

She closed her eyes, but the unmistakable image of a human skull laying on the floor would not leave her sight. She shivered again and looked up and down the street. *Perhaps they didn't leave.*

Mustering her courage, Stephenie slowly approached the window again. She forced herself to look at the mass on the floor. Wiping away some of the dirt on the window, she could make out the arms and runners of a rocking chair mixed with what was likely clothing and the decayed bones of the person who's head had rolled several feet away after the chair had collapsed. Bits of hair and desiccated skin clung to the skull, which was fortunately staring away from the window. *The person died sitting in a chair and no one came to remove or bury the body?*

Stephenie sniffed the air and thought about the strange odor she had been noticing since she had entered the city. It was a musty sweet smell. "Is this a plague city?" She felt her throat tightening with each breath and again quickly retreated from the window. She turned toward the way she had entered the city, ready to run back to the large doors and flee, but the dryness of her throat and the sound of water stopped her. *If this is a plague city, then I am as good as dead and I might as well die after I've had something to drink.*

Slowly, she turned around and continued down the street, no longer bothering to look into the store fronts. The rot and death they held did not interest her anymore.

She passed several side streets, but continued following the slowly turning main street because the sound of water was getting louder in the direction it was heading. After a short time, the street opened into another large plaza at least a hundred feet in diameter. Several streets exited the round plaza, but at the very center, lit with several points of glowing light was a fountain. Its water pushed up from a center mound and cascaded down several stone statues into a series of white marble bowls. The fountain was a dozen feet high and thirty feet across.

Drawn by thirst, Stephenie quickly reached the edge of the fountain and could feel a cool mist splashing over her. Knowing she would die slowly and painfully from whatever disease had killed the residents of this city, she did not care if the water was poison as long as it tasted fresh. Taking a small sip, she tested the flavor and found it cleaner than what she was used to in the castle. Scooping up more water with her hands, she drank deeply before noticing how dirty her hands had become. After quickly rubbing away the dirt, she moved a couple feet away and continued to drink until her stomach felt full.

Relieved of her thirst, she sat down next to the fountain and buried her face in her wet hands. She sobbed with frustration and relief in one confused wail. While she would not die of thirst, how was she going to get out and warn her father and Joshua about her mother's betrayal? She cradled her cut arm in her lap and leaned back with her eyes closed. *I've got light and some water, but what good would warning everyone do if I bring a plague to them?* She shook her head. *Damn it, why do the gods hate me so?* Fundamentally, she knew her tie with Elrin, even if a result of her mother's doing, was her real damnation. She could not bring herself to worship the demon god and she dared not seek out the other gods for fear the priests would sense her connection to Elrin.

Opening her eyes, she stared at her foot prints along the cobbled street. A lone trail to remind her that she had to do whatever it was she was going to do on her own. There was no one to help her.

She sat silently staring into the distance for some time. Then she blinked her eyes, uncertain that she was not imagining it, but after a moment, there was definitely a strange luminescence moving down the street. As it grew closer, she scrambled to her feet, recognizing the dim outlines of a human form. The apparition was moving in her direction. She quickly moved away from the fountain, but as it closed on the fountain, it appeared not to notice Stephenie at all. Instead, it held its, *or her,* hands as if carrying something. When it reached the fountain, it leaned over as if scooping up water.

The form was not solid, it was not even complete, mostly just a head, arms, and a vague sense of a torso and upper legs. However, Stephenie moved a step further away when a mass of water rose from the pool around the fountain as if held by a bucket. Suddenly the water splashed back into the pool and the apparition faded into nothingness.

"Hello," Stephenie's voice croaked out in a bare whisper. She looked around, but there was no sign of the ghost. Feeling distinctly uncomfortable, she backed further away from the fountain. However, her uneasiness did not go away, instead it grew as she slowly became aware of a noise that sounded like a large crowd of people growing over the sounds of the fountain.

Unable to isolate the direction, Stephenie quickly left the plaza, heading deeper into the city. She passed by what were obviously a couple of dead bodies lying in front of one building. A moving glow, having a greenish tinge, but no firm shape, hovered between the door and the bodies. Feeling eyes upon her back, she ran down the street, her leather boots softly slapping against the dirty cobblestone street.

After she passed several side streets, she stopped. Bent over and breathing heavily, she was still unable to catch her breath. She tried to push the panic that had built in her mind away, but all she could think about were the dead bodies and the spirits that remained. Eventually, the trickle of blood on her hand drew her attention and she found something on which to focus.

Forcing herself upright, she took a few steps in a circle to try and relax as she used her good hand to put pressure on her cut. After she felt like she could breathe again and her heart was not racing so fast, the slow bleeding of her arm again stopped.

Light headed, she looked around the small square and for the first time, noticed a large building with a grand set of stairs. The three story tall building was surrounded with stone columns and a domed roof. A pair of large bronze doors covered in raised runes stood closed at the top of the stairs. Sculptures and statues adorned its roof and walls. Although not in her line of view, it appeared the very top of the building's roof might be open or at least contain a series of the glowing crystals, as a glow emanated from the center of the roof, partially illuminating the rough stone of the cavern's ceiling.

Feeling a chill run through her spine and the sense of being watched, Stephenie looked around the square for any signs of the glowing dead, but found none. "Josh, what would you do?" She could almost hear his voice, *"if this is a temple to a lost god, perhaps he or she will take pity on you."* She sighed, "never too late to start worshiping I guess."

Slowly, Stephenie moved toward the large building, keeping her right arm against the wall of the closest building. When she had no choice, she moved into the open and quickly ascended the stairs; silently hoping that rushing the steps would not offend the god.

At the top, she moved to the other side of the columns and instinctively glanced behind her as the sense of being watched grew. She looked over the square, but saw nothing. Fighting the prickling feeling of dread crawling over her skin, she turned back to the bronze doors and scanned the tarnished markings. The symbols held no meaning for her. With a silent prayer to Felis, she stepped forward, grabbed the large handle, and pulled at the door.

Startled by the ease that the door opened, Stephenie almost let the handle slip from her hands. However, her initial surprise was quickly forgotten by what she saw beyond the door. Inside the well lit building was a large entry with a curved counter that stood four feet high. On either side of the counter were two stone staircases going up to an open balcony that held rows and rows of bookshelves. Forgetting the ghost near the water fountain, she stepped into what was a temple of a different kind, one devoted to knowledge.

The door closed softly behind her as she walked past the counter to the stairs on the left, noting the dark walnut wood showed no sign of decay as she passed. Drawn by the pull of the books, she barely noticed the intricate carvings on the stone balusters. As the ten foot wide stairs curved to the open balcony, Stephenie fell in awe of the scale of the library. Just in front of the stacks, half a dozen large tables and a couple score of wooden chairs were arranged in a diamond pattern that complimented the stone tiles beneath her feet. Accenting the stone balusters and railing protecting the balcony's edge were a number of stone planters, now filled with nothing but dirt and the dried remains of plants.

Looking back to the stacks, Stephenie counted over thirty sets of shelves that rose at least fifteen feet in height and extended back into the darker recesses of the library. Above her, the building's dome, containing alternating clear and painted sections, was illuminated from stone alcoves. "Joshua, I've found the greatest treasure there could be."

Slowly, she walked around the tables, on which sat a few discarded books that had never been returned to their shelves. The darkened covers showed ample signs of use. She pushed aside a chair and found the wood solid and unblemished with age. "How?" she whispered as she noticed the dryness of the air in the building compared to the dampness that had existed in the rest of the city.

She picked up an open book that was on the nearby table. The paper was strong and only slightly discolored. The ink on the page crisp and not faded, despite the fact that the words conveyed no meaning to Stephenie. She flipped through several pages and then closed the book to look at the title. The leather cover appeared to have just one small word cut and dyed into the surface.

A sudden feeling of dread filled her bones and the book slipped from her fingers as her mind was filled with the sounds of inhuman rage. She turned. The need to run filled her mind; before her was a faded form of a man screaming at her. Unintelligible words slipped through her thoughts and she stumbled backwards as the man advanced with tremendous speed.

Stephenie screamed as pain ripped through her chest. *Please, Josh, don't forget me!*

Chapter 7

Stephenie slowly felt her mind awaken, as if she was simply a detached observer, clinically learning a lesson by observing someone else's mistakes. A sense of incredible agony existed in her body, but for now, she did not feel the sharpness of the pain. Her eyes were closed and somehow she lacked the strength to open them, as if the cold that permeated all of her body had frozen her in place.

She remembered seeing the arm of an angry ghost driven into her chest. She remembered the freezing cold, the blinding agony, and the spiraling sense of falling.

Gradually her sense of orientation slowed its spinning and she decided she was laying down on something hard and uncomfortable. With a greater realization of her surroundings, the pain that had moments before been simply a distant concept erupted in her mind and she gasped and cried out. Her body shook with spasms and her eyes opened to a dim and unnatural light. Her head lolled to the side and her vision slowly cleared. She was laying on one of the wooden tables, the book she had dropped earlier opened for reading.

Whimpering, she tried to sit up and found the effort almost unbearably hard. But determination won and she managed to get her right arm under her and push her upper body from the table top. Her left arm barely responded to her desires.

"I hope I hurt too much to be dead, because if death hurts this much, I don't want to be dead." She looked around, half expecting to see her own body on the floor where she was attacked. So relieved not to find her body, it took a moment for her to notice that she was a long way from where she had been attacked. She was no longer on the open balcony, but instead in a small reading room that was twenty feet by ten with a single open door looking out onto the stacks. The eight foot high ceiling held a couple of points of brilliance that provided the dim illumination.

"Okay, I didn't walk here." With growing apprehension that she might still be dead on the open balcony, she forced herself to sit up fully. Fighting against the dizziness, she slid her legs over the side of the table, determined she would be able to walk. However, before she could slip from the table, the dim and transparent form of a head and shoulders appeared before her. Too weak to jump, she could only suck in air in response.

Stephenie's terror subsided quickly as strange words filled the room. As the man spoke and he moved, his form became more defined with arms, a torso, and the majority of legs. The ghost was definitely addressing her and trying to indicate something, as his hands became almost completely opaque before shimmering again into a dim transparency.

Stephenie looked away for a moment, the ripples of definition and illumination that made up the man's body were disorienting. "I don't understand what you are saying," she whispered through parched lips.

As the words changed, Stephenie looked back at the ghost. She knew he was trying a different language and watching her intently for a reaction. Returning his intense scrutiny, she realized the ghost's face was that of a fairly young man, perhaps only in his early to mid twenties. The tone of his voice also conveyed a youth that Stephenie had not noticed.

"Understand me yet? I only know so many languages."

The heavily accented words of the Old Tongue filled the room. "Yes," she said, unsettled by the thought of talking with someone who was so obviously dead.

"Damn, Denarian," he said, tossing his hands, which lacked any defined arms, into the air. "Damn invader." He had spun away from her and was losing form.

"Wait," Stephenie said, thankful for her father's ever insistence that she learn the Old Tongue. "I'm not an invader."

The ghost's movement slowed and then suddenly she was looking at his face again as the ghost simply reformed facing her. "Who are you? And for the last time, I won't ask again, how did you get here?"

Stephenie leaned away from the glowing face immediately in front of her. "Ask again? You never asked the first time!"

She felt herself become faint from the shouting and almost fell from the table. A cold force gripped her right arm and steadied her.

When she felt more stable, she sensed the ghost speak again. "Had I not asked? Things are—"

"Wait, I can't understand you."

"Answer my questions," the ghost's voice grew cold and was more in her mind than ears.

Stephenie swallowed, but her mouth was dry. "My name is Stephenie." She watched the ghost's eyes which appeared to be more opaque than any other part of him, including the fingers on her arm. "I was lost in the tunnels. I didn't mean to upset your book."

A puzzled expression crossed the ghost's face and then one of understanding. "Your presence woke me. The city was sealed, how did someone who's use of Denarian is so bad get inside?"

Stephenie shook her head. "It's a long story. You wouldn't happen to have something to drink or perhaps to eat?" Seeing his cold expression, she continued. "I got lost in tunnels under the castle, my mother's soldiers were after me. I didn't have any light and I fell and hurt my arm." She tried to raise her left arm as proof, but the movement was stiff and painful. "I found a crack in the cave wall and crawled through into the city." Before she could say anything else, the cold force that had gripped her right arm disappeared with the ghost. She looked about the room for a moment, waiting for the ghost to reappear. "Figures," she mumbled after some time.

When the ghost did not return, she examined the small room more carefully. There were four chairs around the heavy table and a large stone planter next to the door. A small set of shelves against one wall sat empty. On the wall opposite the door was a large painting of a pastoral scene overlooking the sea. "I guess they need something to take their mind off being underground."

After an angry growl from her stomach, she forced herself off the table and into a wooden chair, where she could at least rest her back.

The movement sent spears of pain through her chest and shoulder. Gingerly she pulled her shirt free of her breaches and tried to examine her chest. "No blood soaking through the bindings." Using her right hand only, she freed her chest bindings and slowly unwrapped her breasts despite the pain and exhaustion the movement caused. Once free, she dropped the binding onto her lap and pulled up her shirt again and froze at what she saw.

Directly over her heart and covering most of her left breast was a patch of blackened skin that resembled a grasping hand. Swallowing the fear of what happened, she knew the ghost's hand had reached into her chest just before she blacked out. Touching the blackened skin, she could feel nothing. After adding pressure, sharp pain erupted below her fingers, but the rubbery skin felt dead.

She looked away. "No. I don't want to die like this."

"You should heal yourself."

Stephenie twisted in her seat. The ghost was standing before her, mostly formed, but still quite transparent. Subconsciously she pulled her shirt down.

"I did not mean to harm you."

"Didn't mean to harm me? You put your hand into my chest!"

The ghost cocked it's head to one side. "Yes, but that was before I was fully aware. Your presence woke me from the ular—trance I had obviously fallen into, but it was not until I felt your mind and a strong desire to protect someone that I realized what was happening. Once I became aware, I stopped what I was doing." The ghost moved one pace to the left, but took no steps. His face became more defined and his eyes narrowed. "You are a mage, why did you not defend yourself and why do you not heal yourself?"

Stephenie noticed that the ghost's mouth had not moved during his last statement. "You're not actually speaking, are you?"

"Are you simple in the mind? Someone of your age should understand."

"Excuse me? In case you didn't notice, you're the one who's dead. I don't know what is going on and I am cold, tired, and hungry. If you want to start again, please do so, otherwise leave me alone. Your fading in and out is giving me a headache."

The ghost vanished from her sight and she closed her eyes. *Damn, that was probably not the best response.* With a great deal of effort, she forced herself to stand and almost collapsed. Using the table to steady herself, she waited until her balance returned, then slowly moved from the room. "If everything else in this library is preserved, maybe someone will have left a midday meal."

Outside of the room, Stephenie found herself at the back of the stacks. There were several other doors along the curved wall, which she presumed were other rooms similar to the one where she had woken. Too tired to check, she walked into the stacks and could not help but to stop and look at the many shelves of books. They were fifteen feet high with rolling ladders attached to the tops. Leather and wooden bound books of various sizes filled the shelves. The words on the spines were obviously in various languages and of differing ages.

She continued to slowly glance over the titles as she walked toward the open balcony and the cluster of tables. When a pair of volumes written in the Old Tongue caught her eye, she stopped. "Pelaris, the Rise," she mumbled. "Volumes one and two." She removed the first book from the shelf and nearly dropped it from the weight.

Damn it, she swore. The weakness she was feeling throughout her body was disconcerting, but she would not allow herself to think about it for fear of what it might mean. *I will get out of here and warn Josh.* Leaving the book laying on the shelf, she continued toward the center of the library. It was as she had last seen it, aside from the book that had moved into the small reading room. *If only I didn't need to get out of here,* she mused, thinking how much knowledge was contained in the building.

Sighing, she stumbled to the curved stairs on her right and started to descend. After her second step, she felt herself growing light headed and sat down to avoid falling. "Damn that ghost."

The priests had preached many times about the sins of witches and the evil curses that had been placed on good men. Being damned to forever roam the world as a spirit had been one of the five most heinous curses. "The priests never said that spirits could harm us." She had listened to the sermons; she had no choice but to listen.

However, she had been more interested in learning what she might be capable of and not in learning a moral lesson.

She tried to stand, but her legs lacked the strength, so she remained on the steps for a few more moments. "I've got one light crystal, maybe I should grab a couple more, then head back to the wall and get out of this place. Perhaps I'll be able to find a way back into the catacombs. With light I should be able to find my way back to the surface. I'll sneak out of the castle and warn father and Josh." She closed her eyes for a moment. "After I rest for a moment. I could use a nap."

About to get up and look for something warmer and more comfortable than a wooden table, she sucked in her breath as the outer door opened. Frozen from fear, she watched as a couple of two-foot ropes floated into the library. After a moment she noticed a translucent hand separated from a shoulder and upper body. The ghost, noticing Stephenie, solidified to a mostly opaque bluish green. This time she noted details in the ghost's appearance that had simply not existed before. The man was dressed in what must have been fine attire. A tailored doublet that was not gaudy or over done. Instead it was more utilitarian, but still made of the finest material. Breeches and calf-high leather boots. A sword belt, with only a hint of a transparent sword. His face was clean shaven and his hair short and nicely combed. In all, a very handsome and confident man.

The swaying in his hand drew Stephenie's attention again and she realized what she had mistaken for ropes was really two pale white snakes. Their lack of movement told her they were dead.

"Where were you going?"

Stephenie heard the words in her head again and knew the ghost was somehow speaking into her mind. *Can he read my mind?* The stories she learned growing up about ghosts lacked any real substance and mostly had been filled with moaning and the suffering of the damned. *Can you read my mind?* She thought again, this time in the Old Tongue.

"If I should want, I could. But the effort is more trouble than value." The ghost moved toward her, the dead snakes swaying in his outstretched hand. "You have failed to answer the question and I know I asked it this time."

"I was leaving. I have to get out of here. Please, I meant no harm. I won't bother you any further."

The ghost's head cocked ever so slightly to the side. "You do not want to go outside the library. It would be unsafe. You obviously are unskilled, though I know not how someone your age should be so helpless."

"Unskilled?"

"As far as I can tell, you have done nothing to actively draw upon your power, which I sensed resisted me on a subconscious level when I attacked you."

"And why did you try to kill me?"

"I told you, I was unaware. Based on how much Arkani has decayed, I would expect many years have passed. What is the year?"

"The year? It's 435."

"That means nothing. What about the Givolar calendar?"

"The what?"

"It doesn't matter. What is 435 based upon?"

Stephenie paused, uncertain how the ghost would react. "It is when Felis and the other gods took control of the region from the witches and warlocks."

"Felis? This means nothing. Any other calendars? Significant events?"

"My family has been on the throne for over three hundred years." She frowned. "They say the elves were driven into the Rim Mountains about one thousand years ago."

The ghost nodded and started to fade slightly. "So I've been stuck in this library for more than a thousand years." He reached out a hand to Stephenie. "It does not feel that long. But I imagine I've been unaware of anything for a very long time."

Stephenie stared at his left hand and then to the right hand and the blackened heads of the snakes. It was his right hand that had been driven into her chest.

He frowned. "I will not hurt you. But you look unable to stand on your own." After a moment more. "The snakes were all I could find for you to eat. There is nothing left in the city. We died because we had run out of food, trapped here forever by your ancestors."

"What?"

"Take my hand and let us retire to a reading room. I do not want to desecrate the outer library with snake guts."

"Do you expect me to eat a raw snake?"

"No. If you showed any knowledge, I would expect you to cook the snake, but you have all the behavior of a simpleton. However, I will assume things are no longer as they should be and take care of it for you."

Growing cold on the stone steps, Stephenie gave in and reached out for the ghost's hand. She half expected her own hand to pass through his slightly transparent fingers, but instead they felt solid and returned her grasp, easily pulling her to her feet. "Why is it your hand is solid now, but before you simply appeared and disappeared?"

The ghost rolled his eyes and drew past and partially through her, pulling her up the stairs. "I am dead; however, my energy has remained coalesced, just insubstantial for physical interaction. But even children know it is a simple matter to control force."

"So you're a warlock?"

"If you are pronouncing the word correctly, then I have no idea what it is you mean."

"How is it we can speak with each other?" Stephenie asked as she allowed herself to be led back to the reading room.

The ghost noticed the book she had pulled out earlier and tsked. "Really? His work was trite, those two volumes are worthless reading."

"Please. I don't know who you are or what is going on. What do you want with me if you are not trying to kill me?"

The ghost turned around, but continued to move toward the reading room, his legs no longer moving or fully defined. "You are the first person I have had a conversation with in over a thousand years it would appear. Everyone else has been dead and lost in the trance that slowly overwhelms the dead. It should be obvious that I mean to engage you in discussion."

Stephenie stopped; the ghost's hand and left arm faded into a vague haze. "I don't have the time. I need to get out of here."

"My dear, you have nowhere to go in your current state. Had it not been for the fact that your mind reminded me of Sairy, I would have killed you. As it was, for a time, I was not certain I had not."

"I need to warn my brother."

"You need to eat." The ghost turned away and headed into the reading room.

Stephenie looked over her shoulder and wondered if she would be able to make it out of the city before the ghost came back and forced her into the reading room. The rumbling of her stomach and the smell of cooking meat decided her mind and she followed the ghost into the small room.

"How?"

"Not now. Eat." The skin of the snake parted down the length, exposing sizzling meat.

Chapter 8

Stephenie awoke slowly, her body ached and sleeping on the stone floor was not helping. She was very tired and wanted to drift back to sleep; however, the insistent need to empty her bladder was not going to be ignored much longer.

She looked around the dimly lit reading room and did not see the ghost. There was a pitcher on the table, next to the remains of the snakes. The unseasoned meat had not been unpleasant, but now that her hunger was abated, not something she immediately wanted again.

Moving slowly to her feet, she felt the strain in her chest at the effort. *What did that damn ghost do to me?* She yawned, trying to catch her breath, but it seemed that there was just not enough air for her. Despite her need to relieve herself, she was also parched. Carefully lifting the pitcher, she took a deep drink. She put it down with a little less grace, but did not spill any of the cold water. Feeling better and determined not to urinate where she stood, she moved forward, using the table, chairs, and then the door frame to steady herself.

She glanced along the back wall of the library and wondered if the ancient builders had thought to put in chamber pots. She followed the wall to the right as it curved around the perimeter of the stacks. She passed several reading rooms before the wall led her back to the grand staircases. Feeling too weak to go down the stairs to the main landing, she stumbled over to the nearest planter. It was about two feet high and filled with dry dirt and a dead plant. She looked around once more and decided to simply water the plant.

When her bladder was empty, she felt a little better. She looked around and still could not see the ghost. "Hello," she called timidly. "You here?"

When no answer came, she sighed and then moved toward the nearest stacks, looking for anything with words she could recognize. She traveled halfway down the stack before finding a section of books written in the Old Tongue. Choosing one at random, she walked back to the open area with the collection of tables. Carefully picking a chair other than the one that the ghost had presumably been using, she sat and opened the book.

Scanning a few pages, she slowly began to puzzle out the language that had been passed down through the aristocracy and the churches of Felis and the other gods. She found the words similar, but a bit different in form, as if the style of writing had changed slightly.

"That author is a slightly better choice. The subject though is uninformative."

Stephenie looked up and found the ghost standing beside her. Her mind, a little calmer than when she first encountered him, seemed to sense his presence just slightly. "You asked me questions yesterday, now it is my turn."

"You are not in tune with the daily cycle. Though, I will confess, the lights of Arkani appear to be mostly out of cycle or simply dead themselves. Why is it you are so unskilled, simple of mind you do not appear?"

"Excuse me, I believe it is my turn to ask questions."

"The tunnels from Arkani are mostly collapsed. I noted the bridge leading to the upper chambers was still partially—"

"What is your name?" Stephenie demanded.

The ghost paused. A wave of opaqueness passed over his face and chest, but faded before it reached his arms and missing lower body. "My name I have already provided."

Stephenie closed her eyes and lapsed back into Cothish to curse. She took a deep breath and looked up at the ghost who was intently studying her with his blueish green face and eyes. For a moment, she wondered what color his hair and eyes were in life. She resumed in the Old Tongue, "you have not told me your name. Just like earlier, you seem to have forgotten just what you've said and have not said."

The ghost seemed to breathe or at least his chest rose and fell. The nearest chair moved back and the ghost simply appeared in the seat before her, his arms mostly opaque and resting on the table. "My name is Karyvarti Jenxeviq. Most people had called me Kas. You will have to excuse my manners. I am still waking from what we would call the ular. I have no knowledge of a word for it that the Denarian have."

"Denarian?"

The ghost's jaw drew hard lines. "That is what you are, no?"

"I'm from Cothel."

"Well, then your ancestors are likely the spawn of the Denarian. You speak the language, if with a heavy accent."

"We call it the Old Tongue," she said with a bit of hesitation. "It's hardly spoken by anyone. Look, my name is Stephenie. I don't know what happened here Kas, but I need to leave."

"You cannot leave."

"Why?"

"The city is full of the dead. I do not think you would be able to keep them at bay. Some of them have roused slightly from the ular."

"What is the ular?"

"If you would stop interrupting the conversation, I would have already explained it to you."

Stephenie sat for a moment and then raised her eyebrows, waiting for him to continue.

"Very well. The ular is a word in Dalish. Loosely it translates to a mind numbing trance that the dead will fall into after so much time has past that they have no real connection to the living."

"I don't understand."

"I did not fully until it happened to me. For many years I remained aware, as did several others. We conversed and studied and tried to carry on a semblance of a life. However, year after year passed and many had already let slip their conscious thoughts and simply continued to relive aspects of their living life. They fell into a loop of sorts, simply repeating the same events again and again for eternity."

"That sounds terrible."

"We lose awareness of the world of others and of even ourselves. It is inevitable, if you were to live long enough, you might also detach yourself from the world even outside of death."

"You seem normal now." Stephenie blushed, "I mean, normal for someone who's dead." She shook her head. "I have no idea what is normal for the dead. I don't know what I am saying."

The ghost chuckled. "Your presence changed the environment, it disturbed my ular. But as one wakes from a long night, it takes time to become aware of what was real. I remember feeling rage and knowing my enemy was before me. I simply tried to stop the noise of your beating heart."

"And it still hurts by the way."

"My apologies for what happened, but I was hardly aware of my actions. It was not until your feeble attempt to push back with your powers roused me further into coherent thought that I became aware. Your mind and presence reminded me of Sairy, a woman I had loved before she died. I did try to reverse what I was doing."

"But that does not explain why I can't leave."

"There are thousands of us here in Arkani. Based on the time you say has passed, I am certain I am the only native left who has not fallen deep into the ular. Your presence in the city itself could disturb those out there, drawing them to an awareness of your mind. They would fall upon you and kill you."

"What's to stop them from finding me here?"

Kas smiled, "this was my library, or at least of those that remained, I was most attached to it. Even before I fell into the ular, I was usually the only one of the dead who would come here. Besides that, the building is somewhat shielded. The magic that protects the interior will hide your presence."

Stephenie sighed. She closed her eyes and thought of Joshua and her father. "I have to warn them. I will just have to risk it."

"I do not understand the language you are speaking."

"My father and brother need to be warned about what my bitch of a mother has done. Thousands of people could die. We are fighting a war and my mother just undermined all the support and supplies for the armies."

Kas remained stationary for several moments and Stephenie almost thought he might have fallen into a trance. Then he moved his arms and leaned back, in almost a natural movement. "Interesting. The descendants of the invaders are now fighting for their lives."

Stephenie cleared her throat, feeling slightly parched again. "Kas, I don't know what happened here. You obviously think I am responsible for some reason, but honestly, I've nev—" Stephenie paused, realizing that she had actually killed someone. The cold chill of fear entered her spine. "Kas, when I was trying to escape my mother, I killed someone. It was not my intent, but I was scared and trapped and I let loose my witchcraft. I just wanted them out of the way, not to die. Will they become a ghost and try to kill me?"

He leaned forward again; his eyes becoming more opaque than she had ever seen them before and Stephenie thought she could detect a hint of brown under the unsettling glow his form held.

"Stephenie, what is witchcraft? Do you mean magic? The power that you seem to have little to no understanding of?"

"I guess. You said before you don't know of Felis, but what of Elrin, the demon's god? I mean the god of the elves."

Kas shook his head again. "You are very strange. I do not think the world would have changed so much. The elves I knew never worshipped gods, at least none specifically. They honored nature and the natural order. As did most of the people of my time."

"But the gods give us power, their priests can heal or create fire or move things without touching them. I've occasionally been able to move small things. My mother did something very bad when she was carrying me and she was cursed by Elrin and so I was born with powers like the elves have. I can do things the priests can do, but I don't get my power from a holy symbol."

Kas shook his head again and slowly disappeared, "it is like talking to a brain damaged child." His words hung in the air after his body had ceased to be visible.

"Kas!" Anger at his comment lent her strength and she quickly stood and turned around, searching for any sign of him. However, weakness quickly overwhelmed her and she had to use her arm to support herself.

Damn it, how am I going to make it to father and Josh if I can't even stand up. She switched to holding herself up with her right arm while she tried to flex her left hand. Moving her fingers drew forth more pain from the cut on her arm.

Carefully, she peeled off the blood encrusted cloth she had wrapped around her arm. Concern over infection melted away when she noticed what should have been a long deep cut was now a red line about eight inches long down the outside of her forearm. The injury still hurt significantly, but it was healing quickly. "My witchcraft." She shook her head and switched to the old tongue. "Magic?" she voiced the word Kas had used. "I really don't understand Kas. It's not my fault."

She looked around and waited, but the ghost did not return. "Nothing I do seems to work the way it should." She glanced down at the book she had pulled from the shelves; it no longer held any interest. Knowing that she was not strong enough to get herself back to the crack in the wall and climb out, she decided to explore a little more around the library.

Slowly, she walked through the aisles of books and felt a little of the wonder return to her. Never before had she seen so many well kept books in one place. She tried to count the number of potential languages based on the types of characters she observed on the spines and estimated that there were at least a dozen or more languages she would need to know to read the books.

She found a series of cabinets against the outer wall on the right side of the library. Despite the fact that the contents likely belonged to someone not quite completely dead, she opened the doors to look for something useful. Inside, she found stacks of blank paper, lap desks, quills, and many bottles of dried up ink.

Closing the cabinet doors, she went back to the main entrance of the library and descended the stairs on the right hand side. She avoided the large outer doors and chose instead to explore the large counter. There were a couple of comfortable stools waiting to be used. Many stacks of ledgers, both empty and partially filled sat on shelves under the counter top. As well as small notes, written in a language Stephenie could not read. They sat, waiting for the attention of someone who, it would appear, would never return to complete the task. She found more blank paper, pens, and ink. "This much paper", she shook her head, "I could sell it in Antar and afford to buy a public house." She closed her eyes and sighed. She wondered if Jenk, Samuel, and Doug would become spirits to haunt her for failing them.

Sighing, she noticed a couple of small steps down to a door that was just on the inside of the left staircase. Feeling a little better after moving around, she descended the two steps. The door was made of wood and covered in a high gloss varnish that made the grains almost iridescent. Turning the handle, she pushed open the door and looked away as light suddenly filled the dark opening.

Blinking and squinting to get used to the sudden change in illumination, she examined the small room under the main stacks. The room had only a seven foot high ceiling. There were three wooden doors, none of which were as ornate as the one she had just opened. The light emanated from the the center of the ceiling and was too bright for her to get a good impression of what was generating the illumination.

Stephenie walked slowly to the first door on the left and pulled on the handle. The door swung open, and as with the chamber she was standing in, the room suddenly became bright with illumination. She gasped and released the door, which slowly closed on its own. A shiver ran down her spine and she tried to put aside the memory of what she had seen. However, the piles of dried bodies, stored much like firewood would not leave her mind. It had taken a moment to make sense of the hair and leathered skin. It had not been what she had expected and the feeling of being watched was incredibly strong. She looked around, and seeing no one in the bright light, she quickly left the room, shutting the door firmly as she exited.

She glanced at the large doors leading outside the library and hesitated, she had seen lots of ghosts out there, but staying in the library meant staying in a building full of bodies.

"Rest is what you should be acquiring."

Stephenie turned. Kas' mostly transparent form was behind the counter. "There are bodies down there, under the stacks. Are all three rooms filled with bodies? Are you down there?"

Kas shook his head and moved in her direction, with the faint outline of legless feet materializing and disappearing with each contact of the floor. "It seemed the best place to put the initial dead. We feared disease. The library keeps things dry and preserved. So we made use of some of the rooms on the first level to hold the bodies. We still had, at that time, hope."

Stephenie could feel the sense of defeat in his words. Her skin still tingled with the sense of dread, but for the moment, she was not overcome with panic to get away. "I really don't understand."

Kas moved past her and up the stairs. "Come, I will try to explain. Though you seem to lack even basic concepts." He did not wait for her at the top of the stairs, but simply drifted out of her sight.

"Damn it," she mumbled in Cothish and then climbed the steps. She did not see him when she reached the tables. Closing her eyes, she tried to open her mind to sense the ghost. After a moment, she thought she might be able to feel something in the reading room near the back of the stacks. Reluctantly, she went back to the room with the dead snakes and pitcher of water. Kas was waiting for her, sitting in a chair. Feeling thirsty, she took a drink and then sat down. The exertion of the exploration was catching up to her.

"Arkani fell in a war long ago. The Dalar kingdom, which we were a part of, as well as the other countries to our west, faced an invasion from the Denarian empire. The elven wars were nearly over and many of the human cities had wrestled control from the elves. In Dalar, we supported a faction of the elves that had not been bent on war, but as the invasion continued, most of the elves had retreated with their families to the north east or far to the south.

"When the Denarians arrived, we retreated into this city underground. We knew we could seal it and expected to be able to withstand the invasion force. Once inside, we used our magic to further seal the doors, walls, and all entrances. We expected the Denarians to try to break through our defenses. However, instead of doing that, they simply decided to seal us in as well. Their magic, combined with ours, created a barrier that could not be breached. We tried to break out for a while, until we realized it was impossible.

"There were several thousand of us here. After time, we ran low on supplies and people started to die. It was a terrible time, people struggling with the desperation of being trapped forever and slowly starving. Many people took their own lives, thinking it would allow others to live longer.

"It was shortly after the first people started to die that it was noticed that the dead had not fully died. Our energy or spirits did not disassociate. Instead, they remained trapped in Arkani as well. The living trapped until they died, the dead trapped for eternity thereafter.

"Mages have searched for ways to carry on after death for all of history and a few had managed, but in the act of trying to preserve our lives, we managed to preserve a whole city through death."

Stephenie cleared her throat. "I don't understand. Dying here means you will live forever as a ghost?"

Kas shook his head and looked toward the left wall for a while before turning his gaze back to Stephenie. "The power that sealed us in is obviously broken. The outer wall is cracked. I would imagine that the dead would easily disassociate now, if something interrupted the cohesive forces holding them together.

"We tried it with the first few spirits, but they simply reformed." He leaned forward. "It is common understanding that only an exceedingly strong-willed individual with a significant skill would even have a chance of holding together the energy that their body contains during death. The energy in most people simply disassociates. It scatters and disperses."

Watching her, he shook his head. "Have you had no training at all?" he asked, a bewildered contempt in his voice.

Stephenie leaned forward. "Kas, I don't know what your world was like, but I grew up with people like me being shunned and burned. The priests control everything around the Sea of Tet and if they knew about me, I'd be dead."

"Is this more nonsense about curses?"

"Well, as I understand it, my powers come from Elrin, who is supposed to be a demon god the elves worship. My mother, the damn bitch who will get my brother and father killed, had done something evil and against the gods while she carried me, that is why I have these powers of Elrin."

Kas shook his head. "This is what people today believe?"

"It is what I have always been taught. My mother would have killed me, except she feared the curse on me would fall on her if I was to die."

"Magic is not conveyed through curses. If your ancestors had the capability to do magic, they can pass that capability on to you by the fact that they gave birth to you. There is no other reason you would have the ability to use magic." He looked away. "What stupidity."

"What about the priests? I have always been told they get their powers from the gods."

"We had no gods that would break the laws of nature and grant powers to people. Either they are new or something else you do not understand."

Stephenie slumped her shoulders. "The priests have been around for ages. They have metal statues blessed by their gods that pass power on to the holy symbols the priests use."

Kas stood and appeared to curse, though Stephenie did not understand the words. He moved quickly about the room, drifting at one point through the wall and then the chair before coming to a stop in front of her. She looked up into his eyes and for a moment grew afraid of the intensity of his face. After a moment, he relaxed and he sat down again in the chair he had been using.

"What was that about?"

Kas chuckled. "I do not know why I allowed myself to get angry. The power of stupidity is insurmountable. Besides, I am dead, what care should I have?"

"I'm sorry I'm so stupid, but I can't do anything about it if no one will teach me."

Kas leaned forward. "My comment was not about you specifically, but a generalization of people as a whole. Who would have ever thought that those using an augmentation device would become considered gods, or more precisely, the priests of gods? This is really something to consider and study. What kinds of lies and events could lead to an entire society of people losing even the most basic understanding of the world."

"I really am tired of saying this, but I don't understand what you are saying."

Kas smiled at her. "Considering you are speaking the language of the Denarian, albeit with an accent and some odd word usage and inflections, I will assume that you do not understand the implications of what I have said, not specifically the words I have used."

Stephenie glared at the ghost, certain she would like to slap him if her hand would not pass through his face.

"My point, young Stephenie, is this. The people you believe to be priests are nothing more than magic users that are using a means to extract energy from another world. These devices were constructed to help give people access to more power without taxing their own physical bodies so much.

"It was several years after the initial discoveries were made that the nature of where this energy was coming from was brought to light. You see, the construct and link to the other world formed some kind of magical trap. The initial team that created it believed it was just pulling some energy away, like a small tap in a wine barrel. However, the truth that was later revealed was that it was more like a bear trap and a being in that world was caught in it. The power drew away the life energy of that being. When the being died, the power stopped until something else fell into the trap."

"You mean the priests are getting their power by killing someone in another world?"

"By someone, I hope you mean a general living creature and not a human or elf or one of the others in our world. If so, that would be correct. We do not know the nature of the creatures that were being killed, the world that was being tapped was very different than our own. Most people, after learning the truth rejected these augmentation towers and stopped using them. The elves almost completely. There were still several groups of people in my time that refused to give up this source of energy, claiming need, right, or simply desire. These people tended to be subjugated when possible. Many countries banned the use on principal. The Denarians did not."

"Then how did they become the ones in charge?"

"That was the point of my comment earlier. It would be an interesting study to trace back the history. My guess is the Denarians conquered and their legacy remained."

"Kas, that is all well and good, but I really don't have time to study the hows and whys. I really need to warn my father and brother about what has happened. Can you help me?"

Kas looked at her for a while before responding. "I am dead. While I am now more a creature of energy than anything else, I do not have the same abilities I had when I lived. You need to heal yourself if you do plan to leave here."

Chapter 9

Stephenie awoke and it took several moments before she realized she was sleeping on a table. The stone floor had been too cold, if not really any harder. She sighed as she sat up, still very groggy and feeling quite dehydrated. Sitting on the floor was the pitcher of water and what appeared to be three new, if not smaller, albino cave snakes. She started to turn up her nose at the dead snakes, but her stomach was growling and she knew eventually she would end up eating them as she had the other snakes.

Getting to her feet was a little easier than it had been the last time she awoke. Her chest, arm, and ankle still hurt a lot and it took some time to catch her breath, but she was not as winded quite as quickly. *Small miracles.* Drinking the cold water made her feel better. She went out of the reading room to make use of the chamber pot she had fashioned out of the planter, then returned with a couple of books she found on the stacks. However, there was already a book on the table.

"This is a Dalish to Denarian guide. You should learn to speak and read a reasonable language if you intend to gain much from this library."

"Kas, I would love to explore these books, but I don't have the time. I need to find a way out of here. I'm sure with a couple of your lamp stones, I could eventually get back to the surface."

He frowned at her. "Your mind is quiet, but I think that is more a factor that your thought patterns are not quite normal. You might have a chance of escaping the city unnoticed, if you are lucky, but you would improve your chances if you learned to shield your thoughts. However, the agony you expose when you are moving would likely draw attention."

"How do I heal myself?"

"Well, first you need to eat. You cannot heal without fuel, not unless you are extremely powerful and skilled."

"The snake is not the best tasting food."

Kas blinked out of sight and reappeared sitting in the chair he had been using. "Your witchcraft, as you call it, is nothing more than your ability to channel and direct energy. Bending it to your will. What is heat?"

Something I don't have enough of right now, she thought sarcastically. Her clothing was a thin cotton, quality material, but primarily good for summer, not cold underground caves. "Heat is fire," she said after a bit, realizing Kas was not going to say anything until after she did.

"Incorrect. Heat is the result of excitement. If you direct a form of energy at matter, you can cause it to become more excited. Or perhaps the term vibration will work for you. Rubbing your hands together makes them warm."

"Okay," she said, wanting to take his advice and do just that, except it would hurt her left arm to even attempt it.

"Objects, physical things are made up of smaller and smaller pieces. If you get these very small pieces moving against each other, even if they are moving ever so slightly, they will warm, and if they warm enough, to have more heat than the surrounding matter, or your body, then they will emit heat that you or the colder matter will absorb.

"Fire is the result of air combining with gases that come off certain types of matter when they get hot. The resulting reaction produces what you call fire."

"How do I do that?"

"Do what? For what purpose?"

"Generate fire. I want to cook the snakes. You did something to them yesterday or whenever that was."

"It was likely one and one half days ago, but the passage of time is hard for me to track, even as conscious as I am now. But more importantly, you do not want fire. This is a library. You simply want heat, not too much heat or you might get a spontaneous ignition of fire. But in my day, we cooked the meat until it was done, we did not char it until it was burnt."

Stephenie exhaled to keep from saying something rude, then realized she did not know anything really rude in the Old Tongue, so she cursed in Cothish before turning back to Kas. "Please explain to the simple child how to heat the snake meat so I can stand to eat it."

Kas grinned and leaned forward. "In your head, you have a part of your mind that can influence the energy around us. Your eyes see light, your skin feels heat. Light and heat are just slightly different forms of energy, different wavelengths of energy. This part of your mind can interact with a slightly different form of energy. In my day, perhaps thirty in one hundred could use the energy or magic as it had been called before it was better understood. For the elves, it was more like nine out of ten. Do you know if these ratios have changed?"

"Kas, I have no way of knowing. But I am hungry."

He nodded his head and Stephenie noted he was far more complete and opaque than he had been at any time previously. "You have tapped into this energy, I felt it when you resisted me. I sense your subconscious usage of it from time to time. You have ability, but you know less than nothing, because the lies you do know prevent you from understanding the truth."

"Okay, I get it, I'm a simpleton. Tell me what I need to do."

Kas shook his head and with his more defined features she could see his annoyance. "I am not saying you were simple of mind. Just ignorant. Obviously, ignorant enough not to understand the difference."

Stephenie took a deep breath. "I must be losing my mind, I am arguing with a dead man."

Kas shook his head again. "I will not take the time to correct your premise on arguing, perhaps you do not understand the language enough to use the words correctly. However, let us focus on you generating heat. I will not explain how you can generate a low power field that will control the higher power field of energy around you. Instead, you have functioned on instinct this far in your life, so let us see what that provides you." Kas actually rose from his chair in a far more living motion than Stephenie had seen him perform previously. "Calm yourself and try to reach out with your mind to feel the energy around you. It is part of you, part of the stone, the books, the tables, the stacks, and even the air. The energy is part of everything. Some things give up the energy more readily than others. Some things store more energy than others, think of it as density." He shook his head after watching her reaction. "Like weight, but that is technically incorrect.

"It is trapped, like the juices of an apple. There is a surface tension like the skin of the apple. Once broken, it more easily flows." He turned his head slightly to the side. "You still have apples, green or red fruit that grows on trees and about the size of what used to be my hand?"

"We still have apples. At least during the summer and fall. You had seasons when you were alive, right?" She sighed. "Sorry, but thinking about a nice juicy apple does not make these snakes any more appetizing."

He grinned, not appearing to have taken offense. "Have you ever been aware enough to sense the energy around you?"

She hesitated. "Yes. I often feel there is something around me, perhaps an extension of myself. I feel it more during a storm or leaning against the battlements of the castle or the walls of the keep. I can almost touch what is there."

"You can touch it. You are absorbing small amounts all the time, pulling it into your body. You become something of a depression or hole in space which the energy will drain into. You need small amounts of energy in you to generate the fields that channel the energy from one place to another. You can control the variations of the energy, the types, what it does, and the impact it has by varying the field your mind creates.

"What you do not want to do is channel all the energy through your body. That is how most people start, but it is very hard on the body and can kill you if you channel too much energy. The skilled use the energy to create fields. However, that is more difficult to master.

"Now sense the energy around us, tell me what you feel. Close your eyes if you must. It may take a while for you to distinguish the energy from the objects."

Stephenie wanted to keep her eyes open to spite the dead man, but practicality overrode her stubborn nature. She took a slow, deep breath with her eyes closed, wondering what lunacy she had succumbed to that allowed her to listen to a dead man and play with what was likely her own damnation. The thought that perhaps this was how the demon god really did work, confusing and deluding people into accepting his power crossed her mind, but she was curious and hungry enough that it did not remain.

"What do you sense?"

Stephenie frowned. She tried to clear the random thoughts from her mind and simply feel. She put aside the fear and inhibition that had always kept her from really trying to use her witchcraft. After a moment, she took another deep breath and allowed her mind to open up. A presence she knew to be Kas was close by her. It was like, but yet so different than when she felt anyone living. It had been what she had started to sense before, just that now she felt the dead man with much more clarity.

"This thing, I don't know how to describe it, but it almost feels like everything is radiating—something. Like it has an aura. Is that what I am supposed to feel?"

"Yes, actually it is. You are a hole in the world, a cold spot where heat or energy will move. Be careful to limit how much you pull into yourself. Many unskilled and ignorant people have simply burned out their bodies and minds. Some have more tolerances than others, but no one can sustain large amounts for any length of time. Consider moving a finger through the flames of a candle compared to holding your hand in a bonfire."

"Okay, so how do I cook with this?"

Kas chuckled and Stephenie opened her eyes. "Ever the eager girl. You—"

"I'm seventeen and I've been learning to use weapons for the last ten years. I—"

"Ever the eager young lady," he said with a wide grin.

"Now that you're nearly solid looking, you really don't look that much older than me."

"I am vastly older than you. I died more than one thousand years ago by your reckoning."

"Ya, ya, but at what age and you don't remember much of any of the time in between from what you've said, so really, does it count?"

Kas appeared to take a slow breath. "I was twenty five when I died. As a result of your people I might add. So perhaps, you might consider not trying to remind me of reasons I should kill you."

Stephenie turned to face him. "I'm sorry Kas. I just don't like people assuming I can't do things because I'm a girl or don't appear to be that old. I'd have been married three years ago, if the people I'd been promised to didn't keep dying." He raised an eyebrow and Stephenie decided to continue. "When I was born, my mother didn't know what I was, and they planned to marry me off to some prince in the southeast. He was two years older than I and died within six months of the promise of marriage. The next prince I was promised to, when I was five, survived the arrangement one whole year. The last one died nine months after the promises were made. Finally, they decided to stop finding me people to marry. My mother kept accusing me of killing them with curses."

"Back to the curses again?"

"I'm just saying that is all I ever knew. I'm sorry that you were killed. But I have no way to know if anyone in my family line was involved in any way."

"We shall see. As nobility, you are more likely to be a descendent of the Denarian or a descendent of one of their puppets." Kas slid to the left and faded slightly, losing feet and most of his legs.

"Wait. Please don't leave. I need to learn this. I promise to be nice."

He solidified and looked at her. "I apologize, I was drifting into thought, not necessarily leaving you intentionally. Before I did die, it was something we observed of the dead. They would lose track of the current situation and time, stopping a conversation and then picking it up hours later as though only a moment happened, not aware that the people they had been talking to were no longer there. We were unable to explain fully the reasons, but we suspected it was some amount of disassociation that was occurring in the energy that remained of the person. Fluctuations in the energy fields that the dead seemed to be more susceptible to."

He looked down at the snakes. "Use your instincts and try to direct energy into the snakes. Try not to draw too much into yourself, but imagine connecting a line of energy from a source outside of you and into the snake's bodies."

Stephenie closed her eyes again. She could sense the aura of energy coming from all around her, internally, she could almost visualize it. She could even sense the snakes, seeming both cold physically as well as limited in energy. The floor and walls seemed to have a lot of stored energy, the air less.

She tried to imagine the energy flowing from the floor at her feet to the snakes. She thought she could almost see a tenuous connection from her feet to the snakes, but nothing seemed to be happening. She felt her hands tingle as if she had slept on them too long.

"You cannot force the energy to move, you must give it a channel through which it can flow."

She opened her eyes, steadied herself by leaning on the table, and shook her hands to restart the blood flowing, which sent pain through her left arm.

"I don't know what I am doing. Nothing is working."

"If you simply give up this easily, then you will soon be dead and no longer my concern."

Stephenie glared at the ghost. She did not appreciate the condescension in his tone. She looked back to the snakes and took another deep breath. She wanted energy to go to the snakes. She sensed it all around her, but Kas had been correct, she was unable to force it. Deciding to work backwards, she imagined a low spot of the floor where the snakes were lying and then visualized a trough or irrigation channel leading down from the air into the snakes bodies.

Almost immediately, she sensed a shift in the energy around her, it was subtle, but there, like watching dust illuminated by a ray of sun twirl about in a gentle breeze blowing through a window. She concentrated on the snakes, imagining a larger hole and a deeper slope. There was a slight sizzling. Stephenie ducked and turned her head, knowing to move just moments ahead of the imminent explosion.

When she opened her eyes and looked back to the snakes, there was a scorched mark on the floor. Bits of burnt and charred flesh covered the walls, ceiling, floor, as well as her own body.

"What did you do?" Kas demanded. "I told you to be careful."

Stephenie looked toward the ghost, uncertain how much wonder had been in his voice. "I did what you said, tried to make a channel for the energy to flow."

He looked her over, as if seeing her anew. His head flashed toward the snake and then took the time to turn back toward her. "That was way too much energy," his voice this time filled with definite wonder. He shook his head and smiled. "You might consider eating the bits you find. I do not know how many more snakes of sufficient size I will find."

Stephenie held her exasperated face for a moment longer, then sighed. Nothing in her life had ever really gone exactly to her plans. Picking off some unidentified remains from her shirt, she found something that looked like meat and took a quick bite. It was a bit rubbery and held a slight fishy taste, but to her hungry stomach, was definitely more palatable than nothing.

Giving up on being proud, she slowly knelt down and started finding bits of meat and putting them in her mouth and quickly swallowing. Long bits of skin, bones, as well as the heads and tails she tossed into a pile over the scorched floor stones.

She took several drinks of water to wash down the increasingly cold and less and less palatable meat. When she had as much as she was willing to stomach, she used a bit of the water to wash the snake remains from her face and hands. She knew there were bits of snake left in her hair, but she did not have a mirror and so she would pretend to ignore them for the time being.

When she was done, she noticed that Kas had left at some point. She tried closing her eyes and searching for him with her mind, but could not sense him nearby. She had not noticed his departure and wondered if people more attuned to magic were more sensitive than her.

Slowly she rose to her feet and wobbled. She was incredibly drained and felt a weakness in her limbs and body. Cursing softly, she climbed back onto the table and laid her head down on the small pile of books. She fell asleep almost instantly.

Stephenie awoke with a headache and a sore back. The room had darkened at some point, but was slowly brightening after her movement. She looked around, noticed a fresh pitcher of water and quickly moved to get a drink. Her hands and skin felt incredibly dry. She thought about the dried and shriveled up corpses in the rooms below the main set of stacks and shuddered. The building was definitely drying her out.

She drank more than half the water, which seemed to help her headache slightly. Putting the pitcher back on the table, she picked up the books, including the translation guide, and slowly walked back into the main stacks. She opened her senses as she walked, but sensed no one near her. "Either I am alone, or not doing it correctly," she mumbled. After a moment, she called out to Kas, but no response was returned.

Shrugging, she decided to take a more careful review of the bookshelves, looking for books that she might possibly be able to read. She spent some time, moving slowly due to her injuries and general weakness. She found a section on basic energy control. The first book she pulled from the shelves appeared to be very old and worn. She flipped through some pages, finding diagrams and drawings with many symbols she could not recognize. The text on the page was written in the Old Tongue, but while she could read the words, the meaning was beyond her. She picked out a couple more books and found them equally unfriendly.

Frowning, she moved down the shelves a little further and picked out another book. It was nearly as worn as the first, but lacked the diagrams. She started to read the first page and thought the book might be intended for someone just having learned to read and study magic. "Perfect." Struggling to rise on her sore legs and ankle, she walked to the central area with the tables and sat down to read.

She got up a couple of times to relieve herself as well as retrieve the pitcher of water, which she finished to the last drop. The book was not overly exciting, but she was learning that the author was intending to make sure the reader understood beyond doubt that magic was anything except magical. The author, a Ritalnish, which Stephenie thought to be male, was explaining that magic behaved in a very predictable manner and everything that happened could be explained and described mathematically. She grinned at one page that showed examples of a proof that Ritalnish said would explain the fundamentals of much magical theory, but would not be the subject of the book. The strange symbols and diagrams were similar to the other books she had thumbed through.

"Mathematics were never this complicated," she mumbled. She was proud of her skill with mathematics. Joshua had taught her how to calculate the amount of draw needed on a trebuchet for stones of varying weights and to adjust for the distance and location of targets. She had been good at that, but the numbers and symbols on the pages of these books were completely foreign.

She continued to read, taking breaks every so often, but staying focused on trying to understand the book. Sitting back, she wished for the hundredth time that the library had more comfortable chairs. Her father's library had a very comfortable chair that was stuffed and large enough she could curl up in it. He had told her when she was very small that she used to completely curl up as if she were a cat and sleep there for hours. Stephenie only vaguely remembered doing as he had described, but the memory of her father brought a tear to her eyes.

She pushed the book away and looked about for the now umpteenth time for Kas, but she could not sense the ghost. She frowned, wondering if he had fallen into that ghost like trance he kept describing to her. She did not understand the dead man, but strange as it was, he was her only contact with another sentient being and she missed his presence.

Stephenie awoke feeling worse than when she had lain down to rest. Her mouth was dry and her head was throbbing. Slowly she moved herself from the table top to the closest chair. She looked around and noticed the pitcher was where she had last left it, still empty on the floor.

She forced herself to walk back to the large group of tables in the hopes it would drive the rising panic from her mind. Kas was her only connection with anything and if he was gone, she would have to venture out of the library on her own. "So damn thirsty," she mumbled.

She closed her eyes and balled up her right fist, her left arm ached too much if she moved it. She opened her eyes, but Kas had not appeared and she could sense no one in the library with her. Sighing, she sat down in front of the book and started flipping through the chapters she had not read, hoping to find some explanations on how to do the numerous things she had already read that magic could do.

She had read that those with sufficient skill and power could reform matter to their whims and that made her think of creating food and water. However, the author had made it clear that it would not be something he would cover in the book. She skimmed a section on telekinesis, which she learned involved moving things with her mind. The reading of emotions and thoughts she also skipped. She stopped again when the author started talking about healing and dove into those pages.

After some time, she pushed the book away again. Healing involved so many of the other skills, even a little bit of reforming matter. The author alluded to the subconscious mind being able to direct a person to what was wrong and how to perform the healing, but frustratingly enough, did not provide concrete examples or explanations.

She closed her eyes and slouched further into the hard chair. Allowing her mind to drift, she tried to let her subconscious instinctively realize what was wrong with her body. She slowed her breathing and concentrated on her arm. *I know what is bloody wrong there, a deep cut from a sharp rock.* She tried to put aside the twisted ankle and injured ribs, hoping that her arm would spontaneously heal itself.

She remained sitting quietly for many minutes before she sensed a growing presence appear in the library's entry. She sighed, hoping

Kas had brought some food and water with him. Opening her eyes, she slowly rose to her feet and walked toward the balcony. The presence seemed to be fading in and out of her awareness and hovering in the middle of the entry area, but not near the floor. She squinted her eyes, searching for any sign of Kas. After a moment, she thought she saw a faint illumination reflecting off the far wall, but his form was not visible.

"Kas, even if you don't have food, I am dying for something to drink."

Stephenie's skin started to crawl and she instinctively stepped back. There was a hostility in the air. Almost a taste in the back of her mouth that was not the result of poorly cooked snake and a lack of hygiene. "Kas?"

Stephenie stepped quickly to the left as she felt a chill fill the air. Where she had been a moment before was the head, shoulders, and arm of a person she did not recognize. Rage emanated from the form. Except for the eyes, the facial features were so translucent that it was impossible to focus on what Stephenie was sure had been a man.

She stumbled backwards, barely avoiding the hand that had reached for her, but managing to keep her feet. "Get away from me," she shouted as she flung the chair that had been in her way at the ghost. The chair flew through the man's head without visible impact. The ghost advanced quicker than Stephenie could move, blinking into existence inches from her. She felt pain rip through her left shoulder.

Screaming, she tried to twist away. She felt the ghost move with her, his energy a cloud that was moving to envelope her. She wanted the ghost and its energy to go away. Knowing she was about to be killed, she tried imagining a hole or depression in the energy field on the other side of the room and formed a link from that depression to the energy of the ghost.

For a moment, she felt the burning in her shoulder increase, then suddenly it vanished as a faint bolt of lightning flashed between the floor and the field of energy before her. She fell backward in reaction to the subsequent crack of localized thunder that rumbled within inches of her.

Landing on her rear and right side, she glanced in the direction of where she had hoped to draw the ghost. She sensed a presence still in the room, but it was vague. Slowly it began to form again and Stephenie shuddered at the overwhelming sense of rage.

"Damn it Kas, where are you?"

She swallowed and tried again to tie the ghost to the floor, linking the energy of the dead man to a place further away from her. This time, she tried to imagine a bigger channel to draw away the energy she could almost see.

The rage coming from the presence grew, then faded as did the sense of a consciousness that had accompanied the presence until both seemed to go away. Stephenie released her concentration and carefully laid her head and shoulders on the cold floor. She could not remember ever feeling so utterly drained.

After some time, she forced herself to sit up. She was fairly certain she was alone. With significant effort, she stumbled to her feet and went over to examine the floor where she had placed the energy drain. The stone floor was discolored, cracked, chipped, and still quite warm.

She sat down in the nearest chair and pulled off her shirt. Her shoulder was blistered and red, as if burned from the cold, but not as bad as her chest had been. Frowning, she unwound the binding around her chest and examined the blackened hand print on her breast. She touched the discolored flesh, but could not feel it until she put pressure on the area. She checked her shoulder again. "I just don't need to be covered in claw prints."

After wrapping the bindings around her chest again, she put her shirt back on and returned to the book she had been reading. The thought that lightning would likely be a very effective way to deal with her mother stuck in the back of her mind.

Stephenie awoke to the sound of Kas' voice in her head. Her body ached and her neck was stiff from having fallen asleep slumped over the table's edge. "Where have you been?"

"I was exploring and I must have lost track of time. How long was I gone?"

Stephenie wiped the grime from her eyes and turned in her chair to face the ghost, who was nearly complete in form. "I have no idea. I'm about to die of thirst and hunger is all I know." Spying the pitcher on a nearby table, she quickly retrieved it and drank half of its contents before turning her attention back to Kas.

"There was a ghost that came into the library."

Kas moved toward her a step. "Are you okay? Did the ghost notice you?"

She grunted and pulled the collar of her shirt to the side to show her red and painful shoulder. "When I move my arm it feels like I am grinding the bones together. It's great to be here. Every few days something else tries to kill me. And since there really is no curse that will fall on my mother, I'd have no pleasure at dying anymore."

"I brought you something more pleasant to eat."

Stephenie looked around and noticed three dead rabbits on the floor, next to an old dagger. "Where did you get those?"

"I told you, I was exploring. I have not been far from this library for hundreds and hundreds of years. I see many of the tunnels that used to lead to the surface have collapsed. However, there are still gaps. It would be possible to get out."

Stephenie forgot the rabbits and her hunger for a moment. "Really, I can get out? I was thinking I could use telekinesis to lift myself back up to the passage I had fallen through. Then make my way back into the castle. But if you found a way out."

"Stephenie, I doubt that you would be able to master any such skill in the near term. Your better bet would be to crawl through the collapsed passages. However, your ribs and arm will be a limiting factor. You will need to heal before you have the strength."

"Kas, I need to warn my father and brother. If I don't there will be hundreds or thousands of people that will die." Her stomach rumbled and she glanced back to the rabbits. "You could lift me back into the passages, yes? You have the ability to move things, you moved me from the floor to the desk in the other room."

"Stephenie. Eat first. Tell me about this ghost who injured your shoulder. I see a scorch mark on the floor. Did you do that?"

She went over to the rabbits and picked up the dagger. The blade and handle were covered in dirt and debris. She knocked and scraped the blade against the edge of table and watched in surprise as a clean and sharp blade materialized from beneath the grime and dirt. The metal appeared to be some kind of darkened steel, but no rust marked the blade.

"Where did you get this?"

"It was mine when I was alive. The blade has some limited intelligence, but you will not likely feel it."

"Intelligence?"

Kas sat down, making an effort to generate a sigh. "Yes, anything that is enchanted or magical as you might now refer to things, must have some amount of limited intelligence imbedded into the object. It is that intelligence that allows the power or magical properties of the object to remain active. Otherwise, the object would lose the enchantments as soon as the person who created it stopped providing power to it."

"I don't understand. You mean this dagger can talk?"

"Of course not. Stephenie, there are years worth of teaching you should have received. That dagger's enchantment is to remain sharp and strong. It does not burst into flame and is not a large sink."

"Sink?"

Kas chuckled. "I should learn to keep my own thoughts focused and to task."

He leaned forward. "A sink is like a reservoir or battery—please do not ask," he added raising his hand. "Think of it as a storage device that can hold and trap energy for ready release. You hardly understand anything about magic, I will not confuse you more with talk of energy sinks."

"I'm not stupid Kas."

"No, you are ignorant. Ignorance can be fixed with time." He stood and moved over to her to watch as she butchered the rabbits. "You do seem to be somewhat skilled at that."

Stephenie grinned as she was careful to toss aside the offal without contaminating the meat. "My brother was fond of hunting and insisted that as a soldier, I would need to know how to feed myself if necessary. He'd make me cook up whatever we caught." She looked up at Kas and smiled. "I think it was more because he didn't like doing it than to teach me anything."

"I will admit that I never butchered an animal. My family was well off enough and I had a living that did not involve manual labor. Most of those who are skilled with magic fall into that category. I would not expect any prince or princess in my time to have such skills."

Stephenie wiped her brow with her right shoulder. Cutting up the first rabbit with a severely limited left arm was somewhat challenging. "Most princes and princesses now would not be able to do this either. My older sisters were very proper, if not simply bitches. I liked Kara a lot, she was the oldest of us girls. She was kind and never understood why our mother hated me. She's dead now. She was killed by the invading Senzar army.

"There was this ship that came up the coast, she was married to the crown prince of Esland, which is on the Endless Sea to the West. They claimed to be emissaries as I understand it. In an audience, these emissaries killed all of the royal family including my sister. They declared themselves rulers of the country and within days, more than a hundred ships had landed." Stephenie sat back with the half skinned rabbit between her legs.

"They started to advance their forces through Esland, my other sister Islet, who is just less than two years older than me, she's married to the crown prince of Ipith, which is just to the north of Esland. Well, she heard of what happened and they sent their forces into battle as they sent word to my father. Their soldiers and priests found that the invaders had witches and warlocks in their numbers. Magic users," she corrected. "They were strong and powerful. But we had more soldiers than the Senzar did, and the invaders were pushed back to the coast.

"My father sent forces, as did Durland, Urmas, Selith, and a few others. But more ships landed and hit squads of their magic users started going after leaders. They captured Islet and her husband. They demanded that my father and others withdraw or they would kill Islet." She took a deep breath and wiped away some tears that had clouded her eyes. "It pains me to say it, but I know withdrawing would not save Islet. There would be nothing that could. My father and brother said as much themselves."

Stephenie went back to skinning the rabbit. "My guess is my mother tried to make a deal with the invaders. Sabotage my father and the war in exchange for Islet. I know that supplies that should have been going to the front were held up. I think my uncle's troops that had arrived were here to take the supplies north and not to the Greys."

"What is it these invaders are after?"

Stephenie shrugged. "I don't know. They made their way to the Grey Mountains and were moving into the northern part of the range the last I heard. There really are no good passes, not for an army. So if they wanted to get into Cothel, they'd have to go further north around them, like my father and Josh did, or they'd have to go south. Going south would be a long trek, through two more countries and nearly back to the Sea of Tet and the straights. Not much information has gotten back to me recently. My mother has done her best to make sure of that."

"These Grey Mountains, are they in the middle between the seas?"

"Yes." She watched his contemplative expression for a moment. "What is it? Do you know something?"

Kas turned his attention back to her. "I know many things, but for your specific meaning, I am not sure. I've been dead a long time. Much could have changed. However, there was once a very powerful magic user that made his home in that mountain range. The invaders who ultimately killed me had originally been trying to take control of Gimtar's holdings. They were repelled in my day, at least before I died. Perhaps he outlasted them and they are back to try and get his possessions now."

"What can we do?"

Kas raised his eyebrows. "We?"

"Something needs to be done!"

Kas appeared to sigh, but there was no movement of air. "Stephenie, these invaders of yours are likely descendants of those that defeated my people. There is probably some ironic justice that your people are suffering at their hands, but I am growing fond of you and do not relish your suffering. But regardless, even if these invaders have had a similar drop in intelligence and understanding that you seem to suffer under, they would out match you."

"But you know so much. You could help."

"Stephenie, I know more than you, but I am one person."

"You're already dead, what do you have to lose?"

"My body is dead, but my consciousness has lived on somehow. I could lose that. It sounds odd, but I do fear losing what little I have left."

"So you can be killed...again."

Kas shifted his position slightly. "The energy that holds my consciousness could be disrupted enough that I would not remain as I am."

"Did I kill the ghost that attacked me?"

"I have no idea. I would suspect that you did not, but I was not present and even then, I am not sure I would know. I may be dead, but that does not make me an expert of all things pertaining to being dead. You, I presume, are not an expert on all things living?"

"Please help me Kas."

The ghost looked away and then met her eyes. "I have been helping you. It is not possible to learn all you need to know in such a short period of time."

Stephenie leaned toward the ghost. "Please. I need to get out of here. I can't stay here. I have to warn my father."

Kas shook his head. "This is a bad idea. Your presence here has caused a slight rise in the awareness of the others. You try to walk out of the library and it will draw attention. Before you can attempt this, I will need to teach you how to generate a field around yourself that will hide the energy signature your mind and living body produces. You will also need to learn how to move objects, which requires yet another type of energy field that will interact with the attraction all matter has to other matter."

She allowed herself a small smile. "Thank you."

"Do not thank me yet, the effort and success or failure will be yours."

Chapter 10

Stephenie rubbed her tired eyes. The words on the page she had been reading were blurring and she could honestly say she had no idea what the last three pages of the book had said. Pushing it away, she rose and stretched. She had slept three times since Kas had agreed to help her further, but she suspected more than three days had passed on the surface.

She sighed. Kas had been no help with time, claiming every time she asked that in his current state, he had trouble marking the passage of time. The lights in the library did not help; she found some remained on all the time, others never illuminated, and still others would react to her movement. The four times she walked up the spiral stairs to the dome with the large clear panels to look at the city also did not help. The city lights, which she could see clearly, were illuminated in a random pattern that Kas had indicated occurred because minor differences in the nature of each crystal had caused them to drift in their cycles.

I'm coming Josh, Father. Please hang on until I get there.

Her ankle was much stronger, the cut on her arm was only sore, and her ribs just ached when she turned too quickly. Her subconscious mind was directing energy to heal her body. However, she still ran out of breath far too quickly and her chest would ache after any significant effort. "Kas, why'd you have to try to crush my heart."

She looked around, but knew the ghost was not present. The exercises that Kas insisted she perform had improved her sensitivity to him and the other ghosts, which from time to time, she could feel outside the library. She had felt one inside the library the prior day, but it did not seem to notice her presence.

She picked up an overdone and dried out piece of rabbit meat that she had left on the table. "That's one decent thing about the library, it dries everything out faster than it can spoil." She chewed on the meat as she took a drink of water. "Of course, I'm nearly as dry as the parchment here," she mumbled, wishing for some lotion to rub on her chapped hands.

She put the pitcher back on the table and looked over at the last piece of meat that was left of the rabbit Kas had brought her the day before. She took a deep breath and held out her hand. She tried to ignore Kas' explanation of the forces that caused objects to fall to the ground because the ground has so much more mass than anything else. Instead, she felt herself draw energy into her body from the air. She felt the ripples of the energy coursing through her arms, chest, and mind. She tried to do as Kas had explained, modifying the natural fields and forces that caused the world to behave in one fashion and use those rules of nature to her benefit.

She saw the meat vibrate slightly as she fooled the world into believing there was something very dense in her hand. Suddenly the meat flew to her hand, but it moved too quickly. She had used too much force and the meat hit her chest with not an insignificant force.

She cursed as the pitcher of water tumbled over and the liquid water flew into the air. Turning away, she moved her hand toward her body and grunted with the impact of the ceramic vessel which landed in her lap as water drenched her chest and arms.

"Damn it!" Her ribs and chest throbbed from the impact.

"You needed to narrow your focus further. The more energy you use, the narrower the field must be, otherwise, you'll have everything in the room flying about your head."

She looked up to see Kas standing over her. "I'm never going to get this right." She frowned at him. "And how is it you always show up just as I screw something up?"

He shook his head and a chair moved across the floor with perfect timing as he sat down. "Stephenie, you have potential, but it will take years to master the skills you are trying to learn. Raw power is one thing, but someone with much less physical ability to channel energy through themselves can easily defeat someone stronger if they have the control to make better use of the energy."

"Kas, I know that. It's the same for using a sword, I'm not as physically strong as the men, but I was quicker and was able to anticipate and think ahead."

"Your ability with magic has undoubtedly helped you there, adding strength, balance, speed, and intuition of your opponent's subtle, but not visibly noticeable movements. But more importantly, do not worry that you ended up drenched in water. You are far from the first. And believe me, water is much more pleasant than a chamber pot."

She returned Kas' grin. "A chamber pot?"

"A full chamber pot."

"Well, I needed a bath and this library will have me dry before I know it."

"That it will."

She sighed, feeling better for Kas' presence and odd companionship. "Being what I am in this time is a death sentence. Those priests who tap the power from those other worlds, they have driven everyone to think I am evil and need to be burned." She forced a short laugh, "of course, perhaps this is all a delusion and maybe I am succumbing to Elrin's influence." Looking up to meet Kas' gaze, she allowed herself a small smile. "If it is, I would not trade it. You have given me more than I could have ever thought I needed; a chance to feel that there is not something fundamentally wrong with me. I hated always being fearful and having to hide myself from absolutely everyone. I've never once been able to talk about any of this with anyone. I am not even angry with you for having tried to kill me."

Kas tilted his head slightly. "That is good, since it was not my fault and I assume no responsibility for it." He softened his expression. "In truth, I cannot remember clearly a time when I was not anxious or fearful of the future. You have also been good for me as well. I will miss you very much."

Stephenie tensed, "what do you mean miss me?"

"I cannot leave with you and you have been desiring your departure. I sense that even the library will not shield your presence indefinitely. The others are becoming more aware. While a long way from self-aware, I have noticed what could be subtle changes in their behaviors. Though truly, only a few day's time is far from enough to have any real empirical evidence. Perhaps what I have noticed is purely cyclical and normal. But, also the library is not a good place to spend weeks of time without periods away from the preserving nature of the building."

"Come with me. Please Kas, you can come with me."

He rose to his feet, but then passed through the arm of the chair as if it was not there. "I am dead. There is nothing on the surface. Your world is changed. I do not understand any of the languages and things do not look as they should."

"You'd have me. I can teach you and you can teach me."

"Stephenie, while that has appeal, it does not change the fact that I am dead and you are not. In time, you will grow old and die, but it is very unlikely that you will end up with a fate like mine. You will want someone else living. You will not have need of me. In time, I will fall back into a trance and lose awareness of reality. Then perhaps I will relive our time together over and over for eternity."

"Kas, please. You are the only person who has any understanding of me. Don't you turn me away. Please, I am begging you, come with me."

Kas appeared to sigh. "There are some things that must be done before you leave. Let me find you some books that will help continue your education. I loathe the thought of the books leaving the library, since that will shorten their existence, but there is scarcely anyone who will miss them at this point."

He drifted into the stacks, more transparent than Stephenie had seen him in days. She stared as he searched through several titles, pulled a couple of books out. Unwilling to accept his refusal, she felt her arms and body tensing in impotent anger. When he returned with nearly a dozen books floating in the air beside him, she wished he was solid enough for her to slap. "You are a callous—" she searched her mind for the word in the Old Tongue, but could not think of one. "Bastard," she said dropping into Cothish. She let go of a stream of curses and then turned away from him.

"Stephenie." She refused to acknowledge him. "Stephenie, I am not doing this to be mean, but to be kind. There is little the dead and the living have in common. I know, I lived in a city mixed with the dead and the living for far too long. It was not a good thing."

She turned around, feeling tears trickle down her dry and chapped face. "You are my only true friend. The only one who knows what I am and accepts me. My own mother despised my existence because of what she thought I was."

Kas looked at the tall pile of books and sighed. "I think there may be some things to wrap around a couple of books to protect them and make them easier to carry. Obviously, you will not be able to take all of them, I will select a couple. Perhaps one day, if you survive and learn to shield your mind, you might be able to return. I will try to remain aware."

Stephenie turned and walked away. She disappeared into the stacks and then went into one of the reading rooms, shut the door, and sank into a chair, burying her face in her hands. *How can he do this to me?* She was uncertain why, but Kas' refusal felt worse than when Joshua and her father had insisted she remain behind with her mother. The sense of abandonment left her hollow.

She took a deep breath and tried to push away the emptiness. "I've only known him a few days." She closed her eyes, "and the bastard did try to kill me." She thought for a moment about staying longer in order to learn more, but she also knew her father and the army were at a greater risk every day she waited.

"Stephenie."

She looked up and noticed Kas standing before her. "I do care for you, which is why I cannot come with you. But there is also the secret of this city and the potential for the ghosts to find their way out. Someone needs to watch and try to keep things calm. If these angry spirits left and went to the surface, many living would die from their pent up rage. They would not likely be aware of the time that had past and would see those above merely as invaders who killed them and their loved ones."

Stephenie took another deep breath and nodded her head. "I'm sorry Kas. I should not have reacted that way. I just thought—it doesn't matter." She wiped her eyes and stood. "You've found a way for me to get out and perhaps one day I will be able to return."

Kas smiled. "Yes, that would be nice." He extended his hand, "come, I have a couple of books prepared. We should gather a couple of things and get you out of the city. I will show you a way to the surface that will take you away from the castle and into the countryside. I did not explore all the passages that led to the old castle above ground, but I found some of them appeared to be recently blocked. The ones I will show you appear to have collapsed a very long time ago, but there is enough room that I was able to bring in the rabbits and I think you should be able to crawl through them."

"So, you mean for me to leave now."

"Unless you have a reason to wait around longer."

"Well, unless you brought food I didn't see, I guess I should get started before I starve." Stephenie moved forward to follow Kas, but did not reach for his hand. "I do appreciate everything you have done for me. I just wasn't ready to be on my own again so soon."

"Come, let's get you on your way. I will do what I can to hide you from the others, but it may not be perfect."

She followed Kas out the door, which he had opened instead of drifting through. His body was fairly transparent and Stephenie wished he would have made himself whole for her, but refused to make that verbal request. On the table was still a stack of books, but next to the large pile appeared to be part of a cloak that had been wrapped and tied around a smaller stack of books.

"A cloak from the rooms downstairs?"

"There are four smaller books here, including the one you had been reading. And yes, the cloak is from the rooms downstairs. They have little need of it and it is probably the only building in the city with material that has not rotted."

Stephenie looked at the cloak with a little apprehension, but in the end picked it up. The bundle was not too heavy or large, for which she was thankful, but part of her still wished she could take more of the library and the knowledge it contained. "Thank you."

Kas nodded his head and led her down the stairs to the front door. "We will gather a better light stone than the one you found and some money. I assume that money is still important." Stephenie nodded her head. "I thought so. It would be best to melt and reform it so that there is no impression of the Dalar empire on it. If you were more skilled, it would be easy enough to simply apply heat and force to fashion the marks of your own country. However, that will take much time to learn. Instead, you might simply want to melt the faces off. We do not want others to see it and somehow decide there might still be a city here. The impact of releasing the ghosts and the knowledge hidden in the library would be devastating to your people."

Stephenie, still numb, nodded her head.

Kas said nothing more, and the library door opened enough to allow Stephenie to exit. The outside was considerably darker than the first time she had come through the city. She tried to reach out with her mind to sense others around her, but felt nothing. Even Kas seemed barely there.

"Try to refrain from using energy. I am masking you as best as I can in this form. However, my abilities are not what I possessed when I was living."

Without further comment, he led her down the grand staircase and away from the library. Thirsty, she half hoped they would go by the fountain, but with the bodies and ghosts that had been there the first time, she understood why they did not appear to be heading in that direction.

Instead, she looked around at the stone buildings as they walked down the deserted streets. She suspected this would have been a very grand city when everyone who was living here walked about, talking, and interacting with each other. She could see the beauty in the architecture and construction. The faded and decaying colors on the buildings and tiles looked as if at one time they would have once sparkled and inspired awe. She felt a distinct sadness for what had been lost and wondered if her own world above would see such loss before the war was done.

She stopped the introspective thoughts when Kas walked into a building, motioning her to remain where she was. He came out carrying in his transparent hand a glowing crystal and a pile of coins. "These are both silver and gold. I do not know what the value would translate to in your time, but this would be considered a fair amount of wealth in my time."

Stephenie took the handful of coins and crystal from Kas. They of course were not valid denominations, but based on the sizes and weight, she suspected he had just given her the equivalent of thirty full crowns, which could easily buy her a horse. "It is a lot in my time as well."

"Good. I could find some more, but I do worry that if you have too much money on you, that will draw you trouble. The light stone will illuminate and darken on command. This one is not set up to regulate its own time. You will have to learn to reach out to it mentally and tell it to brighten or darken. For now, I have set it to a soft glow so that perhaps it can be hidden in clothing and not draw attention, but yet still provide you with some illumination. It responds to Dalish, so you will need to use the translation guide I bundled for you once you learn more mental control."

Stephenie nodded her head. She wanted to tell him that he should come with her again, to teach her, but she remained silent. "So, I won't be able to control the crystal until I learn how."

"Yes. Come, we have one more stop before I take you to the crack."

They walked through more deserted streets, but Stephenie stopped examining the buildings. While there was beauty under the decay, it was obvious that the city was very much dead.

After several minutes of walking, in which Stephenie realized the city was larger than she first imagined, they came upon another block of buildings. These looked very much like residential buildings to Stephenie, which Kas confirmed.

"Many of my friends lived in this area. My family had a house above ground, but I had taken rooms here as well, so I could be closer to the college and library. They had sent assassins into the city above and even into Arkani. Sairy was killed in one of the sneak attacks. Many people were killed in several major blasts before we tried to seal ourselves in. My parents, brothers, and sisters left the city above and traveled away. Many people did. I decided to remain to defend

Arkani. Had I done otherwise, I would have truly died a long time ago." Kas sighed, "come."

He led her into one home, the old wooden door had long ago crumbled and fallen off the hinges. Stephenie stepped over the soft wood and into what appeared to be a small entrance hall. Laying as dark masses on the floor, were the remains of what might have been pictures hung from the walls. He moved just ahead and to the right, into a small room that appeared to have the remains of furniture and a carpet. There was a small fireplace in the far corner.

"This was once my sitting room. I would read and entertain the few guests I had here."

He moved over to the far wall and Stephenie noticed the decayed remains of a human body laying peacefully on the floor. The skull was partially bare of flesh and the jaw dislodged. Bits of blackened remains covered most of the bones, but there was hardly anything left but a skeletal outline of a person.

"Kas, why did you bring me here?" A hard edge of anger tainted her voice.

"Stephenie. You want me to come with you. But this pile of bones is what I am. What has been talking to you is just an echo of the past. There is nothing for the dead above. We could never have more than this."

Stephenie closed her eyes, clenched her fists around the bundle of books she was carrying, and took a deep breath. "Kas, you are more than an echo. But I already resigned myself to you staying, this is just mean." She moved to turn away.

"Wait. There is more than just you seeing my dead remains. I wanted you to take something."

Stephenie turned back to Kas and met his eyes, trying hard to avoid looking at the floor, but he bent down, forcing her to see what she did not want to look at. He motioned her to come closer and while discomforted at the sight, she did not feel the revulsion she had when she had awoken after the first fall to find she was next to the dead soldier. Slowly she moved closer, but did not kneel.

"I want you to take the medallion I was wearing. I do not want it to remain forgotten in this place. It was a gift from Sairy and I treasured it greatly. It would honor me if you would take it as a reminder of me."

Stephenie swallowed and looked down into the sunken chest cavity of the body that had once been Kas. She could see bits of a gold chain and something round lying on what would have been his spine. "It's covered in a layer of dead you."

Kas nodded his head. "I look very unimpressive. I died somewhere else I think. I don't really remember. Someone who knew me must have brought me here. I died when there were not that many people left, some of the last to die were actually moved by the dead. Others no one bothered with.

"The first memories I have after waking from being dead were of the library. I am not sure how much time passed between when I died and my spirit, if you will, coalesced in the library. I do not think it was long, but when I went looking for my body, which is an odd thing to realize you are doing, I found I had been placed here."

Stephenie swallowed again. She could see his arm bones laying against his rib cage, but his hand bones were scattered among the items that had fallen into his chest cavity, as if someone had crossed his arms in death.

"Kas, I don't want to rifle through your body."

"Believe me, I will not notice. There is no connection between me and the bones you see."

Stephenie closed her eyes and shook her head. *Damn it Kas, you just want to make this difficult.* Taking a deep breath, she knelt down and reached into his chest, trying to avoid touching the edges of his ribs. Gingerly, she picked up the chain and lifted. It stuck to the rest of him for a bit, then slowly, lifted free as it tore through the desiccated flesh that had rotted around it. The chain held fast for a moment on the bones of his neck, but they separated and the chain came free.

She quickly stood and moved a step back as his skull rolled to the side and his jaw slid to the floor. She looked to Kas to see his reaction, but he was already standing before her and seemed unaware of the desecration she had just performed. She had no intention of putting his skull back the way it was. Instead she looked at the chain and medallion in her right hand. It was indeed covered in his dried

up flesh. She was slightly revolted by the thought of holding it.
Before she could say anything, Kas rubbed his mostly opaque hands
over the medallion and chain, even moving his hands through
Stephenie's. She was about to pull her hand back, but there was no
biting cold when he passed through her.

As if knowing her thoughts, he met her eyes. "The touch you felt
when we first met was as damaging as it was because I was drawing
away all the energy in that part of your body, pulling it into myself.
As we discussed, adding energy heats, removing energy cools, or
freezes."

Stephenie nodded and looked down at the gold medallion and
chain. It was about an inch across and bore the image of a bird on
one side and a mountain on the other.

"I always liked kestrels, so when Sairy found that, she purchased it
for me. We had a great fondness for each other and I have found a
similar fondness for you Stephenie. I think it is fitting you should
wear it."

Stephenie hesitated for a moment, uncertain of her feelings about
wearing something that was just minutes before in the rotted out
chest of the ghost before her. And there was also the fact that it had
been the gift from another woman. Then seeing Kas' expression, one
of sadness and longing, but also of kindness and concern, she smiled
and put the chain over her head. The chain was not overly long,
leaving the medallion to rest just at the top of her breasts. "Thank
you Kas. I don't have anything to offer you in exchange but my
friendship and the dirty clothes I am wearing. I don't think the
clothes will do you much good."

He laughed once and looked down at his body. "No, clothing will
not help. Besides, I think I was at least half a head taller than you. I
doubt they would fit." He turned and started to move toward the
doorway. "Come, I sense others in the area and we should not
dawdle."

Feeling a bit more peace over her situation, Stephenie followed
Kas out of his house, through several more streets, then to the road
that ran along the outer wall, and finally the main door separating the
city from the caves. "What does the door say?"

"You will need to learn Dalish."

"Ya, when I have time. What does it say?"

Kas continued walking and did not look back at the door. "It said you are trapped here forever. At least that is what the words meant to those of us who were sealed in. But literally, it says here lies the grand city of Arkani, jewel of the Dalar empire and home to those who pursue enlightenment."

"Somewhat ostentatious," she said with a grin.

Kas nodded his head, "that was the intent. The city was created at the height of our power and showcased technology and skill with magic that many could never hope to achieve. They brought in elves and the greatest minds around to create the city. The Denarians would have had a great coup. It would have demonstrated they were the masters of the known world. We held them from that by barring their entry. But they could not let us escape. I guess we had a draw, they did not capture the city, but they still killed us. I would imagine that they tried to erase the knowledge of their defeat by pretending we did not exist." He stopped in front of the crack in the outer dome. "At least that is what I would have done."

Stephenie looked up at the hole in the wall. Her arm was now just a little sore, as were her ribs. Her chest still hurt when she moved the wrong way, but at least her ankle was better. *Healing like magic.* She moved forward to climb up, but Kas stepped toward her and helped her up into the opening. She struggled for a bit, trying hard to carry the books and squeeze through the narrow opening. After a bit, the crack opened wider and she pulled the light crystal from her pocket, holding it in her right hand. With the books in her left, she slowly crawled forward.

Eventually she reached the other side of the dome and found Kas was already there to help her down. Once she was firmly on the ground again, she held up the crystal to look around. The chamber was large, but not anywhere near as large as what was on the other side of the dome and so the limited light was able to show most of the chamber.

The crack she had come through was indeed part of a wall that seemed more formed than natural. The wall was smooth, with an arch that was similar to what she had seen inside the city. In contrast, the walls for the other parts of this chamber were natural. A scattering of debris that had fallen from the ceiling and walls over the years covered the ground. She could see the wooden bridge, just barely at the edge of the illumination and her enhanced sight. The broken covered bridge was high above a smooth flow stone that cascaded down the sloped wall that was beneath the bridge. She could guess where she had slid down the rocks and was surprised she had as few injuries as she did.

The bridge led to a series of wooden steps that trailed along the irregular natural stone wall to the base of the dome, which contained a wide street, partially covered with loose rubble. She followed Kas back around the dome to the other side of the door, which was adorned in what she believed was a mirror image of the carvings and images that were on the city side. The street before the door continued to the right, into a large passageway that was at least thirty feet high and would allow two large carriages to pass each other without trouble.

"The stairs led to a secondary city of sorts. There were markets and chambers used for presentations and performances. There were some homes and residences there as well. I will not call them slums, since the area was more expensive than the surface, but it lacked the prestige of Arkani.

"That tunnel was the main passage between Arkani and the surface. It is a long passage, many miles to the surface. People would draw their wagons and goods into the city for sale or they would make the trip to tour the city and see the sites. Along the way, there were smaller caves where merchants would set up carts and even a small set of passages and chambers where an inn and public house were created. That way tourists could stay close to Arkani, but not have to pay the rates that they would inside the city.

"I checked, those areas are all collapsed and destroyed. There are two other places where the tunnel has collapsed. One about a mile down, then again near the surface. The first one is not hard to navigate with the light. You should be able to crawl through the opening with ease. The one near the surface will be more difficult. The passage through the collapse is fairly obvious, so you will not get lost, but you will get dirty. If it has rained in the last day or so, you will also get very muddy. You will find the opening near the sea, in a wooded area. The old road that led to the passage is gone. The opening is covered in rubble and debris. It is not a surprise no one has explored it.

"I found a small village half a dozen miles to the south. If you go west, you will come to a decent road."

Stephenie nodded her head and sighed. "It's probably the road from Antar to Tuner. There are a number of small communities along the road." She looked at Kas' face, trying to remember his features. "I expect this is where you are leaving me."

Kas nodded. "At this point you should be safe. Going further will just make the departure harder for both of us. Take care of yourself and if at some point you learn to hide your presence and you can safely do so, please come back and visit. I will try to remain aware and not drop back into the ular. But time is hard for those of us who have partially died."

Stephenie wanted to reach out and hug the ghost, to hold him, but that was what he had argued, he had no body and there could be nothing more than what was already between them. She forced a smile to her face and placed her right hand, with the crystal, over the medallion laying on her blouse, dimming the light considerably. "Kas, I could never forget you. If I live, I will return at some point. You are the only person alive or dead that I've ever been able to truly talk to about this and this is so much of what I am." She fought back the tears that wanted to surface. "Thank you for everything."

Kas nodded his head and smiled. "You have given me a reason to continue to exist. I will wait for you. But you should now be going. It is many miles you must travel." He raised his hand to wave farewell and then faded from sight.

Kas, Stephenie thought with more longing than she wanted. Taking a deep breath, she turned and headed into the large passage that would lead to the surface.

Chapter 11

Stephenie emerged from a narrow crack between two large stones. She had never prayed truthfully to any god, fearing they would sense Elrin in her, but she made several compulsory prayers to Felis on the journey that the rocks would not shift and crush her. When she was finally free of the subterranean world, she took a deep breath and was rewarded with the smell of leaf litter and trees instead of the cold, damp, and somewhat stale air she had been breathing.

Looking around, she was, as Kas said, in a forest. There was a faint smell of the sea in the air. There were birds in the distance and the light was fading. "And let's be honest, I am damn tired."

She moved away from the outcropping of rocks that were left of the caved-in entrance and found a somewhat clearer area between some large trees. A moss covered boulder sat to one side. "If Kas is right and it's several miles to the town, it's going to be late when I arrive." Her stomach grumbled, as it had for most of the trip through the passage.

She set the package of books down and untied the ends of the cloak Kas had cut up. The material was tightly woven and lined. She put the crystals next to the books and folded over the cloth, but a dim glow still emanated through the threads. Frowning, she uncovered the crystals and gathered several handfuls of moss. Cutting off her right sleeve at the elbow to match what she had done to make the bandage for her left arm, she piled the moss on the remains of her sleeve, put the crystals in the middle of it and wrapped it up. She placed that next to the books and folded over the cloak.

Pleased with that effort, she rose and walked over to a nearby boulder and frowned. The top bulged slightly. She moved away, looking for a large rock that had a shallow depression on the top. After a couple more rejects, she found one that would suit her needs.

She put a silver coin in the depression and then hesitated. Her experience so far with her ability to control her power had been mixed. Fearing the coin would explode as molten metal all over the forest, she picked up the coin and then took several steps back. Having seen a cold and damp rock added to a fire crack and explode, she did not want to risk further injury.

She calmed herself and focused on the depression in the rock, directing energy into the stone. She tried to do it as slowly as she could, but the energy flow was hard to control. She continued to focus as the rock steamed and then smoked as the bits of forest litter and debris burned away. When the stone started to glow she stopped the flow of energy, wiped the sweat from her face, and moved closer on unsteady feet. The glow faded quickly, but when she dropped a silver coin in the depression, she felt the heat radiate from the stone. She watched as the surface of the coin softened and then liquified. After several minutes passed, she tested the metal several times with a small stick until it had solidified again. She knocked the round and now unremarkable bit of silver from the stone to the moist soil.

Wiping her brow again, she sat back on her heals. "Damn, that took a lot out of me." Her mouth was dry and her stomach rumbled some more. If she had a real coin, she would be able to get more value for it, even if it was not recognized. A blob of silver would be worth less, but she hoped she would be able to trade what was a bit larger than a silver crown for several smaller coins.

Not wanting to risk having too little money, she took a deep breath and repeated the process, hoping that she would need less energy to reheat the stone. After she melted three more silver coins, she did the same thing to two gold ones before she felt the first traces of blood in her mouth.

Exhausted, she tried to swallow the unpleasant flavor as more blood ran from her nose. Panicking, she held her head back and pinched her nose. More than one hit to the nose had given her a fair share of bloody noses, but she did not like where this one had come from.

After several minutes, the bleeding stopped. Tired to the bone, and with the light having faded even further, she gathered up the melted coins and put them in her pocket with the few she had from the soldier's pouch. She retied her bundle of books with the hidden light crystals and headed for the setting sun. She wanted to find the road, head south until she found a place to buy some food and a bed for the night. In the morning, she would get more supplies, skirt around Antar, and then head to the Greys. She would find her brother and father and warn them about what her mother had done.

It was well after dark before Stephenie arrived in the small village. Her head was throbbing and she was finding it hard to catch her breath. There were a few dozen buildings along the main road and she had earlier passed what she suspected were farm houses further to the west. Ahead of her was the swinging sign of a public house. Thankfully, she saw light behind the shuttered windows and from under the door. Wearily, she stumbled up the steps and pushed her way through the door.

Inside was a small common room with several tables and benches. A large fireplace with a few dying coals was on the left wall. A small bar graced the right wall. Stephenie had been too tired to even sense the seven people who were in the room, all had looked up to watch her enter. Five of the seven were divided into two separate groups, each seated at different tables. A bar maid went back to refilling the drinks for the larger group, while an older man behind the bar critically eyed Stephenie's dirty clothing and person.

"We don't offer handouts and I have no need of help. If you're coming from Antar, best keep moving."

"I have money," Stephenie replied with more irritation in her voice than she had wanted. Her pounding headache had shortened her temper. "At least what should pass for it," she added. Moving over to the bar, she pulled out one melted coin and put it on the bar. Lowering her voice, she continued, "it's silver. Bigger than a crown."

The older man looked at the piece of metal for a bit, then picked it up to examine it more closely in the light from the bar lamp. After a careful inspection, he looked back at her. "Steal someone's dinner set?" He shook his head, forestalling her response, "ain't none of my business. Times are hard and if you ran off with your lord's silver, not my concern. What you want?"

Stephenie held in a sigh of relief. She suspected arguing her innocence of theft would be pointless. "I'd like a large dinner, an extra loaf of bread if you have it, something to drink, and change, there's plenty of coin there."

The man chuckled. "Fine girl, we can do that. No more than five square back though. I don't know how pure this is."

"Let's make it ten square, I'll be generous and give you the benefit of the doubt." Stephenie watched the man's expression harden. He glanced back at the melted coin again and then grinned.

"Alright girly, deal." He reached below the counter and came up with a hand full of small square coins. He counted out ten and put them in Stephenie's still rather dirty hands. "Tabby, get this girl some dinner and an extra loaf of bread." He picked a mug from under the bar and turned around to the keg behind him. He eventually handed Stephenie the mug of ale, for which she thanked him.

Sighing, she took the ale and sipped it as she walked to the corner of the room. The other people in the pub had gone back to their quiet conversations, but they still would look over at her from time to time. After some minutes, a large bowl of stew and two loaves of bread were brought to her table by the young girl that had been refilling the drinks earlier.

"Where you from?" The girl asked as Stephenie tore into the bread and stew.

Stephenie swallowed the stew soaked bread. It was stale bread and greasy stew, but it was not cave snake or charred and dried rabbit, so it was delicious. "I'm coming from the north."

"Going to Antar?"

Ignoring the question so that she could answer the demands of her stomach with another mouthful of food, Stephenie looked up at the girl who appeared to be about her age, sixteen or seventeen. The girl did not appear to be in any hurry to leave, so Stephenie washed down the mouthful of food and paused in her eating. "Possibly. What can you tell me about how things are? I've not been able to keep up on the local news."

"Oh," the girl said, sitting down across from Stephenie. "You a runaway? I won't tell no one."

Stephenie shook her head. "No. We've had some trouble lately at the farm, it's just me and my father. He's old and really couldn't make the trip, so I went."

"Well, everything in Antar is falling apart. The Queen up and deserted the castle, I hear she took everything of value. She and her army marched right through town. Going back to Kynto they said. Wagons and wagons of goods. Those troops didn't give no care for anyone here, ran over a boy. Not hurt too bad, but left him laying in the dust, they cared all that much. With her gone and the King dead, there's no one to rule the country."

"What?" Stephenie said too loudly.

"Oh, you didn't know? I guess you wouldn't yet. Runners have been riding the land. The Queen's betrayal left the soldiers without supplies and they were overrun. The King's head was put on a pike they say. Antar is in chaos. Everyone is waiting for the invaders and their Elrin loving bastards to come through and take over. People have been fleeing the city."

Stephenie had barely heard a word Tabby had said. Her mind was reeling from the knowledge her father and brother were dead.

"I think they were looking for one of the Princesses to take over, but one was with the Queen, Princess Kara was killed by the invaders, bless her, and Princess Islet is their captive. The rumor is the youngest is dead or as good as." Tabby leaned toward her, "they say Elrin's spawn will overrun us before the year's out." Tabby ran two fingers from her right hand down her left arm to ward off curses.

Stephenie's hands were trembling and she could feel tears rolling down her face.

"You alright? Don't fret, what do people like us know for their rulers. We just say your majesty and your highness and such. As long as they don't sell us off as slaves or kill us, we'll get by."

Stephenie swallowed and nodded her head. "You're right. I just didn't know things were as bad as that."

"Well, I didn't mean to ruin your dinner. Eat while you can." She looked over her shoulder, "I better get busy or Charl will doc my pay."

Stephenie wiped the tears from her face as the girl walked away to refill the mugs at the table of three again. The food had lost all of its flavor, but her stomach still ached. *I failed you father. I failed you Josh. Forgive me, please forgive me, I tried, I was just not fast enough.* She gave up fighting the tears and continued eating mechanically. She had no idea what to do next, but her body insisted on food despite the complete emptiness that filled her soul.

She was not sure when she had finished the bowl of stew or the mug of ale. She had an impression that the mug had been refilled once. Staring at the bundle of books Kas had given her, she came to the conclusion that her mother must suffer. Growing up, she relied on the thought of the curse falling to her mother for vindication and revenge. Having learned that convoluted and illogical event was not going to happen left her without the normal escape she had always imagined. Death no longer held justice. *You need to die mother, not I. You need to pay for what you did.*

She looked up just before five men and a woman walked through the door. Her senses had been raw and muted since she had melted the coins, but despite this, she could tell these people were trouble even before they finished entering the pub.

"Alright, we're here to unburden your souls." The man leading the pack said, his dark hair pulled back into a short queue. Dark and stained leather armor covered a red shirt. Stephenie noted the worn handle on his sword and a dagger on his belt. The men behind him were similarly armed, with one man and the woman at the rear holding loaded crossbows, still pointed up and not at the backs of their comrades.

"Hmm, what delicacy do we have here?" he said, his eyes rolling over Tabby. "We might have to take a little more pay from this one."

Tabby stepped back, fear radiating from her. "You'll leave your hands off me."

He chuckled as the other four spread out to cover the front half of the pub. "We'll just see about that. I like 'em feisty. For now, Gramps," he turned to the man behind the bar, "all the coin you have hidden there. The rest of you, up your pouches and purses on the table." Taking in Stephenie sitting at the back of the room, he added, "just like that dirty little girl in the back. I'd imagine she's got her world in the bundle."

The man was halfway across the room in a flash, his dagger held to the throat of the nearest patron. "No martyrs please." The patron slowly removed his hand from his own dagger's handle. When it was far enough away, the man in leather smiled, moved the blade away from the sweating man's neck, then quickly punched him in the face, sending him tumbling off the bench and on to the floor.

"I'm leaving with everything all of you have. I'll rape the girls myself and leave it at that. Any of you cause more trouble and all of my men will rape them twice before we cut their throats."

Stephenie sensed three people coming in from the kitchen, one was a young boy, dirty from cooking. The next two held drawn swords. She turned back to the leader, who held a big grin and was looking at her with an expression of lust that matched the sickening sense of emotion she sensed coming from him. "You might not be too bad if someone dumped a bucket of water on your head. But as you can see," he added, putting his dagger back into its sheath as he turned back to the rest of the room. "There is no secret help coming from the kitchen. So let's have your valuables on the tables."

Stephenie ground her teeth, knowing this lawlessness was directly caused by her mother. Toppling the government and destroying the hope of a nation would bring out the worst in some people. Slowly she stood, as if she was going to remove the coins from her pockets, but instead she pulled Kas' dagger from her belt and stepped out from behind the table.

"You think you can take me you sniveling coward? You need six men to guard your back?" Everyone's attention turned toward her. She would be dead as soon as they saw the light crystals. Burned as a witch was not a good way to die. Fighting at least gave her a chance to take out a few of them before that happened.

"I'll definitely take you first. Might not kill you straight away, could use some entertainment on the road." He moved toward her, not drawing a weapon.

Stephenie sensed a readiness to protect his groin and suspected he would try to prove his manhood by taking the dagger from her. He was a head taller and had reach and size. As he drew within a step of her, Stephenie quickly reversed her hold on the dagger to protect her forearm with the blade. His attention was drawn by the movement. She moved forward and kicked out with her left foot, slamming down her heal on the top of his foot. At the same time, she punched up with her right hand, slashing his open hand that had been ready to reach for her wrist.

She lifted her left foot, rotated her upper body away, and kicked the side of his right knee. The knee gave a resounding pop and the man fell to his hands and left knee. He screamed in pain, then grunted as Stephenie kicked him in the side, sending him face down and sprawling across the floor.

She sensed one of the men who had come in through the kitchen closing behind her. Dropping low to avoid the sword, she spun around to face the young man. She lunged forward, inside the man's reach and rammed her dagger, blade again forward, into his unprotected groin.

Blood washed over her hand as she pulled the blade free. The young man's face carried nothing but surprise as she wrenched the sword from his hands. Stephenie expected pain would shortly follow the surprise. The kitchen boy was scrambling to get out of the way as the other man tried to grab him to use as a shield.

As the thought that she might be able to make it out alive flashed through her head, she sensed movement behind her. She turned just in time to see the man with a crossbow depress the release. She heard the sound of the string sliding over wood, pushing the bolt from the crossbow.

Cringing, she clenched her fists tightly, desperately wanting the bolt not to hit her. She felt a lurch of energy flood through her, almost on its own, pushing out, burning, and drawing pain. She could sense a wave of energy leave her and before she could register what was happening, the glasses on the bar, the nearest table and benches, and the man in leather armor, struggling to rise, were all thrown backwards, away from her and across the room. The crossbow bolt shattered in mid air and bounced away, as if it had struck solid stone. When everything had settled, Stephenie tasted blood in her mouth and knew it was running from her nose.

No one moved for several moments, then Tabby shook with fear and drew her fingers over her left arm. "Witch. Elrin's spawn," she cursed, looking away to avert drawing the attention of evil. "She must burn or we're damned."

Stephenie felt her stomach drop. She expected nothing less, but to actually hear the girl that had served her dinner and talked to her declare that she should burn for standing up against thieves and rapists showed how twisted society had become.

She put aside her resentment as movement of the crossbow held by the woman drew her attention. Trying to use less energy, Stephenie attempted to push the crossbow away and discharge it into the ceiling. She forced her mind to the task, but knowing she had only moments to act, she rushed. She stumbled as energy poured through her body. With limited control she directed it at the crossbow, but instead of moving it, the woman and the weapon burst into flames.

The flaming weapon tumbled from the woman's hands, discharging into the floor as it fell. Screaming, the woman beat her arms against her face and chest, all of which were on fire. The woman bounced twice into the wall and then fell out the front door. Two of the men closest to her retreated out the door with her while the man with the other crossbow struggled to reload.

Sensing apprehension, fear, and anger from everyone in the room, Stephenie glanced around herself. The other man behind her still stood in the kitchen door and the two people at the far table had risen. She tossed the sword aside, grabbed her books as she ran past, and jumped through the window. The wooden slats and mica panes broke easily and the force of her weight knocked the shutters from their hinges.

She landed on the ground with a grunt, but quickly pushed herself up and lumbered forward, away from the public house and into the night. She headed east, toward the cover of the nearest trees.

Chapter 12

"Damn." Sergeant Henton mumbled between breaths. He raised his hand and slowed his jog to a walk. The men behind him fell into a small group.

"We too late Sarge?"

"It would look that way Corporal." They were still concealed by the shadows. Henton kept them there as he watched the group of people milling about the front of what looked to be a public house. What he saw left him with an empty feeling in his gut. They had jogged nearly eight miles in the hopes of catching the group of thieves and murderers that were hitting small towns. The informant who passed on this location had taken his time doing so. Henton would make sure the informant eventually paid the price for the delay, *once the band is captured or killed.*

"Corporal, keep everyone here for now. I should be safe enough and I don't want everyone stuck on clean up duty. If the clouds hold off, the Mother Moon should give us enough light that we can pursue them." Henton did not look back to make sure his orders were followed; he simply moved quickly toward the group of people around the pub's entrance.

As he approached, he smelled burnt flesh and noted what appeared to be a body on the ground. *Bastards have crossed yet another line now.* As he neared, the sounds of his leather armor creaking slightly and his weapons bouncing against his leg slowly drew the attention of the crowd until everyone was watching him. "Evening," he called out to the only man in armor who carried himself with a sense of authority. "I'm Sergeant Henton out of Antar. I've been chasing a group of murderers. I fear I might be a bit too late. Did anyone see which way they might have gone?"

"Antar's in chaos," an older woman in the back said with a sharp edge to her voice. "King's dead and the bitch Queen fled. In what army do you think you're a sergeant?"

"Ma'am." Henton nodded his head with respect. "I came off The Scarlet, served many years keeping the Sea of Tet safe for Cothel's ships and trade. The King, may he live well with the gods, called me to land while he lived. Despite his death and the problems with the leadership—perhaps due to those problems, I never received orders telling me to let bastards roam the towns robbing, raping, and killing. Until someone tells me to let that happen, I've still got a duty to perform."

The woman nodded her head and he watched her reappraise him carefully. "Well, Sergeant, you are a bit late, but the dead belong to this band of murderers."

He raised an eyebrow and looked down at the dead body. It was badly burned, but appeared to be that of a woman. Taking a closer look, he could see the remains of leather armor on her upper body. "I am glad the town was not caught unaware."

"It was not us," a man said from the door of the pub.

"It was a witch."

Henton looked toward the young lady that had spoken. She made the sign to ward off evil and he appraised her as likely being a bar maid.

"We were in the pub, there were a few patrons, myself, Charl," she nodded to the man in the door, "and Sam in the kitchen. This slip of a girl, not older than me, thin as a willow, her red hair covered in dirt, killed two of them and broke the knee of their leader."

"Really?"

She nodded. "Yes sir. She had gotten upset when I told her the King was dead, but she said she had come from a farm in the north and was heading to Antar. I told her it wasn't safe and left her to eat. A while later, six men and that woman come in, two with crossbows. They demanded everyone's money and said—they said—well, she got up and with only a dagger, moved faster than anyone not tainted by Elrin has a right to."

"I saw her take down that man," Charl said. "He was flat on the floor before anyone could move. Then she took out one of the men that had come in from the kitchen. Dodged his sword, stuck him in the groin, and took the sword right from his hand. After that, she turned and called upon Elrin's evil; stopped a crossbow bolt dead in the air and flung everything about the common room."

The barmaid spoke up again. "That one there," she said pointing to the dead woman, "she was going to fire her crossbow, but the witch set her afire. All but the first crossbow man had fled at that point. I could see Elrin's poison had taken hold. Blood was flowing from her nose and mouth. She looked worn by the evil, but she simply turned and jumped through the window. Took off to the east toward the woods."

Henton nodded his head. "Anyone go after her?"

Several people moved about uncomfortably, then the man in armor spoke up for the first time. "I don't care if Elrin's poison had made her weak, none of us are that stupid."

"What about the leader, you said he was still alive?"

"Ya, broken knee. But a noose will take care of that."

Henton kept his face expressionless. He did not mind the town dispensing justice. It would save him from having to do it. "Okay. I think the main threat is over. Sounds like you've got the leader under control. You might find out where the others would likely have run before you hang him. You can send word to Antar. There are still troops there protecting the honest people."

"What are you going to do?" the old woman asked.

"Me and my men have someone new to pursue." He nodded his head to those present and then jogged back down the street to his squad.

He slowed as he approached the group of eight men. He could just see the corporal raise his eyebrows in the moon light. "Several of the bandits have been dealt with, including the leader. However, we have a lead on another person I would like to catch up with. We'll be moving fast, I want to catch up to her. No one is to engage her if you come across her, just let me know you found her."

Taking a quick glance to make sure those who had not served under him for long understood his orders, he nodded his head. "I just hope we can follow her trail well enough in the moon light," he said as he took off at a jog back toward the pub.

Keeping his men away from the group of townspeople who were dragging another body out of the pub, he circled back around to the side of the building, where the window had been smashed open. Pausing briefly to note the broken slats of wood and the shutters that had been thrown to the ground, he thanked the gods that the ground was still damp and soft from the recent rains.

Taking a quick look to the east, he tried to estimate how the land lay and which direction would be most likely for someone in a hurry to run. Reaching a hand back, he was rewarded by Private Zac handing him the hooded lantern. Opening the shutters just slightly, he noted the crushed grass of someone's hasty retreat, going off in the direction that seemed most logical. Closing the shutters, he kept the lantern and headed off at a fast jog.

Stephenie slid to the ground, her back against a tree. The throbbing of her head was nauseating and she was having a hard time catching her breath. She had never felt as drained and raw as she did now. Any jubilation from having managed to escape the public house alive was truly gone. Her nose had been bleeding on and off since she had run and while it had stopped for the moment, she did not think it would last. What she was experiencing she knew theoretically as being poisoned from Elrin's tainted power. She suspected it might be the after effects of cooking her brain and wondered what lasting damage might result. Kas had warned her that it could kill her, but he had not elaborated. She wondered if perhaps he thought he had explained it all in detail, but simply forgot to vocalize it.

Remaining very still, she tried to breath slowly, but it felt like she was not getting enough air and that was making her edgy. Her only thread of hope was that everyone in the town might be too scared to follow her. It was not a confident hope, just one of desperation and one she knew to have been pointless when she heard, then only afterward, mutedly sensed the approach of a man.

She held her breath, hoping he might pass and not notice her, but as he came around the tree, it was obvious he had tracked her. She looked up and into the light of a hooded lantern. She tried looking away, but her night vision was overwhelmed by the bright flame. She struggled to her feet, her dagger already in her right hand, her left arm clutching the bundle of books to her stomach.

"Easy," she heard the man speak, slowly recognizing his voice. Her mind had opened slightly and her head burned from the effect. She swallowed knowing that Sergeant Henton stood before her and eight other men were in easy shouting distance.

"I'm not here to hurt you Stephenie."

She looked back at Henton, who had lowered and turned the focus of the lamp. She could just see the high features of his face.

"I've got my men not far off, but they should be far enough away they won't hear what we say for now. When I heard the description of what was done in the pub and who had done it, I could scarcely hope it might be you."

"What do you want?" Stephenie said in a whisper. Her sight was coming back and she could see Henton's face clearly as he nodded his head, though she could not sense much emotion.

"I am not entirely sure. You didn't kill me when you could have, though perhaps you tried and simply failed. But I don't think that was your intent. You tried hard to warn me your mother was up to something. Though I could tell something was wrong, I did not allow myself to fully believe your conviction. I feel responsible somehow for what happened." He raised his free hand, "not fully, since it was not my actions, but your mother's, that has put our country in jeopardy. However, perhaps I could have raised an alarm sooner." He frowned, "though honestly I don't know how I could have, since I knew I was being watched."

"Sergeant, I absolve you from any guilt. It makes no difference any more, everyone I loved is dead and gone. My only point in living now is to get revenge upon my mother. If you want to kill me or capture me for what I am, do it. Or let me go and I'll do my damnedest to kill that bitch." She watched as Henton looked her over.

Behind her, someone called out, "Sarge, you good?"

"I'm fine Corporal, just stay put." He had not taken his eyes from her. "Stephenie, you are the last of the royal family available that I would care to see on the throne. You need to come back to Antar and declare yourself queen. Then get the city and the country under control. If you don't, we'll fall into civil war with barons and dukes fighting over land and the throne. That will leave us open to the invaders."

Stephenie laughed once and shook her head. "What are you saying? You know what I am. They'll put fire to me first chance they get. I can't be queen."

"I've told no one and I have not heard anyone say anything about you. If your mother starts rumors, say they are simply to discredit you. I—I would vouch for you. You are what we need. You understand the enemy and can know how to defeat them. We cannot fight them. Even our priests are getting slaughtered."

She closed her eyes and leaned back against the tree before looking back to meet his eyes. "Even you, who, for whatever crazy reason suggested it, are having trouble accepting it. I can hear it in your voice. I can't be queen." She sighed, "my mother would try to destroy me or at least take me prisoner. But if it did come out and even if I said it was lies, the priests would insist on testing me and would find me guilty. There is no point. Kill me or leave me be."

"Princess, the country will fall if something isn't done. I know you are a witch, but perhaps you can keep Elrin's taint from you. Perhaps we can explain that."

She shook her head. "Henton, what you know about witches is just a bunch of lies people have been saying for hundreds of years. I am not evil, at least not more so than any normal person. But it will mean nothing. Everyone is conditioned to believe what they have been told over and over again by those who want to retain their position and power."

"You mean the priests? I have a close friend who is a holy warrior of Felis. Are you saying they have lied?" Henton took a deep breath. "We need to talk about this more. Perhaps there is another way to save the country, but I don't think we can settle this before my men get overly worried. Come with me, I will protect you until we can decide what to do."

"Why?"

"Princess, you tried to oppose your mother, who is a traitor. You tried, I think, to protect me. You were fighting for your father and you just killed some bandits. You've done nothing that I can see as being evil. I will give you a chance to tell me your story. Perhaps we can save this country."

He looked over his shoulder and toward the men who were standing a few dozen feet off into the woods. "Let's not tell the men who you are yet, we'll say you were close to a childhood friend of mine, Ben. I'll call you—"

"You can call me Steph," she said, forcing herself off the tree.

"Sarge?"

"Coming," Henton called out, grabbing Stephenie's right arm.

Too tired and weak to challenge it, she allowed herself to be led by the sergeant. Stumbling up the uneven slope, she was thankful his arm offered some stability.

Near the top of the slope, they stopped. She noted the eight men who had gathered around. They appeared calm and capable, though Stephenie could not sense much of anything through the throbbing in her head.

"Men, this is Beth. She's...a close friend of an old friend of mine, Ben. Fortunately, she was talkative enough to the barmaid, that when they described what happened in town, I suspected she had been in the tavern when the bandits arrived."

Stephenie bit back an angry retort, she did not consider herself a Beth. Her irritation tried to push through the dizziness, threatening to bring her to her knees, but only barely.

"She was punched in the face by the thugs and ran off when the town's people overcame the leader and two others." Henton turned to address the men standing on the left. "Sam, take Ramous, Bones, and Quin back to the garrison double time. Tell them that the leader and two others of the gang we have been chasing are dead and I'd expect the gang will disperse at this point."

"Sarge, what you going to do?" a blond boy asked.

"Ramous, I'm going to take Beth to my parents. She was heading north. She and Ben had a house in Antar, but Ben's at the front and it's not safe in Antar."

"Not safe outside of Antar, Sarge," added another man next to the blond.

Henton continued as though nothing had been said. "My parents are a ways to the north. I'm not going to let Beth try and travel there on her own. But we cannot go several days without reporting in either. So you four will avoid getting into trouble. I'll take the other four with me. On the way back, we'll see if we can track down any more of the gang.

"Look," Henton said, adopting more of a commanding tone, "I'm going to catch a lot of crap for doing this. I don't need to get all of you in trouble with me." He sighed. "I'd avoid the town and head straight for Antar. They've got three graves to dig tonight and none of you want to deal with that."

The man Stephenie assumed to be Sam nodded his head. "We learned that the hard way last time. I use a bloody sword, not a dam shovel. Not my job to dig holes for bastards. When should I tell the Cap you'll be back?"

"I'd say four days at the soonest, private."

The young man whistled. "You are going to be mucking crap out of stalls." He turned to the other three next to him. "Alright, let's get a move on. The night's not getting any earlier while we stand around."

"Good work private. And good luck," he added as they moved off into the forest at a slow jog.

It was several minutes before anyone moved or said anything further. Stephenie eventually detached herself from Henton's grasp, moved to a nearby tree and sat down. She felt too unsteady and worn out to remain standing. She felt everyone's attention on her, but did not care.

"Sarge?"

"Yes Corporal?"

"Well, when you have a moment, I just wanted to run over our supplies with you."

"Quit with the crap, Will. You want to ask him what's going on."

"Fish, you're out of line," the Corporal responded curtly.

Henton cleared his throat. "No Will, I will be upfront with the four of you. The other four I sent back because while I don't have any reason to distrust them, we've only known them for a short time. The four of you served under me on The Scarlet, so I feel I can trust you with more. Right now each of you need to make a decision, will you throw your lot in with me or not. If not, I won't hold it against you. In fact, I'd fully respect it. I'd just ask that nothing more of what's happened here goes any further."

"We talking treason?"

Henton looked over to a red-headed boy. "No. Nothing like that, but the things we will discuss here need to remain secret. If you don't want any part of it, please head back to Antar. Join up with the others and say you didn't want to get your ass in a sling for me."

"I think we're all in Sarge," said a bearded man of no more than twenty. The other three chimed in quickly with their own confirmations.

"Alright. First off, we need to put some distance between that town and us. Then I'll fill you in on the details."

"Like why Ben would have been in Antar, or fighting at the front, or even married to Beth?" The corporal smiled. "Only Ben you ever told us about was living in Pandaras the last you said, getting his kicks off with as many women as he could. This girl's likely pretty enough under all that blood and dirt, but I knew your story was off."

Henton cleared his throat again. "Corporal, I used Ben's name in the hopes that the four of you would know to keep your mouths shut and not make trouble for me."

The corporal smiled, "you know me sarge, I can't resist giving you crap when it's obvious that somethings smells a bit rotten." Gaining a more serious tone, that drew Stephenie's attention, he added, "she going to be fit to travel?"

Stephenie took a deep breath and forced her eyes to remain open. She wanted to say she would, but she could not force the words from her mouth. The corporal walked over and knelt before her. She noted the concern on his face; that one she was sure could be very charming. She turned her face as he tried to put something in her mouth.

"It's just a little something to give you strength." He put one in his mouth and swallowed. "It'll help."

Reluctantly, she let him put the small mass in her mouth. It turned immediately bitter and, following his command, she swallowed it.

"Give it a few moments and you'll feel much better. Now let me wipe the blood from your face."

She sat quietly as he slowly and gently used a wet bit of cloth to clean her face and neck. As he moved to her hands, she felt herself grow more aware and able to focus. She took a deep breath, her head was still throbbing, but the dizziness had seemed to pass.

"What'd you give me?"

"Not a clue," the corporal chuckled. "I get them from a man down near the docks. Always tells me not to ask, so I don't. They work, but you don't want to take too many for too long, when you finally crash, you'll feel a thousand times worse than you do now. But the Sarge wants to move and I didn't think you would be able to without a bit of help."

She nodded her head. "Thanks."

"Don't mention it." He grinned again, "I mean it. Strictly speaking, we're not suppose to use things like that."

"Corporal, she ready to travel?"

The young man looked at her with questioning eyes. Sighing, she pushed herself to her feet. She was not nearly her normal self, but was feeling better than she had since she left the caves. "Yes, Henton, I am ready to travel, at least for a while."

The corporal winked at her and then turned back to Henton. Without a further word, Henton started off at a reasonable walk and Stephenie fell in behind him with Will remaining just a step behind her.

Chapter 13

"Sarge, she's still out and the rest of us are done with our rack time."

Henton opened his eyes. He had not been sleeping, just resting his eyes. Concern over what he was doing had kept any truly restful sleep from him through the whole of the morning and now it was early in the afternoon.

Slowly he moved into a sitting position, the four men left to him from The Scarlet all watching him expectantly. They had all saved each others lives multiple times in the last year and a half, now he had asked them to get involved with a witch when he could not tell them what she was. But he knew that their options were limited. Nermin, his holy warrior friend, had confided in him that the invaders were far too powerful for any of the priests. The power of Elrin's evil was washing over Felis' faithful like the breaking of the swell of a massive tidal wave against a sand castle. If she could not provide Cothel's forces with the knowledge of a weakness, then all would be lost.

"Men, you know when we delivered those damn Kynton soldiers to the castle, I got myself mixed up in a mess."

"You never said much of anything about it. We heard you were babysitting some spoiled princess and had some cushy job."

Henton looked at Douglas and thought to order him to shave just because he did not like looking at the stupid beard the boy had decided to grow. Instead he shook his head. "I was ordered to keep Princess Stephenie locked in her rooms. The Queen, I had understood, wanted her controlled. You see, I happened to be the reason she had not managed to escape the castle. If she had, perhaps things would now be different.

"Will, what do you think you know?" Henton said, noting realization dawning on his corporal's face.

"I'm taking it Princess Stephenie was not killed or secreted away like the rumors have it. The soldiers that were kicked out of the castle and sent to guard the streets talked a bit, saying the Queen was always a bit of a bitch to her daughter. I saw a young conscript get the crap kicked out of him by a couple of ex-castle guards for talking ill of the Princess. Seems they were quite fond of her."

"She has a very commanding personality," Henton said with a grin.

"And a pretty face when not covered with blood and dirt?" Will asked slyly.

Henton watched Fish glancing back and forth between Stephenie and Will. His jaw had dropped and he had not found cause to close it yet.

"Yes, Will. She had a very pretty face when she had not recently been beaten, which the Kynton soldiers had done to her once I turned her back over to them. But that is not the point. The point is, with the Queen turned traitor, the King and Prince dead, her other sisters dead, captured or fled, she is actually now the Queen. At least as far as I am concerned. The problem is, getting her back into the castle without getting her killed by someone bent on trying to usurp the crown. That, and convincing—"

"I told you I am not going back to the castle. I'm going to kill that bitch who destroyed my family and this country."

Corporal Will, rose to his feet, turned, and executed a bow. "Your Highness."

Henton took a deep breath, but remained seated. "Your Majesty, I had hoped to fill in my men and then talk with you privately about what the next steps are."

He watched as the others, uncertain of themselves, slowly rose and gave Stephenie a bow, most of which were not executed with any skill. Stephenie did not appear to notice, she simply glared at him, irritation and a bit of anger creeping through the exhaustion that filled her features.

"You intended to use these men to convince me when I told you already it would not be possible."

Henton stood. "Stephenie, you are the last of your line. It is your obligation to take the throne. Just as it was my obligation to serve in the navy because my father decided I should, you have an obligation, no matter how much you might not want it. You might even find you like it."

"My father and brother need to be avenged. I am not fit to rule and you know it."

"Your Highness?"

Henton and Stephenie turned to look at Zac, his red hair in as much disarray as hers. "I'm not sure your brother, the Prince, is dead."

"What?" Stephenie and Henton demanded in unison.

"Ma'am, you see, I heard rumors from some soldiers who had managed to escape the front lines. They were people I had known when I was growing up and so I didn't report them when they came through to get what little they could before heading south to try and avoid the fighting. They gave their all and the front was lost."

"Private, please, tell me what you know about my brother and father."

"Ma'am," he said, bowing his head again. "Your father, I know people who saw him fall. May he live with the gods forever, the heathens took his head. But your brother, these men say he was on a special mission, trying to sneak across the lines. He and his men were captured, several were killed, others left for dead. For a while, my friend was a captive with your brother. No one said who he was and the heathens simply assumed they were all just spies or common soldiers, no one had rank and they were being taken away to be slaves."

"Slaves?"

"Yes ma'am. My friend was injured and they thought he'd die. They didn't bother healing any of our men, but those healthy enough were taken to work on the west side of the Grey's. Seems the invaders are mining and digging. Perhaps there is gold. Your brother was last seen alive and healthy and no one knew who he was."

Henton saw Stephenie's eyes were alight as she looked toward him. "You want someone back on the throne, it would be my brother. He's the rightful heir and he knows what he's doing. Help me rescue him and you can help save the country."

"Your Majesty, we do not know that he's still alive. We know you are and you are here, within easy distance of the throne."

"If I am your queen, then obey my orders. Help me rescue my brother and put him on the throne."

Henton cursed and looked away. *Why is it that people can't see reason?* He looked up to meet her eyes. "This is foolish. We have to cross hundreds of miles of countryside, skirt around the Grey's, get through enemy lines, find your brother, figure out a way to rescue him, then get out, get back here, and hope there is still a country left for him to rule."

"Henton. I know what we are up against. But as I said, I cannot take the throne. So, if you want someone reasonable on the throne, you need my brother. If we were an army, we'd not be able to do this. But a handful of men could do it. We'd just have to be careful, fast, and avoid being seen. Definitely dump the colors and maybe even the armor to avoid the insignia, but we could cover it with some nondescript tunics. There's enough of us that I would think most thugs would leave us alone and we aren't carrying anything of value anyway."

"Aside from you."

"I can hold my own. Six people can move quickly and quietly. Perhaps even borrow some horses."

"You steal some horses and you'll have hangmen coming after us. You'd need to be able to jog all day for many days." Henton shook his head. He could tell it was a lost cause to argue, but he could not simply leave his concerns unsaid. "I'm a sailor. I can't tell you where we are going or even how far it is."

"It's about four hundred miles to the northern edge of the Grey's. Perhaps another fifty to get around to the west side and hopefully my brother. Half would be on roads, the other half across open prairie and some forests. Mostly west, but a little south. We do a forced march, assuming we can pick up food along the way, we should be able to press hard and do twenty five to thirty five miles a day. That means thirteen days at best and say twenty at worst, if we can't quite average twenty five miles a day."

"You've thought about this," he said, feeling a slight change in his level of confidence.

"I studied maps and planned and prepared. I'd have made the trip myself long ago if someone had not stopped me."

He could hear the tinge of accusation in her voice, but did not see anger or hate in her eyes. Just desperation.

"Look," she said, turning to face everyone in turn, "I can't pay right now, what money I have on me we will need to save for the journey, just in case. But I can promise you that I would make sure you would all be promoted to the rank of personal guard. It pays well and I would make sure that none of you are cheated. We just need to survive this and get my brother out." She took a deep breath and moved closer slowly, continuing to look everyone in the eye. "I know this is risky and I know there is a good chance we might all end up dead. But, if we do nothing, a lot of people will die and the country will fall to the invaders or be torn apart by internal struggles. I can imagine a handful of dukes and barons who will all make claims to the throne. My brother can salvage the country. He's the best chance. I don't know what we will find when we get there and I won't take it personally if none of you want to come. Just know that I could use your help and would be grateful for anything you are willing to do."

The last she said looking directly into Henton's eyes. He did not turn away, but he knew the other four were watching him closely and would follow his lead. Two ten-days of constant forced march to put himself on the front line of a war that was lost was terrifying in the insanity that it represented, but he knew she had a point.

He finally turned his focus to his men. "Not one of you would be a coward to say no. You've given more sweat and blood than truly your obligations require. If—"

"Sarge, if you're going, count me in," Corporal Will interrupted.

"Same, here", the other three added.

"Okay. I guess that is decided. Your Majesty, we can't refer to you by title or even treat you as a lady. If we do this, I expect that you'll need to suffer the indignity of a common soldier." He could not help but grin at the relief that was on her face. "You said to call you Steph earlier. I propose that we all address you as such. Everyone will need to call me Henton. We lose our rank at this point. Considering we are for all intent deserting our posts without leave, we really do not want to draw attention in that manner." Henton sighed, "Steph, the Corporal is Will or William."

"Call me Will Ma'am."

"That one with the stupid grin is Michael, but we all call him Fish because he's always stripping down and jumping in water."

"Ma'am," the tall man said, bowing his head slightly.

"Douglas is trying to look ten years older with that beard and Zac's the one that has friends all over the place."

Stephenie nodded to each one in turn. "I really appreciate this and yes, please feel free to call me Steph. I hope we can all get to know each other better. I've always been fond of the guards I've had and you might have heard I can be difficult, but that really is only if someone is trying to lock me up and keep me from doing what I know needs to be done."

"Well, Steph, we are past noon, I propose we find a town, one you've not been in, pick up some supplies, and put some distance between us and the coast. We've got a lot of days to cover and the more time we give things to fester, the worse they might get. You well enough to travel?"

"I'm a bit famished. I've gone a while just eating half cooked snake and rabbit. But I'll manage."

Henton picked up his small pack and pulled out a chunk of cheese and some dried meat. "None of us are equipped for an extended journey. We've got a day or so of food and our water is mostly gone. No blankets or rain gear. We'll have to make do with what we have and pick up some things. I've got a few coin on me, I imagine the men do as well. Are you well off money wise?"

"I've got a little and some bits of gold and silver. But it's not stamped, so we might have trouble trading it. There should be several towns along the road to East Fork. The town of Telling should be the first safe one to stop at. Probably three or four hours to the west from here."

Henton nodded. "Okay, but only two people will go into town. I'll go with Fish when we get there. The rest of you will have to wait out of sight. The less people see us together, the better."

He turned west and started heading through the thin forest, trusting everyone to fall into step behind him. This was crazy, but he had to admit to himself that a witch on the throne was a terrifying proposition. If it did come out, the country would be torn apart by that just the same as doing nothing. The crown prince was a better choice. Then he swallowed, *what if the prince was a warlock?* He would need to ask Stephenie when he had her alone.

Stephenie was feeling the toll on her body when they finally slowed from a jog to a walk. She was not the only one panting and working to catch their breath, but she was the most winded. She had jogged farther and much harder with Joshua, but her chest was tight and her limbs felt like logs.

"You okay?"

There was obvious concern in Henton's voice; Stephenie was unable to see his face, bent over as she was. She tried to claim she was, but could not get it out. Instead she nodded her head weakly and continued to pant.

"We can take this slower."

She shook her head no and forced herself to stand up straight. "No. I don't know how long it's been since the last you saw me, but I've not been eating well. I must have lost some conditioning."

"As well as some blood, based on the state of your cut up and stained clothing." He took a couple of deep breaths himself and surveyed the others. "I can smell wood smoke, so we are not far from Telling. Fish, you're with me. Steph, if you can give me some of the money you have, we'll go get us some supplies. The rest of you, remain here. We should not be too long."

Stephenie nodded and handed her pocket full of money and flattened silver to Henton. He appraised it quickly and put it into his pouch without comment. He was gone before she could sit down to rest.

"Ma'am, can I get you anything?"

She looked up into Zac's blue eyes, darkened by the fading light. "Water," she mumbled, wondering just how long it would take and if she would ever heal from what Kas had done to her.

The young man was back before she had stopped wondering, having gathered everyone's water skin. "It's not much, but this is what we have left. And here are some biscuits I had been saving. They're sweet; got some funny spice and some sugar in them."

Gratefully, she took the water skins and drained what was left of two of them. She looked at the cookie and the rumbling in her stomach overrode the guilt she felt in taking something that would have likely cost the private a fair sum. "Thank you Zac," she mumbled as she chewed the hard, but delicious treat.

"My pleasure Ma'am."

"Please, call me Steph. Everyone needs to get used to that. I'm just a grunt as my sister would say, not fit for the dinner table at family gatherings." Zac appeared a little taken aback by the comment. "My father and brother encouraged me in the less feminine pursuits," she added with a smile, "and they never had trouble dining with me."

"Ma'am, I mean Steph, I couldn't see how someone could be troubled to dine with you. We heard some rumors, not from Sarge, I mean Henton; but from other soldiers who had worked in the castle, they all loved you. They said you could best the arms master if you ever tried."

She smiled, warmed that there were some people still who liked her, at least while they did not know what she was. "They exaggerate, but I am glad for the compliment."

"What happened to you?"

"Ya," Will interjected, "if you don't mind us asking?" He came closer, handing her a piece of bread and some cheese, which she gratefully took.

Stephenie glanced once to Douglas, who was squatting next to a tree and watching the woods, but definitely listening to the conversation. Zac she knew was her age, Will maybe two years older, and Douglas' beard could not truly hide his youth. The three of them were like many of the younger soldiers she had grown up around, outwardly confident, but unsure what to make of her. She could read it in their body language and just sense the undercurrent in the air.

"I was spying on my mother and was found out. I ran deep into the catacombs under the castle and managed to lose them, as well as myself. I don't know how long I was under there, but being lost in the dark and struggling to find food took a lot out of me."

"Well, its been just over a ten-day since the Sarge came back to us. The next day the Queen left," Zac said, his eyes glued to her. "You went that long buried in the ground?" He shuddered.

Stephenie thought back to Kas and Arkani; despite her desperation to warn her father and brother, she had allowed herself some peace and enjoyment with Kas and learning about herself. "It was not as bad as it sounds. I did get a bit beat up and was famished, still am a bit," she added, "but looking back now, it was not as bad as it could have been. Definitely frightening at times, but as long as I didn't let myself get panicked, I was able to push through."

"You've got my admiration," Will said, shaking his head. "I wouldn't have done that well. On ship, we've always got someone watching our back—"

"And watching us using the pot," Douglas added from where he watched.

Will nodded his head, "but alone in the dark?" He shook his head, "no thank you."

"Well, I appreciate the support. Looking back is always easier than when you are in the middle of it."

Douglas rose to his feet and turned toward her. "Not to be rude and all, but hearing stories is one thing, seeing is another. You appear to have survived well enough, but you really think you can fight?"

Zac was on his feet in a flash and face to chest with Douglas, who was a good head taller. "I won't have you disrespecting her!"

Douglas kept his focus on Stephenie and quietly waited.

Stephenie could feel the tension coming from Zac and Will, overriding anything that Douglas might have been feeling. She took a deep breath. "Douglas, I respect your concern. I won't lie, I'm not what I was before—before I got myself lost underground. I am having a hard time keeping my breath and I feel so weak at the moment. It scares the crap out of me, but I don't have a choice. I'll recover or I won't. I know how to fight and I think I killed at least two people in that town, but it left me drained."

Will moved a step closer and into her line of sight. "What happened in that town? Sarge said the town's folk killed a couple of them and were going to hang the leader of that gang."

Stephenie swallowed, feeling very stupid for bringing up something that tied her directly to witchcraft and not keeping to Henton's story. She decided she could not go back now. "I was trying to get my first real meal in days and learn what was going on. I was just sitting there, reeling from hearing my brother and father were dead."

"Your brother might still be alive," Zac added, no longer confronting Douglas, but moving back to her. She sensed a strong protectiveness from him.

"Yes, but at the time, I didn't know that. These men came in, started demanding money and threatening to rape the barmaid and myself." She looked toward Douglas, trying to ignore the indignation on Zac's face. "They had the back door guarded and several people at the front door. I had my dagger, that's all. I goaded the leader into getting in close. He was probably your height Douglas." She took a deep breath, unhappy about having to kill the boy that had come up behind her, he was Zac's age. "I reversed my dagger, slashed his hand, stomped on his foot, broke his knee, and then sent him sprawling across the floor. One came up behind me with a sword and I got in under his reach, stabbed him in the groin, since there was a gap in his leather there. I took his sword from him." She closed her eyes, remembering the smell of burning flesh as the woman burst into flames instead of the crossbow moving as she had intended. "I escaped by jumping through a window."

Zac was on his knees, almost reaching out with his hands to comfort her. "There were nine of us going after that gang. Didn't the town's people do anything to help?"

She smiled at him, forcing down the memories. "It's past. We've got far more important things to do, like rescuing my brother."

She looked up at Douglas, who nodded his head. "I was not trying to be rude Ma'am, and I'm not going to abandon this mission, but a man will have doubts."

"Well, you shouldn't. The Sarge—Henton, trusts her, and so do the rest of us. If you didn't want to come, you could have gone back with the others."

"Zac, calm down." Will raised his hand to stop the outburst that Zac was about to unleash. "Douglas wasn't completely out of line." He turned to Douglas, "if you do have doubts, you might want to raise them more tactfully."

"I said I had not—"

"Please, everyone stop arguing." Stephenie mustered the strength to stand up. "Douglas, I understand your concern and I've taken no offense. So please, Zac, Will, I appreciate your desire to protect my honor. But we have to trust each other and that includes trusting that we are able to question and doubt without being made an outcast or shunned. Your concerns Douglas, I have them myself. I was hurt under the castle. I fell and landed badly. I'm not whole, not yet, but I will push through it and do what must be done.

"None of you have to come and I respect all of you so much more for your decision to do so. If any of you change your mind as we go on, I will respect that as well. I just ask that nothing you hear along the way is repeated. I don't want to risk the rest of us because of something someone says."

"Ma'am, I'm with you all the way."

"Thank you Zac. But I mean it, if anyone changes their mind, I do understand."

Douglas nodded his head and went back to watching the woods.

She glanced at Will who smiled at her. "You should get some rest. The three of us will keep watch until Henton comes back."

Chapter 14

Stephenie awoke slowly in the morning. She had two blankets under her and one over her. Zac and Fish had each one blanket and had shared those with the others as they had taken watches overnight. Henton had only been able to buy some meager supplies from Telling without drawing too much notice and despite her arguing that she did not need three blankets, none of the others had paid any attention.

Realizing that the sun was already casting a red glow over the horizon, she also knew that none of them had woken her as promised for guard duty. The twinge of irritation at being treated differently faded as she realized just how tired she had been. *And perhaps it was because I've been injured,* she thought, hoping their skipping her was not because she was a girl or a princess. She would have a talk with Henton at some point if it happened again.

Lifting her head drew the attention of Zac, who quickly came over. "Can I get you anything? I've a bit of a bread and meat the Sarge brought back. Saved you some."

Stephenie stretched her shoulders and smiled at the red head. "Thank you. That sounds good."

"You might also want to get cleaned up," Henton said from across the camp. "There is a stream not far to the north. If someone sees us on the road, your hair might draw some attention." He tossed her a brown shirt, which she caught. "Don't throw out that thing you have on, but it is looking quite worn...and missing the sleeves."

"Thank you," she said to Henton, and again to Zac as she took the food from his hand.

"We've filled the water skins, so don't worry about keeping the stream clear."

It was several hours later before Henton called a stop to their march, which had been a mix of jogging and a fast walk. Stephenie felt stronger for having eaten some additional food, but was glad for the rest. She had munched as they moved and had run out of food and water some time earlier.

Her back was also a bit sore from the bouncing of the books she had put into the pack Henton purchased for her. She had noted his apparent desire to question her over her bundle and was glad he had not actually vocalized the question. While the books themselves would not be overly suspicious, the glowing crystals would definitely cause her trouble.

"Eat and rest a bit. Give Will your water skins and he'll refill them in the stream before anyone decides to splash around."

Stephenie looked up at Henton as she handed the empty bladder to Will. "I can carry a bit more food and supplies."

He watched her for a moment and then shook his head. "Did you eat your whole share already?"

"You can have some of mine," Zac said, already on his feet and coming over to her.

She looked at the redhead and shook her head. "No, I thought you had only given me a portion. I won't eat someone else's share as well."

"Steph, I won't eat it. Besides, you've been half starved and injured. Please, I want to give it to you."

"Zac, you eat your rations." Henton, shaking his head, brought over his small pack. "Yes, I had only given you a portion of your share. I'll make sure to buy some extra until you're back to normal. Considering you didn't eat much when you were in the tower, I imagine these last couple of days have been the first real set of meals you've had in a while."

She smiled, taking the bread and cheese from Henton, knowing he was lying about having held back her share. "I had no way of knowing when someone might put something into the food. And quite frankly, I really didn't know if I could fully trust you."

"What about now?"

She took a deep breath, trying to feel his emotions, but as always, he was quiet and reserved. "I trust you. I trust all of you. It's not something easy for me, but I do."

"Here, here," Fish said. "To our band of crazies."

She smiled and sat down to eat Henton's food and tried to ignore the frequent glances and looks the others continued to give her.

They walked and jogged well into the evening, having skirted around two other towns, with Henton and Will having stopped at the second one to purchase some additional supplies. The night was cool and everyone agreed there would be no fire. In the middle of the night, Stephenie awoke to Henton shaking her shoulder.

"The others are out, let's have a bit of a talk."

She got up slowly, stiff from the effort of the last couple of days. Quietly, she followed Henton through the camp, the light from the Mother Moon providing more than enough illumination for her to see clearly. When they reached a small river, several hundred feet away from the others, he stopped and turned to face her.

"Okay, before we go all the way to the mountains, I really need to clear a few things up with you."

"Okay," she said, unsure if Henton had seen her head nod.

"Is your brother like you?"

"No. He's not a warlock. I'm the only one, and honestly, he doesn't know. My mother was the only one who knew, which was why she hated me so much."

"And you have not sold your soul to Elrin."

Stephenie swallowed, missing Kas and understanding his repeated accusations of ignorance. "No. I was born as I am. Henton, there are things about witches and warlocks that people just don't understand. Most of what people believe is not true."

He pursed his lips for a moment. "If you were born this way, that would mean, assuming what people believe, that your mother committed some mortal sin that caused you to be cursed with Elrin's touch. I can see why she would not want to harm you and keep you close. She, and everyone else, would believe that the curse would transfer to her."

"Yes. Except that she thinks she found a way to stop the curse. I'm not sure how, it really doesn't matter, because it doesn't work like that, but she planned to sacrifice me and eat my heart or something like that. I think she was also trying to sell out my father and brother to the Senzar forces. I think she was planning on getting Islet back from the invaders in exchange. So she had her brother's troops take everything of value and leave our troops without supplies."

"Well, we know she did that. The caravan left to the west, then turned north outside of Antar so most of the people in the city would not be aware. It was cunning, but traitorous. If she ever came back, most of the loyal soldiers would probably try to hang her."

"You'd all have to be in line after me. I'm probably weak and somewhat cowardly in that I really don't like hurting people, but that bitch needs to die for what she did."

"Not wanting to hurt people does not make you weak. I've seen your handy work and even felt it. You don't appear to hesitate when you have need."

Stephenie bit back emotions that threatened to undo her composure. "I had not intended to kill the man that was with you in the hall. I did not intend to hurt either of you. I just needed you out of the way. He was the first man I've killed. Since then, I've directly killed two other people and was present when a third died. I don't like to think about it, but I will do what's needed to protect myself and those I care about."

"As I said, not a coward. But I need to understand what you can do and what we are up against. On The Scarlet, Lord Nermin, my friend, the holy warrior of Felis, handled any warlocks or priests on enemy boats. My instructions were always to stay out of the way and if possible, kill them before they knew I was trying. I don't think me or my men will have that luxury at this point. We don't want the others to know about you. I kept them away from what you did to that gang, initially because I didn't want them to get caught up digging graves, but once I learned you might have been responsible, I didn't want them to know."

"Thank you. I don't think it would go over all that well. I'm actually quite surprised that you accept me as well as you do."

Henton looked away for a bit, then back to her. "I've never been one to accept everything everyone says, but it is not easy for me you being a witch. If I had not picked up a certain feel for you before I learned what you can do, I don't think we would be talking right now. I don't think you are evil. The thought of what I might be getting myself into scares me, but honestly, you are the best hope for this country." He raised his hand, "okay, perhaps your brother is a better hope, but we have to be realistic, he might not even be alive at this point. However, putting you on the throne would be a risk, at some point, someone might find out and then the country would again be without a ruler. Your brother, if he's not a warlock, would definitely be a safer bet.

"Plus, you are the youngest of your family and the least well known. You have not been paraded around lately and to be honest, a fourth daughter when the first born is a prince, means you really are extra."

"Thanks," she teased, not really taking it as an insult, since she had known that already for the better part of her life.

"But, I need to know what you can do. I know you can smash people into walls and burn them to death. Can you make people do what you want? What kind of spells and curses can you cast? What's in that bundle you have bouncing on your back?"

"Henton, I know what the priests say, believe me. I know what mothers say and the stories told by soldiers around camp fires. I believed many of those things myself up until a short while ago, so I'm not going to try and convince you otherwise. I'd love it if you'd give me the benefit of the doubt and even more so if you would consider perhaps that what's been said over the years about Elrin and witches and warlocks are actually lies. However, I won't respect you less if you don't."

"You mentioned this the other day."

Stephenie felt her pulse increase and a lingering hope creep into her chest. "It's all lies Henton. There is no Elrin. The power that I have is not from some god and it has nothing to do with the elves. The priests and I share similar capabilities because those of us who can use this power just have the ability to do so. The priests are also making use of a secondary source of power from outside this world, but it is not that of the gods. The old gods, the very old ones that people have forgotten, might still exist somewhere, but the ones we currently worship, they are not the sources of the power."

"Stephenie—"

"Just consider the possibility of what I am saying. I'm not the first to make those statements. I've heard them before, by people that are called heretics and usually end up dead, but please, just consider that there might be a possibility it is true."

Henton remained quiet for a long time and Stephenie felt her hope move from her chest into the pit of her stomach and turn to fear. She tried to reach out with her mind as Kas had tried to teach her. She felt a bit of fear and apprehension coming from Henton, but it was muted as he had always been to her.

"I'm sorry. I've said too much. But to answer your question, I don't cast spells. I can manipulate energy that surrounds and penetrates all of us, including the ground and the air. I'm not very good. I've not learned much control, but I can move things, when I don't cause them to accidentally burst into flame. That woman...I had not intended to burn her, just push away the crossbow she was going to shoot me with.

"I can heat things. Make them real hot and once I made something cold. The only other thing I can do right now is get a sense of when someone's about."

"What kind of sense?"

Stephenie swallowed, glad that Henton was listening to her, but worried about the cold and mechanical sound to his voice. "I could sense every one of your guard changes in the tower. I could feel them walking up the stairs a couple of floors below me. I applaud how random and quiet you tried to make them so I wouldn't know when they were happening."

"And how'd you get out of your room."

She grinned, his voice had thawed a little with curiosity. "There were some loose floor boards in my back room. In one of the support beams of the floor, I had a carved-out section with a rope and a change of clothes. I simply climbed down to the storage room below and snuck out. Then went into the catacombs and across to the kitchens for supplies. I was going to go over the wall, but I saw someone come into the castle and go to the keep. I thought I might overhear something pertaining to the front. It turned out to be one of the Senzar mages—or warlocks. He sensed me in the secret passage adjoining my mother's study and that's what set the chase going.

"I tried to escape into the old tunnels and got lost. A guard had followed and found me, but we fell through an old bridge. He died in the fall. I don't feel responsible for his death." Stephenie took a deep breath. "From there, I wandered in the dark, falling again and getting hurt." She hesitated. She considered mentioning Arkani, but could not bring herself to trust Henton that much. "It was a long time before I managed to get out. But in the process, I managed to learn a bit about myself."

"And your bundle? You were not carrying that when you went past me. Anything of use in there?"

"Just some books. Old books that talk about magic." She took a deep breath. "I told the others that I will understand if any of you change your mind about helping me. I won't hold it against you."

Henton took her forearm in his hand. "Let's get back. I don't want to leave the others alone too long." He paused and she returned his gaze in the darkness. "I need time to digest what you've said. I'm not going to leave you. But, I need time to think about it."

By the end of the next day, having eaten and drank more than anyone else, Stephenie was feeling much stronger. She no longer felt winded and the others had commented, with even a bit of envy, that she was less winded then they were after a day of jogging and marching. Henton had sent Will and Fish into one of the towns they passed along the road to buy more food, insisting that they all needed to eat a lot to keep up their energy. That evening they had a small fire and roasted a couple of chickens Will had included in the purchases. Nothing was left of the meal.

The following day, they stayed on the road, passing several groups of travelers heading to the coast, riding the wave of fear coming from the west. They asked a couple of questions of those fleeing the rumor of the invading army, but no one had seen anything for themselves, aside from their own countrymen turning rogue.

Henton avoided most questions and ignored warnings to turn back, opting instead to cut the conversation short and continue their quick pace.

Just after the sun crested the high point for the day, the road grew close to the Uthen River. A wide, but slow channel of water bargemen used to transport minerals and raw materials from the Duchy of Uthen down toward the coast.

"The road will turn north and follow the river. My plan was always to cross around here. If we can find a barge in the next couple of miles to ferry us across, so much the better, but otherwise, I had planned to swim it. We'll be off the main road, but I'd rather head almost due west and get to East Fork and likely save a day of travel."

Stephenie watched as the others surveyed the river. She expected the waters to still be a bit cold. When she had planned for her own travels, she had not been intimidated by the cold, knowing that her powers always kept her warm enough when she swam in the sea. However, with five other men, she might have to adjust a bit if they were not up to the cold.

"I'm game."

"Fish, you are always game to strip down for a swim, but the rest of us can only really stay afloat. Sarge only made sure we'd not sink if we fell in, he never wanted us to be as much a freak as you."

Henton shook his head. "As much as I don't like to refer to you as a freak Fish, I have to agree with Will. Steph, we need to find a barge. That's too far for the men to swim, not to mention, everything you are carrying will get wet and ruined."

"Clothes will dry Henton," Zac said. "And, we can always get warm with body heat on the other side."

Stephenie sensed Zac's underlying motivation and desire for her, but chose to ignore it for now. Her original plan also did not have her carrying books. "Agreed Henton, we follow the road until we find a barge and hope that we can convince them to ferry us across. The worst that can happen is we follow the road and cross the bridge at Denington and fail to cut that day off."

"Well, assuming that we can get across, we might also want to find some food first. We'll need to carry more if we are off the main roads, we won't be able to just stop at the next town to buy more."

Stephenie nodded her head as Henton picked up the jog again, following the road still to the west. It would be an eighth of a day's travel before it truly turned north and started to take them out of their way.

The day was getting into the late afternoon before they neared a small town called Venla. They had seen two barges pass them earlier in the day and neither had chosen to acknowledge their calls from the bank.

"Jim was from around these parts and he said bargemen were a suspicious and greedy lot. Wouldn't save a man from drowning unless there was sure profit to be had."

"Douglas," Henton chastised, "you know Jim never had anything good to say about anyone. So you can't judge based on two barges who didn't want to pull to shore to find out just what a group of armed men wanted."

"Could have put Steph on the banks and had her flash her pretty smile."

"Fish, you take that back!"

Stephenie put her hand on Zac's arm. "He's only teasing. Besides, if this keeps up, I'll flash whatever it takes to get us across."

Henton raised his hand and everyone quieted and stopped. Ahead of them and down in a valley was the walled town of Venla. Inside the walls, there were several barges tied up along the river next to a number of large wattle and daub buildings with thatched roofs. Further inland, and along the road, were a couple dozen smaller buildings. Another dozen buildings, small farms, and corrals were outside the walls. "I think we'll all have to go into the town. We can reprovision and arrange for someone to take us to the other side of the river. We'll avoid our real names here I think. Let's go with what we used in Myt when we were getting into trouble.

"Will, Fish, Zac, you three get us at least four or five days of rations. You'll probably have to get some larger packs to carry it. Also get something that's been oiled to protect it. I think we'll be seeing rain tonight or tomorrow if those clouds keep up like they are. Let Fish do the buying, he's better than I am. Besides, he still has the coin from the last stop. And don't split up."

"Thanks Sarge."

"Karl, if you please." He corrected, then turned to Douglas and Stephenie. "The three of us will arrange passage across the river. Steph, we're also going to need to break more of your silver."

"Can we stop at the temple?" Douglas asked. "I'd like to make an offering if we have time."

"Sure, two turns of the glass should be more than enough time for you three to get the food and supplies."

"Should be, Karl," Will added with emphasis, Fish and Zac standing behind him.

"Then let's get moving, time's a wasting."

The East gates to the town of Venla were open, but there were six guards on duty. "What's your business here?" a man wearing the colors of Duke Richard Burdger demanded as they approached. Stephenie wondered why Burdger's men were outside the duke's duchy, but held her tongue as Henton stepped forward.

"We're heading west and need some supplies. We're taking news to the families of some of our friends who have recently died. It was our deathbed promise."

"You have money to buy supplies?"

Henton pulled a pouch out of his shirt pocket and jingled the coins inside.

"Okay, been having trouble with deserters and thieves."

"We're neither."

"You look army."

"We were, but have leave. Besides, it'd be a bit foolish to desert toward the fighting."

The guard chuckled and waved them into the town.

Inside, Stephenie looked around at the people with their hurried pace and worried expressions. There were many soldiers about as well as fearful citizens. Will, Zac, and Fish silently broke off and continued along the main road toward what appeared to be a small market area among the larger group of buildings in the town.

Henton veered left, toward the river and warehouses. In a normal year, spring goods and supplies would be making their way east, down toward the coast, with the hopes of being put on ship and traded across the sea or ferried north or south to another port in Cothel. The war had seen a larger movement of supplies to the west instead. However, it appeared that the uncertainty of what lay in Antar and eventual payment for the goods had left things languishing. Stephenie noted numerous crates, barrels, and piles of hay in and out of the warehouses. There were a number of barges and bargemen around, but none of them appeared to be loading or unloading much of anything.

Stephenie trailed just behind Henton, with Douglas on her left. She glanced his way, sensing a wariness in him that she did not know how to place. Of all of Henton's men, he was the only one that watched her as one might watch a stranger in their home. She could not be certain, but his unease felt directed elsewhere for the time being.

Stephenie came out of her contemplation when Henton slowed to a stop next to a group of men standing idly by the wharf. The eight men straightened slightly and Stephenie felt their eyes linger on her a little too long, reminding her of the leering stares her mother's soldiers had given her. The soldiers she befriended before the war had never looked at her as merely an object and she had to push down her irritation.

"We'd like to arrange transportation across the river," Henton said, a slight hint of irritation in his own voice.

"We're not going nowhere. No pay, no work."

Henton shifted his stance slightly to address the brown-haired man that had spoken. "We just need transport across the river for six people and some supplies. We'll pay for the effort, a small amount of work could give you enough coin for a couple rounds of ale in the tavern."

"Nothin' on the other side of the river."

Henton took a deep breath. "Not that it's any of your business, but my sister and her husband live on the other side of said river. They're but just over a day to the south. I'd like to save the time of walking all the way to the nearest bridge. I'm offering eight square for a quick and easy trip. Better than standing around doing nothing."

"Make it a crown and you've a deal."

"I'll do it for ten," a thin man near the back said as he moved forward despite the angry glare from the brown haired man. "When do you want to leave?"

"As soon as my companions purchase a few supplies." Henton, pulled a small group of square coins from his shirt pocket and handed over all but two coins. "I'm Karl, this is Glenn and Beth."

The slim man took the coins and put them in his belt pouch, then shook Henton's hand. "Baltic's the name. I've got the small craft down past the wharf." He pointed to a wide, flat bottom boat with six oars angled up off the ground. It was obviously not designed for heavy cargo and Stephenie suspected this man serviced some of the smaller and more shallow tributaries, bringing smaller loads into town for others to haul away. "I'll get my crew ready while we wait for your friends."

Henton nodded to Baltic and ignored the angry stares of the other men. He led Stephenie and Douglas in the general direction of the small craft. However, the three of them remained in an open area where there was no one else in near proximity. "Will should keep the others moving. Then we get out of town before those other men take issue with us."

Stephenie watched as Baltic gathered three other men to his boat and started to move around the few crates that were still on board. After they finished and sat down to wait, she turned her attention back up the hill to the town proper and started watching the town people as they went about their tasks.

There was a definite unease in the movements of people; a fear and uncertainty held barely in check by resignation or perhaps an unjustified hope for something better. The invading armies were not here yet, so panic and retreat was not filling the streets, but it was apparent that most with the ability to leave had already left.

Stephenie sighed, feeling the weight of failure on her shoulders. The plight of those unable to flee should not be ignored by those with responsibility. She had heard the arguments from certain lords and advisers that it was healthy to cull the herd from time to time. If those too weak to survive persisted, they would drag down the rest of the populace and the country. She even agreed with the premise to a certain extent, but neither her father, nor Joshua, nor her own heart, carried the cold disdain and indifference that others in power seemed to be able to call forth.

"I still think you could do more good by taking charge than running off on an errand that is nearly certain to result in your death, as well as ours."

Stephenie turned her head slightly to look at Henton, whom she had felt come up quietly behind her. "I don't need you trying to make this harder. You know why I can't. I don't like what is happening, but I am not ignoring it, I am actively trying to address it."

He raised his hands. "Peace. I just saw the way you were looking around."

Stephenie shook her head. "I am trying to be realistic and hope I am not growing callous. But, I can only help these people in certain ways."

"No. If you ever stop showing the concern I have seen in you, I will let you know. And then I will leave you to your own ends. I am here because I see you really do love your country and people. Not because I think it will give me a chance at money or influence. Most likely, I'll end up dead if the truth be—"

Stephenie cut Henton off with a subtle change of posture. Her focus was up the hill toward a group of men that had been talking to a handful of barge men. She turned toward Henton, shifting her back toward the men. "I think I was recognized."

"Who?" Henton asked, but did not turn toward the group of men.

"Lord Elard is up there. He's Duke Burdger's son. For a time he thought to court me, but Joshua put him straight. His father was generally a friend of my father's. That would explain why the Duke's men are here, but not why they are guarding the gates."

"Glenn, got a moment?" Henton said, casually summoning their companion. When Douglas grew closer, he added. "The group of men up the hill behind us, in the Duke's colors, they coming this way?"

Douglas, playing his part, turned back toward the river and looked at the barge that was being prepared for them. "Nope, I noticed they watched me coming over, but have started up the hill toward the town."

"Perhaps you were not recognized," Henton said to Stephenie.

She shook her head. "He knows or at least suspects who I am. I could tell."

"Is he trouble?"

Stephenie shrugged. "His father and mine were friends, at least I think so. Elard was always a bit proud and full of himself. But, I can't have him tagging along with us, that would not work. Nor can I have him drag me back to Antar. We have to rescue Josh."

Henton nodded and took a quick glance up the slope. "The others are likely still shopping. Will should keep them on task, but I don't know how much longer they will be. For now, you and Glenn get on the barge and try to avoid being recognized. I'll keep an eye out." He looked at Douglas, "sorry, have to skip the temple I'm afraid."

Stephenie stood in the flat bottomed barge facing the far shore. She found it difficult to keep her eyes off the town and its people, but it was better to keep her face hidden at this point. Douglas was facing her side, sitting on the wooden side rail. She assumed it allowed him to keep a watch on her and Henton at the same time. The bargemen were not currently on their vessel, instead, they were lounging in the shade of a nearby building and out of casual hearing.

"You carrying state secrets?" Douglas asked after a while. "Never hardly let that pack out of your sight."

She turned to face him and sat down on the worn planks below her. "No, just some books that might be useful later. Nothing too special."

He nodded his head, but did not say anything further.

"No one ever calls you Doug," she observed.

"My father named me Douglas, not Doug."

Stephenie waited a moment to see if he would elaborate further. When he did not she added, "my mother named me Stephenie, but my father and Josh—Joshua," she corrected, "always called me Steph. I just started liking it better."

"Girls should not be soldiers."

Stephenie sat up straighter, as did Douglas.

"Look at how Will and Zac are behaving. Even Sarge—Henton, is getting all protective. Someone's going to get hurt. Fish is the only one that doesn't seem to be prancing about. At least not more than his normal foolish self."

She opened her mouth to say something, but paused for a deep breath. "Well, what do you think we should do about it? Aside from me running off on my own and trying to lose you and the others, who I think might just try to follow me, you have any ideas?"

Douglas also opened his mouth and then grinned. "Smart-ass woman. I shouldn't of called you a girl." He shook his head, still grinning slightly. "I got nothin'. I just stand by what I said, girls make men think about one thing and it ain't fighting the enemy."

Stephenie smiled in spite of herself. She could sense Douglas had softened slightly and was not so tense. "I agree in part, but women can and have led armies many times. I've also known some women mercs, but they acted just like the men." She lowered her voice, "in cases like this, to be honest, I don't know if any of you would be chosen to be my personal guards. It does require detachment from both sides. You might hear stories of a princess falling in love with one of her guards and the two of them riding off to an isolated tower to live their lives in secret to avoid the king's disapproval. But the reality of it is far colder. If I was to fall in love with one of my guards, then I might put myself at risk to keep the guard from doing his job, which is potentially to die protecting me."

She took a deep breath. "Douglas, I have never enjoyed thinking about the role my protectors have to take and wish everyday that I would not need any and that I could just have simple friendships. And I have had friendships with just about everyone who's protected me, but there is always that painful undercurrent of truth waiting to emerge and ruin people's lives." She took another deep breath. "I desperately hope those who were protecting me before my mother turned completely traitorous are safe, but I fear the worst and blame myself."

She turned her head back toward the far bank and the fields of swaying grasses that covered the rolling hills. After a moment, she turned back to Douglas. "I know that does not fix what my presence is doing to Zac and the others, but honestly, I am not trying to lead any of you on."

He looked at her a moment more and then nodded his head. "I didn't say you were doing anything intentionally. But every stallion in the pen is going to prance around when a mare comes near." He looked back up the hill. "Looks like the others are on their way."

Chapter 15

The tall grasses dragged at Stephenie's legs. She knew that it was her magic that kept her going when the pack on her back should have long ago pulled her to the ground. The books plus food and other provisions were heavy and she knew that the others, despite claiming she was carrying an equal share, had taken some of the burden she should have.

She sighed with relief when Henton called a halt to their travels as they passed a stand of trees surrounding a gully and dry stream bed. It was growing dark and although they had a bit of a rest in Venla, Stephenie had been traveling hard and her head was aching from both the physical and mental effort.

"We keep the normal rotation for tonight," Henton stated, his own pack already sitting next to a tree. "Cold rations and no fire."

"What do you want me to do?"

"Steph, I want you to get some rest. You are keeping up better than I could ever have imagined, but I can see the toll you are under. Stretch a bit, then eat, and get some rest."

She nodded her head, too tired and with too much of a headache to argue.

Stephenie rolled onto her side again, unable to find a comfortable position. The days of sleeping on the hard wooden table had not yet managed to make the cold ground any more comfortable. After a couple of minutes, she returned to her back.

She had gotten some rest earlier in the evening, but now she just could not drift back to sleep. Opening her eyes, she looked up into the sky and could see the thin haze of clouds that was passing over the large Mother Moon, bringing some extra darkness and allowing the dim stars to brighten. Recognizing the nagging feeling in the back of her mind, she took a deep breath and concentrated on reaching out and feeling with her magic.

Quickly, she rolled over toward Henton and shook his shoulder. The sergeant immediately opened his eyes, but said nothing. "There are a dozen men approaching slowly from the north and east," she said as quietly as possible.

He said nothing as he crawled away from his blanket toward Fish. He gave her a quick hand gesture, that she interpreted as wake the others in her direction. Sensing the closing of the men in the grass, she crawled to Will and shook his shoulder. His eyes opened. She held out her hand, fingers spread and flashed it twice in front of his face, then pointed toward the east. He nodded his head, grabbed his sword, and rolled over to Zac. A moment later, the two of them were moving quietly to the south.

She felt Henton behind her and when she turned, he appeared to be signaling her to move west, away from the camp site. She removed her daggers from their sheaths, pressing the flats of the blades against her forearms to conceal the metal, and moved toward the dry stream bed further in the trees. Halfway there, she heard a startled cry of a man, then the sounds of steel against steel. With her magic, she could feel her companions engaging the approaching hardened and purposeful men. They were outnumbered more than two to one and while her warning might give them the advantage of surprise, it would not last long.

Ignoring Henton's command, she moved quickly toward Zac, who had three men engaging him. As she closed, one of the men turned toward the noise she was making and she could clearly see his blue eyes despite the darkness. She could also sense the underlying discipline and training of a professional soldier.

The man swung his sword up and Stephenie went low and stepped forward. Reversing the grip on her right blade, she drove it into his thigh. He howled in pain and tried to back hand her with his left hand. Knowing her reach was limited with her daggers, she stayed close, raising her own left forearm to block the blow as she twisted her right dagger when she drew it out of his thigh. His gauntlet slid across her blade and the pain she had caused limited the force of his blow.

Standing up, she carried her left arm up, driving the pummel of her dagger into the soldier's chin. Dropping the dagger from her right hand, she reached across herself and grabbed the sword from the soldier's slack hand.

Stunned, the man staggered back and fell. Twisting, she firmed her grip on the sword and blocked a thrust from the man who had been standing next to the first soldier. The soldier stepped forward and slammed her face with his gauntlet. Slightly stunned, she instinctively brought her left arm around and blocked the soldier's sword, grunting with the effort of deflecting the blow.

Her vision clearing, she swung her stolen sword at the bearded man's left leg, which he easily deflected. Sensing subtle movements, Stephenie let her sword drag slightly as she reversed the grip on her dagger. As the man moved in close again to punch her, she twisted away from the blow and struck out with her dagger. The man's own force drove him into her blade, which sliced into the side of his unprotected neck, sliding roughly over bone and then up and through his ear.

She stepped back as Zac, having dropped the third soldier, now drove his own sword into the man's back. The soldier, crying out in pain, tried to twist around, but Zac put his foot to the man's back to free his sword and the soldier ended up face first on the ground.

"You okay?" Zac asked, a bit of panic in his voice.

"Behind you," Stephenie responded as another man slipped past Will and was coming upon them. Stephenie pushed Zac to the side and met the soldier's thrust with her sword. Dropping low and to the left, she turned the man's attention away from Zac with a sword thrust. The soldier moved in the direction she led. She followed the thrust with a feint and a flash of her dagger. The soldier, off balance, moved to block her weapons and was too slow to avoid the real thrust of her sword that went into his right armpit. The man staggered back as Zac moved in and finished him with a blow to the head.

"Bastard!" Zac swore, wiping a bit of sweat from his face. "You okay?", Zac asked again, coming up on Stephenie's side.

She took a deep breath and reached out with her mind, trying to feel who was still around them. She grimaced as the sense of pain and agony overwhelmed her. She tried to push down the emotions, but could not weed out the emotions of the injured to clearly sense the situation. She exhaled and turned to Zac, nodding her head. "I'm fine."

She watched Will move off in the direction of the others. Slowly she felt the level of agony and pain dwindle and she allowed Zac to escort her to the sounds of Henton and the others, who were responding to a call to sound off. By the time she reached the others, there were only two men not part of their group that she could feel.

"I told you to stay back," Henton said angrily.

"I'm able to hold my own and Zac had three men on him."

"I'd have taken them," Zac said casually.

Henton took a deep breath, then turned toward Will. "Fish has a graze on his chin. Anyone else injured?"

"I've got a small cut on my arm and Douglas took a solid blow to the chest, but his armor held. Probably will just bruise."

"Okay, clean up your cut and question those we have left. Zac, take Fish and police up the bodies." He looked quickly to Stephenie and waited for a reaction, "if there is anyone else out there, call out, we don't want you taken by surprise."

Stephenie shook her head slightly.

"That blood on your shirt?"

She looked down, noticing a slight burning on her side. "Just a small scratch."

He shook his head. "Zac, Fish, watch the captives until Will is ready, then count up the bodies. Stephenie, I'm not having you get sick because you got cut and didn't bother to clean it out."

"I'll take care of her," Zac offered. "She saved my life, it's the least I can do."

Henton glared at Zac. "I'll take care of it. We're all soldiers here, but I'll not ask Steph to have her breasts stared at and ogled." He turned back to her, "I promise to be as quiet and polite as possible, but you want to be a soldier and fight when you don't—or didn't, have a sword, you will just have to suffer the consequences."

"It really isn't—okay, fine." Giving in under Henton's gaze, she followed him away from the others. Once out of their hearing, she continued with her protest, "really, it will heal just fine. You should have seen the cut I had in my arm, barely even a scar now."

"Steph, sit." He pointed to a fallen tree.

Even in the dim moon light, she could see the look in his face and knew arguing would be pointless. She pulled up her shirt and sat down. Noticing the bloody binding around her chest, she pulled the end free and unwound it. Sensing surprise from Henton, she looked up. "What?"

"I didn't mean to stare, but what happened to your breast?"

She grinned and lowered her shirt somewhat. "That was done by a friend."

"You let someone tattoo you?"

"It's not a tattoo. I think it was frozen. The feeling has started coming back, but it's still blackened and that doesn't seem to be changing."

"It looks like a hand print."

Stephenie looked up. "You want to check the cut? My arm's getting tired holding my shirt up."

"Sorry." Henton knelt down and started looking at the slice on her side. He poured some water on to a rag and started dabbing at her side. "Who got you?"

"To be honest, I think it might have been the second guy, but I don't really remember. I didn't notice the cut until you mentioned it."

"It's already closed up. If there's cloth in there, I'd have to cut it open again to get it out."

"What I am means I heal fast."

He sat back and she lowered her shirt.

"Look, I'd appreciate it if you kept the hand print on my breast between us. It's kind of personal."

"Who froze your breast?"

"A ghost. His name is Kas and it was not so much that he was going for my breast, but my heart. It's getting better, but I've been feeling winded and tire a lot more quickly than I used to."

"You mean you going all day with a heavy pack would not normally wear you out?"

"Not as much as it has. I've been falling back on my abilities to get me through the day and that's been giving me a headache."

"I hope you destroyed that ghost for what he did."

Stephenie shook her head. "He's a friend now. He didn't know what he was doing. I miss him. He saved me when I was lost under the castle."

Henton sat back on the ground. "You are something. Those soldiers would have easily overwhelmed us if you had not woken everyone in time. We owe you our lives."

"They were Burdger's men. I sensed it from them. If it wasn't for me, I doubt they would have come after us."

"Well, we'll have to find out what Will has learned. I'll let you wrap yourself up. I will need to keep up appearances in taking care of your wounds, otherwise the others will start suspecting something."

"Okay. And I guess I owe you a belated thank you for not taking away my door. It's one thing for you to get a peek, but I'd have been really uncomfortable if I had other people watching."

He chuckled and got to his feet. "I doubt I would have taken your door permanently. I didn't trust those Kyntian soldiers. Get dressed and we can see where we are at. We'll probably need to move and put some more distance between us and Venla."

Stephenie knew the two captives were dead before she returned to the others. She had felt a sudden panic and then a slow diminishing of the mental presence of the men from where she had been. The men had come to kill them, she knew that much; sensed it from those she had fought. However, the reality of killing the injured soldiers did not quite feel right.

When she joined the other five, the bodies of the men had been dragged away and the metallic scent of blood and urine was in the woodsy air. There was a pile of equipment in the middle of what had been their camp.

"Steph. I've gone through the gauntlets and armor, I think just about everything will be too big for you. There are some bracers for your forearms that should fit and perhaps a leather jerkin, but it has colors on it. Since we wanted to avoid that, we might just have to leave it."

"Thanks Will," she said, taking the bracers.

"We've got some more money and some jewelry that we can probably trade. So we should be a little better funded now. No real food, just bits and pieces of things and some water skins. They were told to come kill all of us, especially you, and come back."

"Damn pieces of crap were supposed to bring back your head as proof," Zac said, indignation radiating from him.

"Zac, she didn't need to hear that."

Stephenie shook her head. "It's okay Will. I know they were here because of me."

Will shuffled his feet a bit. "Well, I don't think your Duke's boy told them who you were. They thought perhaps you were some enemy of the family. None of them knew your name or any of our names, other than what we gave in town."

Henton cleared his throat. "Okay, I imagine that come first light, the Duke's son will be expecting his people to be returning. At best, we can hope he might wait until mid-morning before sending someone to investigate. Perhaps on horse. We're a few hours away on foot, but we need to put more distance between us and Venla.

"Steph, I've already asked everyone, but none of us are master trackers. Other than trying to lose our tracks in streams, I think our best option at this point is speed and time. Unless there are any tricks you know."

She shook her head. "Not my specialty."

"Okay, then gather up our things and let's get moving. We'll take a few breaks and catch a little rack time during the day, but we'll assume the worst and until we cross a road or something that can hide our passing, we need to keep moving and watch for pursuit."

* * * * *

While they marched into the morning, Stephenie kept looking over her shoulder and into the rising sun, waiting to see the shadows of men on horses. The morning dragged on and no shadows appeared, so her mind wandered into the topic of what she would do if she did encounter Lord Elard. He had sent a dozen of his men to kill her, knowing that if he did, he was killing a member of the royal household. It was traitorous, but more importantly, she found it to be personal. Not only was he going to have her killed, but he was willingly going to have her five companions killed as well. That fact nagged at her until she was finding it hard not to want to turn around and confront the man that at one point had been interested in marrying her.

"No use fretting about it."

Stephenie looked up and met Douglas' eyes. He had drifted back and was marching beside her. "Revenge can wait."

"How did you know what I was thinking?"

"We've all been there. I was just waiting until it was obviously on your mind."

"He obviously was trying to secure the throne for his father and he gave no thought to what the impact would be. What of the people? What of you? He simply was going to have you killed because you were there and would have known the truth. Someone that cold inside doesn't deserve the chance to rule. I know it's naive to think like that, but it doesn't mean it's not true."

Douglas forced a laugh. "You aren't like most people. We've seen plenty of people die for someone else's greed."

"Well, I intend to stop it when I can. But you are right, I'll put it from my mind for now. When I can come back to it, I'll do something about it then."

"Good."

Chapter 16

They marched long and hard for the next two days, avoiding the few homes and villages they saw across the plains. Before they reached the city of East Fork, they crossed the main road and headed northwest. East Fork was the seat of the Duchy of Lists and the home of Duke Richard Burdger and his son Elard. The choice meant taking a longer route and likely wasting time trying to find another barge to cross the Altain River.

The Altain River was narrower, but stronger than the Uthen they had crossed at Venla. East Fork, which was far from being "easterly" in either the country or along the river, was named that by the early settlers coming from the west because the settlers had decided that was as far east as they cared to go. The difficulty with East Fork was that Duke Burdger's castle guarded the river fork and the two bridges leading to either the west or south. The next closest bridge was in the city of Warton, more than one hundred miles north. With a group of horsemen they had twice dodged in the area, they considered the chance that someone was watching and waiting for them at the bridges to be too great and the consequences of being captured far too grave.

They spent most of the second day trying to coax passage across the river and it was not until it was nearly sunset that they managed the feat. The short barge trip cost them nearly a silver crown and no one doubted the barge captain would tell anyone who asked that he had seen five men and a woman on the far side of the river.

Because the barge was heading south toward East Fork, Henton marched them well into the night, relaxing when the grassland close to the river faded into thick forests that were not yet cut and shipped down stream. After another turn of the glass, they quickly set up camp for the night, with all but Henton and Stephenie grumbling about sore muscles and unreasonable working conditions.

In the morning, they rose before dawn and continued their march through the deciduous forest in a mostly westerly direction. Stephenie and Henton debated the merits of stopping at Vantar for information and supplies. Vantar was the seat of the Duchy of Crowns, but it would be a slight detour south unless they decided to try to find a pass through the Grey Mountains, as opposed to going north around them.

They finally decided to have Will, Fish, and Zac purchase supplies at a small village along a back road through the country and then they would stop at the village of Ten Stones, where Zac was raised before being sent to serve in the navy. The village was a day north of Vantar and just over three days to the west. It was close to the border of the country of Selith, but a small enough town that an invasion force would likely ignore it for larger and fortified cities such as Vantar. However, it was close enough that they hoped to get information and Zac promised supplies from his family.

After four exhausting days of marching, two of which were wet with a cold rain, they finally approached Ten Stones. Everyone had listened to Zac talking about his family and home for the last four days and when Henton called a stop to their march, he nearly had to grab Zac's collar to restrain him.

"Steph, you'll meet my parents, right? I mean we won't tell them who you are, but I can introduce you, right?"

She tried to force a grin, but she had already agreed four times since they started that morning and she had lost some enthusiasm. "Of course, Zac."

Henton cleared his throat. They were standing in a small clearing on the east side of a series of hills. "You sure this area is not used much Zac?"

"Not often. Just stay up in the rocks here and you'll see anyone before they see you."

"Okay. We've not seen people following us these last couple of days, but we've left one muddy trail to follow if they are still behind us. Zac, you and Fish can take Steph to meet your family. Spend a couple of hours if you want, get information on what's been happening and pay your family for any supplies you can get. We'll need several more days of food. I want the three of you back here well before the sun sets. We don't want your parents insisting you stay the night and we want a couple more hours march before we crash for the night."

"Man, Sarge, you wanna wear a few more inches from our feet don't you. I know I'm taller than all of you, but making me shorter won't make any of you better looking." Fish grinned, "aside from you Steph, the rest of these lugs just look funky and they'll look all the worse two inches shorter."

Stephenie grinned, barely keeping from laughing.

Will tossed Fish an empty pack. "Fish, you ain't seen yourself in a mirror lately. Drag yourself a couple miles on your face and you might wear off the dirt sticking to you."

Henton cleared his throat again. "Will, Fish, enough." He turned toward Zac, "I'm counting on you to not get carried away. Don't tell your parents too much and make sure they know they need to keep it quiet that you were here."

"You can count on me, Henton."

Stephenie thought she heard Henton mutter something under his breath, but before she was certain, he was waving them off. She had to nearly run to keep up with Zac, who was dragging her along quickly. They were soon on the other side of the ridge and making for a back road leading through the village.

"You'll like my sister Steph, she's a year younger than me and always was considered a bit of a tomboy."

"Zac, you just need a good man to swoon her."

"Not you. You're a dirty bastard."

"Oh Zac, my dance card is filled for now, but perhaps when this is all done, I'll properly introduce myself."

Stephenie grinned, "Fish, you can be terrible."

"Oh, my Lady, you must have been talking to all the jealous husbands, or perhaps all the ladies who want me as a kept man."

Stephenie looked at the stupid grin on his face and giggled. "Even when I know I should find you offensive, you make me laugh."

"It's charm, my friend, pure and simple charm."

"You're just full of crap," Zac grumbled and Stephenie had to bite her lip to avoid smiling at the teased discomfort she felt from Zac. The two of them would banter quietly for hours but neither of them took it too personally.

As they passed by a field with a series of houses in the distance, Stephenie was pulled out of her introspection. A wagon pulled by two horses was passing along a line of trees and pulling out onto the road they were traveling. She felt half a dozen men and sensed a wrongness about them. A coldness and detachment she normally only felt from hardened soldiers. "Hold up," she said, but it was too late, three of the men were already moving toward them.

"Move not!", the lead soldier called in broken Cothish.

"Run Steph," Zac said softly, drawing his sword.

Fish put his hand out to push her back behind him, but did not draw his sword.

The tall, dark-haired man on the left grinned and then Stephenie felt the energy around her pulled away, sending a slight chill through her body. Before she could react, a wall of energy slammed into the three of them, knocking them all from their feet and backwards on their rears.

"Now, you squirm in pain," said the man on the left, his Cothish much better than the first man's.

Zac was struggling to his feet, his sword still in his hand. The other two soldiers had drawn their swords and were now only a dozen feet away and closing quickly.

Stephenie watched the mage wave his hand and saw Zac's right hand fly up and hit him in the face, the pummel of his sword smacking his cheek bone. "Stop, we've done nothing wrong," Stephenie called to the Senzar soldiers.

"You are escaped soldiers or fools, you are slaves now."

Stephenie felt a weight crash down on her from above, knocking her back to her knees. Zac and Fish had both collapsed completely to the ground, unable to even kneel. She sensed a fourth man approaching from the wagon. A sickening pleasure emanated from the soldiers at the terror and frustration from Zac and Fish.

Taking a deep breath, Stephenie drew in more energy than was already coursing through her body and pushed back against the force holding her down. The sadistic pleasure of their mage turned to anger and concern as he realized Stephenie held power herself. Sinking a gravity hole behind the three men, she dumped energy into the field she created, not trying to be subtle.

The two soldiers were yanked back as if a horse had run them over. The Senzar mage stumbled in the direction of the gravity hole, but was able to hold his feet.

Stephenie felt the weight on her go away and she stumbled toward her own gravity well before stopping the flow of energy. A moment later she had the briefest sense of a line of energy between herself and the mage. Instinctively, she jumped to the right just as an arch of energy leaped from the mage. The energy hit her left forearm, spinning her around. With a detached certainty, she knew her arm was severely burned and perhaps bleeding. However, there was not yet any pain overwhelming her. Instead panic was filling her; Kas had not taught her to fight someone else with magic, let alone defend herself. Instinctively, she knew her only chance was to strike quickly and with as much force as possible.

Sensing, and almost visualizing, a tiny thread of energy spring into existence from the mage's mind to her chest, Stephenie barely had the time to recognize the change that represented another blast of raw energy. Already on the ground, she could not physically move to avoid what would be a deadly strike. Without conscious thought, as the massive arch of energy formed, she linked the flow to the thin thread leading to the mage, hoping to draw the energy away like a river diverted by cutting a channel into it's bank.

A moment later, Stephenie blinked and then exhaled. The sound of the mage's skull exploding and ripping out part of his chest followed just ahead of the spray of blood and flesh that covered the road, trees, and people nearby.

Everyone had frozen for a moment, unable to completely accept what had just happened. The fourth soldier that had been approaching from the wagon was the first to move, rushing forward with his sword. Stephenie sucked in energy, and mimicking what she had sensed the mage do, she unleashed a flood of energy toward the charging soldier. An arch of blue-white light flashed from the air in front of her and slammed into the soldier's chest, sending him flying ten feet in the other direction.

Fish was on his feet and charged the two soldiers that Stephenie had knocked to the ground earlier, quickly knocking aside their swords and ending their lives.

The two remaining men on the wagon had dismounted and were changing direction to run down the road toward the village of Ten Stones and away from Stephenie. Closing her eyes, Stephenie made the conscious decision and drew in more energy. The men were a fair distance away and growing farther every moment. Pushing down the regret she knew she would feel two heart beats later, she unleashed the energy, striking both men in the back of the head. She did not bother moving to investigate, she could no longer sense the terror and fear that had been coming from them.

"You—You're one of them!"

Stephenie turned toward Zac. She felt drained and hollow, but that only took some of the edge off the sense of betrayal she felt coming from Zac.

"You're a witch! You're one of them!"

"Zac, let me explain. I'm not one of them. I—yes, I can do things, but I am not one of the Senzar."

"You—you're one of Elrin's spawn!"

Stephenie shook her head, feeling more afraid now than when she was confronting the mage. "No, Zac. Please understand. I was born this way. I don't worship Elrin. I never have. I am not like that." She despised the perpetration of the lies she had been told growing up, but it would be easier to convince the others if she talked in a manner they already believed. "My mother did something when she was carrying me. Something that drew the curse. It is not my fault. That is why I could not go back to Antar and take the throne. That is why I need to find my brother."

"Who's a warlock as well, isn't he?"

"No. No one else in my family is one. I'm the first and only one. It was something my mother did."

"Zac," Fish said softly, holding his hand out to indicate Zac should lower his blade. "Stephenie just saved our lives. She saved your life before, three on one, that would have ended badly. I'm good with what she is."

Zac shook his head. "No. This isn't right. A witch." He would not look her in the eyes. "No. I can't travel with a witch. I won't let Elrin take me."

Stephenie nodded her head, despite the fact that Zac was not looking. "Zac, I understand. I don't blame you. I thank you for what you have been able to do. You are home, go and see your family. Stay here and protect them." She looked toward the dead, "you might need to escort them away."

Zac turned to Fish. "You going to stay with a witch?"

"I owe her my life. I'm not going to turn on her. I can live with what she is. She's not one of them, she just killed four of them herself."

Stephenie winced slightly at the thought of having killed the last two. The first ones were in obvious self-defense, but the last two were closer to murder than she wanted to think about. "Zac, I release you from your promise to come with me. I just ask that you don't tell anyone about me and the others. We need to find my brother and rescue him and to do that, we can't have others aware of what we are doing."

Zac looked at Fish and then shook his head. "Fine. I won't rot in Elrin's grasp." He turned and started walking down the road toward Ten Stones.

"Fish, you sure?" She struggled now to hold her composure. She could not even look at her arm and needed to sit before she fell. "I won't blame you...if you wanted to leave."

He shook his head, taking her left arm in his and wrapping a bandage he pulled from his pocket around the bloody mess of her arm. "I meant what I said. I'm okay with it. I'm a bit of a bastard anyway. The gods won't take me, so might as well help you."

The pressure he applied by wrapping the bleeding and burnt wound sent waves of pain and nausea through her. After a moment she took a deep breath and barely avoided throwing up. A few minutes later, she looked at the wagon and draft horses still in the middle of the road. "Supplies?"

Fish nodded. "I'd guess they are plundering where they can to feed the soldiers and perhaps slaves, if that was what they were going to make of us."

Stephenie looked at the blood that had already soaked through the bandage and took her left arm and pressed it under her right. "Grab what we can carry. Must get back to Henton. We can't stay here... could be others."

"What are you going to tell the others?"

She took a deep breath and responded slowly, "the truth. You all deserve that much. I'll take what comes."

"Well, if you—Henton already knows doesn't he?"

Stephenie nodded her head as he led her to the wagon.

"Well, I was going to say, you convince him, the others will be okay with it, so I think the hard part is done. He'd be the hardest to convince you're not evil, being as devout as he is to Felis."

Chapter 17

By the time they were getting close to where the others were hiding, Stephenie was leaning heavily on Fish. Her arm was throbbing in rhythm with her head and she was very nauseous. She barely felt the others as she and Fish came around the ridge.

"Back so soon—what happened?" Henton was on his feet, sword drawn and moving quickly in their direction. "Where's Zac? Are you being pursued?"

Fish spoke first, "we ran into a group of soldiers. Damn invaders."

"Zac?" Will asked, scanning the woods for enemies.

"Zac's fine," Stephenie said. Standing taller and releasing Fish's arm, she drew upon her magic to remain standing. "He wasn't hurt. I need to explain." She swallowed and took a deep breath, looking to Will and Douglas. "I never wanted to hide things from you and I don't want to deceive you any more."

"Your arm," Henton said, leading her up the slope and toward the outcropping of rocks where they had been hiding. She followed, too drained to resist, but the knot in her stomach was growing even tighter at the looks she was getting from Douglas. Her head hurt too much to be able to sense much from any of them.

After she sat on a rock, she let Henton pull off the bandage and start the painful process of cleaning the burned and charred flesh of her left forearm. Turning her head away to avoid the ugly sight, she looked at Will and Douglas who's concerned expressions were bouncing between her and Fish.

"What happened?" they asked in unison.

"It's her tale, I'll let her tell it," said Fish. "Though she saved our lives, I will say that."

"We were coming down the road. A wagon was coming out from behind a long row of trees that bordered a set of fields. It was loaded with food and goods and there were six Senzar soldiers. They saw us and ordered us to stop, Zac drew his sword and that's when we found one of them to be a mage—or warlock," she corrected for the others.

Will, Douglas, and Henton stiffened, but said nothing. After a moment of silence, Henton went back to working on her arm, pointedly avoiding looking at her.

"She saved our lives," Fish said again. "That warlock threw us to the ground from a hundred paces and the soldiers were coming at us with swords."

"How'd you escape?" asked Will.

Stephenie took a deep breath, more terrified of their reaction than of the mage she had just fought. "I am a witch," she finally said, and then repeated it louder so they could hear her clearly. "I was born that way. I have never worshiped Elrin, please believe that." She grimaced as Henton pulled some of her shirt from the wound on her arm.

"Then your mother sold her soul to Elrin when she was carrying you. That explains so much. How the evil bitch could be a traitor and rob the country blind when we are fighting a war." Douglas looked at the others, daring them to challenge him. He turned to face Henton; his face stoic and without emotion. "You knew, didn't you?"

Henton stood and stepped between Stephenie and the others. "I did." He glanced back at her and then looked each of the others in the eyes. "I didn't tell you because I didn't know how you'd react. But I can say without doubt, she is not evil. Her concern and desire to help the soldiers and the people of the country is real. I don't understand everything she's tried to tell me and we have not had much time to talk, but she is the best hope for saving Cothel."

Will looked around Henton and at Stephenie. "Your brother a warlock as well?"

Stephenie shook her head. "No. I'm the only one, no one else in the family is one. No one in my family knows I am one, save for my

mother.   And I think some of her personal advisers.   They had
planned to take me with them and then cut out my heart and eat it
because my mother heard she could prevent herself from having
witchcraft should I die if they performed a sacrifice."

Will nodded his head.

Douglas turned to Fish, "you okay with this? Obviously the Sarge
was and didn't bother to tell us."

Fish nodded his head. "Ya. I'm all in. You should have seen her.
She dodged a blast of lightning, just getting it in the arm instead of
the chest. Then from the ground, she managed to flip the next bolt
back at the warlock, blew his head clean off his shoulders and took
out half his chest with it."

Stephenie cringed, not wanting to remember the sudden spikes of
fear and panic the soldiers had as they died.

"Then she shot lightning herself, pure white; a sword of the gods.
Took out three of the remaining soldiers. There were two she had
knocked to the ground that I dispatched with my blade, but she did
all the real work."

"What happened to Zac?" Douglas asked.

Fish frowned. "Well, the fool got all panicky and threw a fit and
didn't want nothing to do with her."

"I told him I understood. I don't blame him. Zac is a good guy
and most people do not understand what I am. Please believe me
when I say I am not like the Senzar or like the stories that are told
about witches.

"I told Zac he should go home to be with his family. He helped
as much as he could and I would not ask him to do anything he
didn't want to." Feeling slightly better, she stood and looked at the
four men before her. "I won't ask any more than you are able to give.
If you are uncomfortable with me and what I am, I do understand
and I don't hold that against you. I just ask that you forget about me
and what I am trying to do, which is rescue my brother so he can
become King. Once I do that, I'll go away and stay out of the way
and not be part of the kingdom. I don't want to risk his honor with
people thinking ill of me."

Douglas shook his head, "I—"

Stephenie interrupted him and turned toward the top the ridge. "There are people coming quickly over the ridge!" She felt them just as they crested the ridge, "a dozen."

The others scrambled for their weapons as Stephenie tried to reach out to the energy around them. She felt the draw of energy from some of the men as it slammed into her. She felt herself falling backwards and saw Henton's legs as her head hit the ground and darkness filled her vision.

Pain crippled Stephenie; a deep throbbing, as sharp spears of agony radiated from her arm and the back of her head. She felt like she was falling, but she knew she was on the ground, jagged rocks were poking her ribs and making it hard to breath.

"She's waking," Stephenie heard a woman say in a heavily accented version of the Old Tongue.

A man spoke and it took longer for her to piece the words together. "She's pretending, cut the throats of her friends until she stirs."

"Quiet. There's no point, no one speaks the language. Besides, she'll know you're not near the hostages."

Stephenie tried to clear her mind, to fight through the pain, but it was difficult. She was only realizing what was said after a moment or two. Her arms were bound tightly behind her. She was dumped on her back, her legs slightly twisted, and her head facing downward. She could barely feel where the men around her were. *Kas made me work when I was half dead, I can do this,* she swore to herself.

Gradually, she felt some people moving about as her head started to clear. There were at least thirteen of the Senzar. She could feel her companions and recognized each one of them, except for Fish. She began to panic as she searched for Fish and realized he was not nearby. Her blood chilled as she realized Zac was next to Henton and the others.

"You here why?" asked one of the men in broken Cothish.

"She's becoming more alert," the woman said again.

Stephenie had pushed the pain further from her. She felt numb, as if she was looking down on everything from above. She felt a change in the energy around her and then felt the effect upon her face as if she had been slapped with a gauntlet.

She let out a small cry of anguish before she could stop herself, more from surprise than the pain of the blow. Slowly she opened her eyes and blinked at the bright sun shining down in her eyes.

"You here why?" a dark haired man asked. He was standing five feet away and slightly up slope from her. The woman and another man she guessed to be mages were standing further up the slope, one of them holding some of her books in his hands. She sensed the other Senzar soldiers around them. Henton and the others were a dozen feet away and lined up close to each other.

"These books are old. She has some crystals that are enchanted with a permanent illumination. We need to take her and these things to Lord Rosling. Perhaps she knows something that can help locate the orb and we can be out of this cursed land sooner."

Stephenie was beginning to follow their strange accent of the Old Tongue more closely, but she forced herself not to react to what they were saying. She only hoped they could not read her mind and realize she could understand them.

The woman had started flipping through one of the books and looked up. "This is in an old form of Denarian, she might understand us."

"Why do you have me tied up?" Zac asked, fear quivering his voice. "I told you about the witch, she deceived us!"

Stephenie saw the man closest to her turn toward Zac.

"You. Tell me. Here, why?"

"We're here to—"

Stephenie heard a commotion around the others, but her head was not at the correct angle to see it and rage was blinding her mental senses. Thinking only of protecting Joshua, she reached into herself, ignored the raw burning that filled her body, and drew upon the energy around her. Repeating the channeling of energy she had done earlier, she quickly formed a line of potential from the rocks a few feet away, through the chest of the nearest mage and into the head of the man with one of her other books.

"Hans! She's—"

Stephenie dumped as much energy as she could into the channel and a blast of lightning crackled as it raced through the air and the first mage. She sensed the second man creating a channel of his own, drawing away the energy and angling it toward the trees behind him.

Uncertain what to do, Stephenie strengthened what she saw as the differential of one end of her channel from the other. Imagining a bigger and deeper pit. The energy that had briefly diverted into the trees, exploding branches and incinerating leaves, bounced back to her original destination of the mage's head. The roar of rolling thunder filled the air as the man's head exploded.

Quivering from the emptiness that she felt inside her, Stephenie noticed energy washing over her, burning her and singeing her clothing. Instinctively, she drew off the wave of energy, pulling it into herself to prevent herself from being burned alive. The pain of drawing in the energy was immense and she almost lost consciousness. Barely able to focus, she dropped a gravity hole below the woman as she had with the soldiers. The concept was easier for her and required less thought. Pushing all the energy she had absorbed into the formation of the hole, she sobbed with relief when the energy she was drawing in stopped.

She rolled to her side coughing and choking. Blood had filled her nose and mouth. With the pressure off her arm, feeling returned and pain radiated from the deep burn. Spitting out the blood in her mouth, she struggled to finish rolling onto her chest. After a moment of dragging her face across the rough stones, she managed to get to her knees.

Blinking away tears of anguish that had run from her eyes, she spit out more blood and looked around. Her numb mind could barely feel anything around her. She sensed the other Senzar soldiers had scattered in all directions when she had taken down the three mages and she was glad to see they had not appeared to return.

Henton, Will, and Douglas had gotten to their feet. They were still down the slope a couple dozen feet. Slowly, she staggered to her feet and moved toward the mage that had been closest to her. His dead eyes staring into the sky, a blackened crater in his chest burned through the leather armor he had been wearing.

Stephenie knelt down and pulled a dagger from his belt with her right hand. Henton was already moving in her direction, his own hands, once bound behind him, now in front of him. He reached her in just a few strides. Taking the dagger from her hand, he cut her arms free and she sagged into his chest as more pain from her forearm overwhelmed her.

After a moment, she straightened and spit more blood from her mouth. The flow that had been running from her nose had slowed, but had not yet stopped.

"You okay?"

She nodded, taking the dagger back and slowly cutting the rope binding his hands. When they were free, he scanned the ridge for signs of the soldiers, then left her to quickly cut free the others. Stephenie watched his movements, then noticed Fish's body laying on the ground. She closed her eyes, but could still see the unnatural angle of his head and the burns in his armor and clothing.

"Free me!" Zac demanded, his arms still bound behind his back.

"What happened Zac?" Henton asked. A sword now in his hand.

"She's one of Elrin's demons! Did you see what she just did?"

"What happened?"

"She killed some of their soldiers with her witchcraft and I could not suffer the indignity of traveling with her. When I saw the other soldiers, I knew they'd blame the town's people for it. I told them that their soldiers were killed by a witch and I'd take them to her. They were not supposed to harm any of us!"

Stephenie had moved closer, biting down the rage that was giving her strength to move. "I saved your life and let you leave. I respected your decision not to want to travel with me, but then you go to their witches and warlocks to look for help? You killed Fish. A good man is dead because you betrayed us."

Zac spit at Stephenie, but did not have the reach. "He's not a good man, he decided to stay with you. He's tainted!"

"No Zac. You are tainted. You went to what you call Elrin's demons and sold out your friends and your country. If you had only harmed me, I might have considered looking the other way. But I can see you would sacrifice those close to you because you are too blind with hate to see what you are doing. You killed Fish! A man that made us laugh and smile when everything seemed so hard. He didn't even get to have a chance to go swimming since we started this journey, but he was still good-natured about it."

Zac spit at her again.

Stephenie swallowed, but did not close her eyes. "I, Her Royal Highness, Princess Stephenie of Cothel declare you a traitor and sentence you to death." She noticed Douglas walking toward Zac, a noose already tied.

"I don't accept your judgment, Witch! You can't do that!"

Douglas put the noose around Zac's neck before he knew what was happening. Zac started to struggle as soon as the knot tightened. Henton helped restrain the young man as they dragged him to a nearby tree.

Zac continued to struggle and curse, but Henton was larger and stronger and easily controlled the bound man as the rope was tossed over a tree limb. A broken branch, a good foot in diameter was stood on end. Henton balanced Zac on the unsteady branch as Douglas tied off the rope.

At this point, Zac was crying and pleading for Will to help him, but Will simply turned away and looked at Fish's body.

Zac was slightly choked, but managing to balance on the three foot high branch that was lodged between a pair of rocks. He turned his venom back to Stephenie. "You evil and vile beast, hiding among us to poison the world! The gods will burn you!"

"Zac, I wish you a swift end in memory of the man I thought I knew." She took a deep breath. Her insides were raw and her body ached, yet she found the strength to draw in enough energy to push the branch out from under him. She heard his neck snap as the rope pulled taught, his feet inches from the ground.

She turned away, unwilling to watch him dangle from the tree. Will, Henton, and Douglas stood before her. There was more blood on her face, slowly running from her nose. She swallowed what had gone into her mouth, unwilling to spit it out.

"I am truly sorry to have deceived you. But what I am is not something I can share without hate and fear coming as a reaction. I can and do fully understand if any of you no longer want to support me. I just ask that you allow me to go on my way. My only goal is to rescue my brother, who does not suffer from my condition. I want nothing more than to free him so he can take the throne and save Cothel."

Douglas cleared his throat. "Stephenie, as I was saying before we were interrupted. I always knew there was something wrong about you. Something you were not sharing. Knowing now what you were hiding explains much." He glanced at Henton and Will. "I am with you to the end. Fish and Henton were convinced and I've seen nothing evil from you."

"Same," Will said. "Steph, I don't understand what you are dealing with, but I won't blame the daughter for what evils the mother did. You say you don't worship Elrin and that is good enough for me. Heck, you just killed three more of those bastards and perhaps you are what we need to be able to fight their evil."

"Thank you," she choked out. She felt her legs wobble, both from blood loss and relief. She struggled to wipe away the tears that started falling from her eyes as Henton moved in her direction.

"Come on, let's sit you down and clean you up." He turned to Will and Douglas as he helped Stephenie cross the rocks to a flatter spot. "Gather up all of our things, including her books. Check those warlocks for supplies and goods. We need to get moving as quickly as possible. We don't know when the soldiers that got away will come back."

"What about Fish?" Will asked as he started to gather their scattered supplies.

"Put a blanket over him. He'd want to be buried in the water if he could, but we don't have the time to do anything proper."

"Thank you," Stephenie whispered as he washed the blood from her face.

Chapter 18

It was well past dark when they stopped for the night and still they managed to travel only a small distance. Stephenie had taken turns leaning on the others and was not able to even carry her own pack. She fell instantly to sleep, leaving the others to take care of the camp.

"Henton, you should have told us."

Henton sighed and looked up at Will and Douglas. He had nearly raised Will, at least from a silly and awkward seventeen year old. The last four years had shown a lot of growth in the young man. He glanced down at Stephenie's sleeping form and back to the others. "I was conflicted. Very conflicted. But I care for my country more than I fear what she is."

Will shook his head. "You were the last person I'd have thought would be sympathetic. What of your ties to Felis?"

Henton grunted. "I've seen her vulnerable and terrified, yet at the same time, she tried to keep me out of trouble. She could have killed me when she escaped, but didn't. I think she is just truly coming into her full powers. But more to the point, I think to defeat these Senzar, and with their witches and warlocks just running over our priests, we need someone like her. She says she doesn't understand them, but she killed four of them in short order and lived."

Douglas tossed aside his pack. "You are not saying to use her and then turn her over to the priests are you?"

Henton sighed. "Perhaps when this started I might have considered it, but no, not now. I gave her my word and it is as good as any word I have given."

Douglas nodded his head. "Good. We'd have issues otherwise." Bending down, he picked up the sword he had placed on the ground earlier. "We need information. We saw lights from a cluster of homes when we were on that last hill. I'll find out what I can, then come back."

Henton raised his eyebrows slightly.

"Don't question me. I understand why you did what you did, but we gave up our ranks when we started this. I'll be back and I won't let slip what we are up to, but we can't simply walk into another group of soldiers. At least not while Stephenie is as hurt as she is."

Henton did not say anything as Douglas walked out of the camp. He wanted to insist Douglas remain, but it was true, they had given up their ranks and positions. He had sold them into their current situation without asking, fearing their reactions. Zac's betrayal and Fish's death was on his head. He had failed to protect his men and had perhaps lost the right to command their actions.

"Douglas will be back. He's a bit angry right now, but he'll get over it."

"Thanks, Will. What about you?"

Will grinned. "Hey, I'm always a bit easier to please. This stuff don't bother me that much. They say in the northeast, people actually have witches and warlocks as advisers."

"She mentioned something when we first found her. Said that Elrin does not really exist and the underlying power the priests use and she uses is the same."

"That's an old argument. Witches and their supporters have claimed that before."

"What if it's true?"

Will smiled. "Then there is even less reason not to support her." He spread out his blanket on the ground. "I'll let you take first watch. Wake me when it's my turn."

Stephenie awoke slowly. Her body ached as much as her head. Even after Kas had tried to kill her, she had not felt this drained and exhausted. She heard the other three talking quietly and for a moment considered listening to what they had to say, but decided that would be another invasion of their trust she could not risk.

Grunting from the effort, she pushed herself up with her right arm; her left would not support her weight if she tried. The others looked over, then rose to come to her. She got to her feet as quickly as she could, not wanting to look weak and pathetic.

"We let you sleep in. You doing better this morning?"

She nodded her head, sensing an uneasiness in the others. "What is wrong?"

Douglas cleared his throat. "Well, seems there are a lot of enemy soldiers about. Generally traveling in groups of twelve or twenty four. Always pulling wagons. They have been raiding most of the lands around here and to the west. Though not killing many. They take food, animals, and some able-bodied people. Though that's limited, since they don't seem to want to rekindle a conflict here.

"People also aren't fighting back. Each group of six generally has a witch or a warlock and no one wants to deal with that. There's been talk that the food is for prisoners and if people don't cooperate, it'll be our people that starve."

Stephenie shook her head. It made sense, but it angered her. "We need to get to my brother."

Douglas looked to Henton and then back to Stephenie. "There are a lot of soldiers out there. Not running into another lot will be hard. Plus, Ten Stones is likely to see a significant reprisal. Apparently, early on, there was resistance in some towns. Those towns don't exist any more."

Damn. She sighed. Biting her lip, she looked to the ground and then back up to meet Douglas' eyes. "Nothing we can do. The people will likely know something happened and it would take a while for soldiers and warlocks to return. If they are smart, they will leave."

"We could—"

Stephenie interrupted Will, "there are four of us and I'm spent. It will take me a while to recover."

"Which makes running into a group of soldiers risky," Henton said. "We have to go around the tip of the Greys and then south along the west side of them. We've covered a lot of miles, but we've got a lot more to go and we won't likely be able to buy supplies from locals. They will be suspicious and will likely talk and that is assuming they have anything to spare."

"You seem to be able to sense them," Douglas said. "How far and what other things can you do?"

Stephenie paused a moment, afraid of revealing too much about herself, but knowing she had no choice but to trust the people who had put their trust in her. Perhaps unfounded trust. "I've been getting better at sensing people. When they are emotional, I can feel them more easily. Perhaps at fifty yards, maybe more or less. I know I can sense the three of you more readily. I'm used to how you feel." Sensing a chill in their emotions she added, "I can't read thoughts. I can just sense if you're angry, frustrated, and such. Not really any more than if someone watched your facial expressions."

Will smiled, "no card games with you."

Stephenie appreciated the humor. "I've never shot lightning like that before. I sensed how their warlocks used it on me and was able to repeat the effect."

"What about crumpling that woman into a pile of broken bones?"

"I've moved things. There is a force that causes all objects to be attracted to one another. I strengthened the force under her. Made it very strong, but localized it to a small area. It's one thing I have been able to practice as we've been marching. I'd move a rock or a tree branch or something."

"And here I'd been thinking we've had someone closely following us," Henton said with a shake of his head.

"Being honest, I really do not have much practice in using my powers. I started to learn a few things after my mother found me spying on her. I didn't have time to learn much and I've not had the time to read as we've marched. I am getting much better at moving things. The first time I really tried, once I understood what I was doing, I had a pitcher of water land in my lap. Before that it was mostly instinctual. Now I have some control."

Will smiled, but said nothing.

A silence hung in the air for a while until Henton broke it. "We still have a long ways to go and a lot of challenges."

"I won't ask any of you to go any further than you want to. I really appreciate what you've done so far."

Douglas stood. "I said I was with you to the end and I am. Discussion ended." He looked about the camp. "We need to put some more miles under us today and I think it will be slow for you. We should move while we talk."

Henton stood as well. "Good sentiment Douglas, but we still need to know where to walk. Do we make for the mountains and try to find a pass? One not being used by the enemy," he added. "Or do we try to dodge them with a longer trip around the north side of the range?"

Stephenie, still favoring her arm, shook her head. "Josh taught me a lot about fighting in mountains. The first thing was, don't, unless you are the defender. Too easy to funnel aggressors down valleys and too hard to take the high ground from someone dug in. We could go for days and end up in a canyon with no easy way out. Less chance of food and I know you guys are more than fit, but even the hardiest men will find the mountains a lot of work. Your legs will be aching the first day."

"And what of witches, they fare better?" Will asked with a hint of a smile.

Stephenie shook her head. "I know my endurance is better than most and what I am helps even more. I was incredibly drained when we first met, most of those early days I didn't have strength beyond my muscles. I've not been to the mountains, but Josh spent time training in the Uthen range and said his legs were like lead. I don't think I would fare much better than any of you. Plus, right now, I feel like I've been run over by a horse and put too close to the fire. Any little thing is just so tiring."

"How long until you've recovered?" Henton asked. "Wearing out witches and warlocks is how the hunters take them down. I don't think they wait around until they've recovered."

She shook her head. "I have no idea. I've not used this much energy before and I am just learning what I am."

"It could be days," Douglas said to Henton. "It took her several days to get a stride in her step once we found her. It might take longer now."

"Well, then I was physically injured. My heart was hurt. It's been feeling better for a while now."

"And what of your arm. The flesh and even some of the muscle is burned away. A normal person would have lost the arm. I've noticed you seem to be healing. And eating," Douglas added. "Will it heal completely?"

She shrugged. "If I knew more I think it would. The people a thousand years ago, before there was all this desire to kill witches and warlocks, could reattach a severed limb. I've not heard of anyone doing that these days. It might heal all on its own." She looked down at her bandaged arm; she could barely move her fingers. "I desperately hope it will heal on its own."

"So, if I understand you correctly, you say we should go around the mountains."

"Yes, Henton, we'll have a better chance of getting food and while we risk running into the enemy, I am sure we'd have a worse time in the mountains and we'd risk running into them there as well."

"How far do you estimate we have to go?" Douglas asked.

"Somewhere between one hundred and one hundred fifty miles," she said quietly.

Douglas cursed softly.

Stephenie nodded and stood up. "I know I'll be slowing us down the first few days. I just don't have the strength right now. But I'd still hope we can get there in less than eight days. If the route was easy, I'd say four or five days, but I suspect it will be difficult."

"And we'll need to keep out of sight of just about everyone." Henton picked up his pack. "Won't be able to trust locals. They will want to save their own skin more than ours."

Will shrugged. "Perhaps we'll run into some of the damn Senzar and can just take their clothes and food."

"Probably not a great idea," Stephenie said. "We want to avoid people knowing about us, and leaving a trail of bodies towards the mountains will be trouble. I'm hoping they will think the ones we just left were from people fleeing. Don't want a second set several days later for them to draw a line the other direction."

Will shrugged again. "You're probably right. That's one of the ways we tracked pirates at sea."

Henton gave everyone a quick look. "Let's put some miles under us while we can."

They had managed only forty miles in the next three days, but they were now able to see the mountain peaks in the distance when the sky was clear and there were breaks in the trees. So far, they had seen the signs of soldiers and the passing of loaded wagons, but had avoided contact with anyone, friendly or otherwise. The three days of travel without resupplying had eaten into a large portion of the food Stephenie and Fish had taken from the wagon at Ten Stones.

Feeling stronger, Stephenie was again carrying her pack with her books. However, her arm was throbbing and any movement of her hand sent spears of pain straight to her head. She tried to tell herself that the changes meant her arm was healing, but the agony of it was eating away at her composure. She tried to comfort herself with the fact that it was just her left arm, but being a one-armed sword woman was a weakness.

As they marched through the thick forest, Stephenie tried to take her mind off her arm and at the same time avoid thinking about Joshua and the mess that was left of their country. That of course, did not leave a lot to think about.

By mid-afternoon, the throbbing of her arm was worse, but a sudden echo in the back of her head overcame the pain and she became aware of a presence moving quickly toward them. She stopped and turned. "Kas?" He was not visible, but she could sense he was within one hundred feet.

Will, who had been following directly behind her, drew his sword and turned when she stopped suddenly. Stephenie stepped around his sword arm as Kas' form slowly materialized into a dim transparency somewhat masked in the dappled light of the forest.

Will cursed and tried to muscle Stephenie behind him as he swung his sword at the specter still a dozen feet away.

Stephenie cried out in pain as Will had grabbed her injured arm, bringing Kas instantly to her side. She cried out again, this time in panic, using the strength buried inside her to put herself between Kas and Will. "Kas, he's a friend!"

She barely heard Henton and Douglas cursing. The drawing of the energy to push Will behind her had taxed her tired body. "Don't hurt them."

Kas stopped a foot in front of Stephenie; his hands at his sides. "You are injured."

She looked at the ghost and smiled. "Have you known me when I was not?"

Kas paused a moment, a fluctuation of light flashing over his form before a grin materialized on his lips. Slowly his body solidified into an opaque firmness, bringing a hint of what might have been color to his eyes. "I feared you were dead. I felt so much pain and terror from you. But your position changed soon after. I needed to know what had happened to you."

"How?"

Kas reached for her chest and Henton screamed Stephenie's name. However, Stephenie only looked down as the necklace Kas had given her rose from under her shirt. He dropped the medallion so that it would be visible.

"You've been spying on me with that?" She put her right arm out to keep the others back. All of whom were talking quickly and with no small amount of fear. Slowly she turned to face them, catching Henton's eyes. Switching back to Cothish she cleared her throat, "Kas is a friend. He saved me when I was trying to escape my mother."

"He's the one who tried to crush your heart," Henton said, pointing to her chest. "He put that hand print on your breast?"

Stephenie sigh. "Let it go. He's a friend. He won't hurt us." She turned back to Kas and resumed the Old Tongue, "so you've been spying on me."

"Not in the fashion you think. Watching you bathe would do little except frustrate me and the medallion cannot do that."

"Well, if you have to know, I've not bathed since I left the caves, aside from a couple of rain showers."

"Than I am pleased I lack the ability to smell you. I am not good with time these days, but you are certain to be rank."

She snorted a laugh and shook her head, "you're just lucky you rotted so long ago your bones didn't stink. That would have been really rank, thank you very much." That brought a full smile to Kas' face. "How is it possible you found me?"

"The necklace. They were considered passé even in my time, but Sairy and I shared a set. We were attuned to them and could sense the other from great distances. I was afraid to leave, but more afraid for you. I was not sure the medallion would bond well to you or not, but I knew at least I would be able to sense where it was and find you if needed."

Stephenie grinned. "Careful, one would think you were getting feelings for me." She did not let Kas respond. "I have missed you so much. I could really use someone to talk to right now." She held up her arm and failed to keep all the quivering from her voice, "my arm is ruined. I took lightning, or perhaps it was just raw energy, right to my arm. It's blackened and burned. I really want my arm back. I really do, Kas!" She blinked back tears that were threatening to form.

He moved closer and his hands took hold of the bandages, unwinding them slowly, as if it took significant concentration for his hands to actually grip the material. Once the bandage was away, the charred and pitted flesh showed hints of bone under a thin layer of burnt muscle and skin. He slowly turned her arm to look at the other side, then released it.

He looked up to meet her eyes. "I've been practicing doing things to appear as if I was living. However, forming the fields and moving them that delicately is quite frustrating." He looked back to her arm. "You will need to put forth effort into the healing if you want to use it again. And the sooner you do, the better the healing will be."

She sobbed despite herself. "I don't know how. I just don't know how."

"What happened? If you had a mage shooting a channel of energy at you, how did you survive?"

She looked around, her three living friends were getting more and more concerned, if less vocal. "I'm feeling a bit hungry, let me make introductions and then I will explain what happened." She turned all the way around, leaving Kas at her back. "Henton, Will, Douglas," she said to each in turn.

"You're speaking their language to him. He's one of them!"

"Will, this is Kas, he's been dead for more than a thousand years. It is not his language, but one he knew, because the invaders that came in his time killed him and his family spoke it as well. If anything, we are likely descendants from those Denarians. Just like the Senzar. I think I remember one of those mages used the word Denarian when they were looking at my books."

"Us?" Will asked.

"Our priests and several members of nobility speak the Old Tongue because of the old documents. My father insisted I learn it. Kas would consider it poetic justice that the descendants of those that killed him are being killed by the descendants of the people we came from. Except he's taken a liking to me."

"She's right Will," Douglas said. "However, I don't know that a ghost makes our acceptance of what is going on here any easier."

"Can we stop to get something to eat? I need to explain what has happened, plus just rest a bit."

Henton, having regained some of his composure, nodded his head. "Will, Douglas, we can stop here as well as anywhere else. Let's make a quick check of the area. I'll stay here with Steph, when you get back I can go with one of you if we need to keep any eye on anything."

Stephenie sighed with relief and let Henton take care of the details while she found a soft spot at the base of a tree and sat down. Kas joined her, more blinking into a cross legged position than actually moving into it. "A couple of days ago," she started, but Kas interrupted.

"Tell me how you survived the mage throwing energy around."

"The first blast, the one that hurt my arm, I felt a connection of sorts between the mage and my chest. I didn't know what was happening, so I instinctively jumped out of the way. The thread linking us left my chest, but I think it looked for something else—"

"A different anchor. Another point of attachment."

"Ya. It twisted and caught my arm. Then a moment later, pain and anguish as the energy ripped into my arm. It hurt and I was on the ground. I sensed the mage create another anchor to my chest, but there was nowhere for me to jump. It was then I noticed, or perhaps just became aware of another thread leading back to the mage. I don't know why, but it felt like that thread was moving in the other direction, away from me and into the mage. It was so small, so inconsequential I don't know that I had ever noticed something like it before, but since then, I've seen them more and I noticed that I generate them as well. I can even sense something similar coming from you right now. Like little tentacles of a jelly fish, but finer and more numerous."

Kas looked at her so intently that she stopped talking. After a moment, he spoke, but she more felt than heard the words. "What you are describing is the fine fields we build to sense the world. They are the control fields we create. They are the eyes we use to sense and feel and pull information into us. For someone who is so mentally deaf as you seem to be, it is quite amazing that you were able to sense these. Even for someone who's been working with magic for years, often these concepts go unnoticed. But do not count on others not being able to sense these threads."

Stephenie nodded her head, not quite in understanding, but in acceptance of what Kas had said. "Well, the second blast of energy, I felt it coming toward me and I didn't want it to reach me. I just reacted, connecting the incoming energy channel with the one leading back to the mage. After the fact, I think I was just looking for a quick way to get rid of the energy."

Kas' eyebrows rose. "You routed the energy back? You bridged the energy back to a control thread? You just instinctively did this?"

"His head exploded. Took off a good chunk of his shoulders with it." She shuddered at the memory. "It was a very disturbing sight." She watched Kas' eyes, "I did. Why?"

Kas almost beamed with pride. "That is something very few people can master and succeed at. The timing has to be precise. Be forewarned, others may be able to do it to you as well, so if you ever sense someone messing with your control threads, block that channel. However, very few even know they exist, or at least it was mostly theoretical in my time."

"I killed three more men, not mages, just after I killed the mage. I shot lightning or energy I guess at them."

"You did what? How did you learn to do that? And lightning is not a completely inaccurate description."

"Well, I saw what the mage did with the fields. I just reproduced it. It left me drained and exhausted."

"I can imagine. You have not learned to be subtle yet. That takes years and subtlety with power normally develops before someone has the ability to draw in too much power." He shook his head. "You could burn yourself up. Overwhelm your body by drawing too much energy through it. We've had that discussion before."

"I killed three more mages not long after the first. Two with lightning. One was by surprise, the other tried to direct the blast away and for a moment, had managed. But I...I guess I just pushed harder. The last one, I used what you called gravity. I made a very strong field just under her feet. Limited to the small area and very attractive. She crumpled into a heap of broken bones." Stephenie closed her eyes and took a deep breath. "I really hated killing them like that. I hated killing them at all." She opened her eyes, "am I becoming a monster? I never killed anyone until the night I had to escape my mother. Now I've killed more than ten people. How can I become something like that? How can I live with their deaths? I felt the life flee several of them. I felt them die. I felt the deaths of others that I didn't kill. I felt their terror."

Kas' face remained expressionless for a while, only fluctuations in his illumination crossed his form. When he finally spoke, it lacked any sound and Stephenie could only feel it in her mind. "You are not a bad person. To defend one's life and those you care about is not an evil act. I do not know the circumstances that led up to all of these deaths, but the very fact that you feel bad about killing a man who was trying to kill you, shows you would not do so lightly. You obviously did what was needed.

"Plus, be glad you are mentally deaf to their thoughts. You would like the killing even less if you were not."

Stephenie pursed her lips and then slowly let out a weak smile; she had felt the concern and pride Kas had for her.

"Regarding the healing of your arm. I will try my best to show you how, since words and reading may be the least effective with you—not that they would not be effective," he added quickly. "You will need food and the fact that you appear to have overtaxed yourself will be a hindrance to your healing."

"We are nearly out of food. We stole as much as we could, but we are still several days from being able to get to where we hope we might find my brother." She looked up. "Oh ya, I forgot to tell you. My mother is a traitorous bitch who's screwed over the whole country, my father's dead, and my brother is believed to be a prisoner, probably digging in the mountains for that old warlock's lost treasure. We have to avoid being seen and we are running out of food."

Kas shook his head in a nearly living fashion. "Just a few things that slipped your mind. Perhaps you should tell me the whole story from the beginning. Then I will see what I can do about finding you food in an unseen manner."

Stephenie grinned.

Chapter 19

Will and Douglas were back well before Stephenie had finished her story. She noted their arrival, but continued telling Kas about everything that happened in as great a detail as she could remember. Partially drawing out the telling to avoid the need to stand up and continue the march, but mostly because for the first time since she had left the caves, she felt at ease in being able to tell someone her concerns, fears, weaknesses, and silly observations. With the others, she knew she needed to maintain some semblance of authority and strength. They were following her, not because she had a great idea, but because she had conviction in her belief and it was something she had to do. It was something she owed to the people of her kingdom. She could not give up the one chance they had at being able to recover in a healthy manner. She admitted the idea of rescuing her brother was a touch crazy and Kas accepted her self appraisal with his normal dry manner that made her smile.

He listened to her whole telling, seldom interrupting, but always attentive until she finally reached the point where she was telling him about his arrival and their current conversation. "I think I can predict where you are going with this line of conversation."

Her smiled widen slightly at his grin. "What about you? What is going on under Antar? Is Arkani safe?"

"It should be. The ghosts do not appear to have noticed your presence in any lasting manner. If no one disturbs it, the city should remain as it is." He rose, not so much in a fluid motion, but a stuttered one of three brief flashes of change. "However, now you have the problem of avoiding people while still gaining sustenance and finding your way. Fortunately, I can help with that. I will scout the path ahead and make sure you avoid anyone you need to avoid. I will also try to find you something to eat."

"We don't want to rob people blind. The Senzar are already doing that."

"You need food, and to be plain, I put your welfare ahead of others. I won't harm them, but I will not hesitate to steal what is needed." Seeing her expression, Kas moderated his tone slightly. "I will endeavor to take only from those that can afford it."

"Thank you."

"You should get walking, I will warn you if needed." He smiled and then faded from sight.

Stephenie watched as she felt his presence drift quickly to the west until he was out of range. She then turned back to her three companions; all of whom were staring at her. She grinned, aware her conversation with Kas had been quite upbeat considering their situation. His presence had simply lifted a huge weight from her. "Well, Kas is going to help." The others said nothing. She allowed her expression to become more serious. "Kas will scout our path for people to avoid and come back to warn us. He will also address our food problem. He promised to try to avoid stealing from people who cannot spare it. So we should hopefully have more food before we stop for the night."

Henton nodded his head. "Until the food is in hand, we still need to ration it. I take it, however, that you really need to eat a lot to regain your strength?"

Stephenie nodded her head. "Kas is going to try to show me how to heal my arm this evening. He mentioned he can keep watch, since he doesn't really need to sleep, being dead and all."

"How is it a ghost is your friend?" Will asked. "How is it he can even help?"

"His death was not normal. As I understand it, it takes someone of immense power to be able to hold together the energy that makes up their essence at death. And very few have ever managed it. Kas was the victim of a lot of mages using magic. It was not an intentional effect. However, he was a mage, someone like me.

Someone who did not worship any of the gods that we know of today. So he knows how to use magic, or witchcraft as we call it. He can teach me."

"He can teach you things people have lost in the last thousand years," Douglas commented, rising to his feet with his pack. "We should keep marching. We've lost enough time sitting. We can talk more on the way."

Stephenie rose as well, but struggled with her pack. Henton came over to replace the bandages around her arm and stood quietly as she addressed Will and Douglas. "I honestly never thought to see Kas again. I am very glad he has come. I hope he doesn't bother any of the three of you too much. I can understand if he does. I was quite uneasy when I first dealt with him. But I was also nearly dead, so a bit less animated. I'll try and teach him as much Cothish as I can so we can all talk to each other."

"We're nearly, if not already, in Selith", Douglas said. "You might teach him Pandar instead. Be more useful for all involved. We'll pass into Ipith and possibly Esland before we get where we are going. The trade tongue is more useful."

Stephenie nodded and fell into position after Henton, with Douglas and Will behind her. She felt bad about omitting the details of Arkani, but with the unease she was now feeling from Will and Douglas, she did not want to risk another betrayal, even if it was not to the extent of Zac's. From Henton, she was not sure what she was feeling. His emotions were always more guarded, and while she sensed unease, it did not seem to be driven by fear alone.

The conversation as they marched lasted only for a short while, since no one really wanted to advertise their presence with loud voices, even after Kas had made an initial report that the area was clear. Once darkness fell, Kas rejoined them to urge them to move another mile through the woods, his glowing form providing illumination to follow. Stephenie took up the rear of the march, her sight being so much more vivid in the dim, overcast light, that she did not have to worry overly much about tripping.

Once Kas stopped, they noted a small glade in the forest with a stream in the distance, flowing quickly in an easterly direction. A pile of packs lay in the middle of the grass-filled clearing, the insignia of the Senzar army visible to Stephenie's sight. She translated to the others that Kas stole them from a group of soldiers encamped five miles to the northeast.

"Five miles is not that far," Henton said, unsure and obviously worn by the hiking in the foot hills of the mountains.

"They are heading east," Stephenie continued for Kas, "and are being sent to investigate and retaliate for Ten Stones."

She could tell Henton was still unsure, but unwilling to argue further. He started making camp. Trying to do it out of her hearing, he arranged with Will and Douglas to take watch even with her assurances that Kas would keep them safe. Stephenie said nothing, aware that a gulf was forming in their relationship.

"Kas, I just wish they could know you as I do."

"Do not fret overmuch. I take no insult, though they will be slower tomorrow for the lack of sleep. But I do not think they will be slower than you."

"Thanks. I really hate being the reason we can't make better time. Though my head has hurt less this afternoon. I stopped trying to constantly search with my mind for people. I am trusting that you will warn us in time."

"That is my intent. Once you have recovered more of your strength, you should still keep a constant vigilance. I will do my best to always protect you, but I cannot be everywhere at all times. I will be able to stay closer if I am not looking for food for the next few days, but—"

"I understand. That was what I meant. My head has just been throbbing and I feel so raw."

"You burned your insides. You are lucky you did not cook your brain and kill yourself."

She stiffened at that description. "Okay."

"There is a concept of conservation of energy. To use power, some will be spent or wasted. You can never get more out than you put in. There is a similar concept with healing, if you damage your body by bringing in too much energy, bringing in more to heal yourself will result in overall more damage done, not less.

"However, you are also injured in a manner not directly related to overextending yourself. Healing your arm will draw energy through your body. Some of the damage from overextending yourself has healed, but not all of it. So, some of your body can tolerate the effort, like a swordsman using his tired muscles, they are more tired, but not torn. However, a swordsman who uses torn muscles will do more damage. This is your condition. You will tire things not damaged, but add damage to things previously damaged. However, you need to heal the arm, so the cost in the end is necessary."

"How do I heal this?"

"I have been trying to think of how to show you, but I lack what I had when I had my body. I think it best that I show you memories of healing. You have some nearly miraculous ability to reproduce things you observe—unless you have been lying about what you did," he added with a grin.

Stephenie took a deep breath. "What do I need to do?"

"You need to let me into your head. It will be against your natural instinct and I am sure if you decide to resist, I will not be able to overcome you, even in your current state. However, it is the only way I think I can show you."

Stephenie swallowed. "I trust you."

Kas frowned. "I know. I would not suggest this if you did not. However, I also have to trust you. I have not done this while being dead and if you get scared and resist forcefully, I may cease to exist."

"What?"

"I am now little more than an energy field held together by my will. A sufficiently powerful field could disrupt my cohesion and kill me. By reaching out to your mind, I will be weakening my own cohesion, at least in theory. Considering, as I said, I have not done this before, and do not know anyone who has done it, I cannot be certain of the effects. I would hate for you to feel guilty about killing me."

"Kas, we can't do this."

"You need your arm. Simply relax and do not fight me. It may be unpleasant, but I will try not to rummage around in your memories too much. I would suggest laying back and closing your eyes."

"Kas, no. I will not let you."

"Stephenie. You will do this. Do not fight me and there will not be that much risk. Just breathe."

She shook her head, but lay back. "You bastard. One day, I will make you do something you don't want to."

"Quiet. Close your eyes."

She took a deep breath and closed her eyes. "I promise. You say no and I'll bring this up. I'm a girl and we can do that, years—" she stopped talking. She could feel and sense the energy around her and the thin, nearly undetectable tendrils emanating from Kas. She held her breath despite Kas' commandment to breathe. The number of threads coming from him was vast and it threatened to overwhelm her sense of personal space.

Slowly she let out her breath and tried to relax as she realized, a number of those tendrils were from her. Little fingers feeling the world around her and the energy potential in all the matter she could perceive. She breathed again, slower and more deeply. The world around her became crisper, more defined, and more vivid.

"Stephenie," came Kas' voice, but it was more than just her name, it was a sense of perception of who she was, or at least his interpretation of her.

Stephenie answered, first with his name, then with more of herself, like releasing the breath held too long, understanding that more than words could be transferred. She felt his presence, more clearly and more painfully than she had before. He was no longer simply near her, but also with her, behind her eyes, in her thoughts. She started to panic, but her fear of hurting him caused her to stop and she forced herself to breathe.

It will be uncomfortable, but I will try to share with you an understanding of healing.

Stephenie inhaled sharply. Her sense of self started to crumble as memories filled her. She felt male and powerful at the same time she knew she was female and completely uncertain. She knew from what Kas had told her and what she had read that healing involved directing energy and forming the necessary material where the body already knew it needed the help. Giving the body the strength and a source of raw components to repair what was broken.

She felt the wave of emotion and pain as an injury long forgotten surged into her awareness. A burn from a fire gone out of control that had scorched and charred the skin of her leg. She could see the blackness that had also burnt the hair from her crotch and the very unfeminine appendage she did not have.

Panic began to seep into her again as separating Kas' memory from her own became impossible. Her sense of self was fading faster, and she almost missed the way Kas tapped into his own subconscious, letting his body direct its own healing without his conscious need to direct it. He simply reacted by providing the energy, and somehow, created the raw materials out of matter already in his body. The last part she barely understood as she felt Kas fall away from her. Suddenly she felt very hollow and empty, as if a great void had formed in her.

Gradually, the feeling of emptiness faded and she opened her eyes. With her right hand, she reached down and felt her right leg and then checked her crotch to make sure nothing changed since the last time she had checked. She exhaled, feeling uneasy and terrified, yet somehow resigned to the knowledge of what had just happened.

She opened her eyes. Kas was above her, apparently kneeling, but he lacked any visible form below his chest and arms. "That was different."

Kas smiled. "Somehow I knew you might say that."

"You had to show me that?" she asked, aware that despite the pain and agony of the memory, she felt slightly aroused by his choice of what he shared.

"Well, I meant to show you my leg, but the burned hair was part of it." He raised his eye brows, as Stephenie realized he did when he was alive and feeling cocky. "I did fully recover and nothing was damaged by the way. Not that it matters now. I'm little more than a decayed lump of bones."

Stephenie shook her head. She still felt like her leg and crotch had been burned, but that was fading.

"It was the only serious burn I ever had. A little youthful rebellion."

"You were twenty," she realized, as other details of the memory surfaced in her mind. "Older than I am now and playing at dueling."

"Well, that is true. However, it was not entirely my idea and I was the one who got injured. The important question is, do you think you will be able to repeat what I showed you and heal your arm?"

Stephenie took a deep breath and closed her eyes. She could still sense an underlying echo of Kas in her, not his presence, but something not entirely her. Something that over time would break down and become one with her, as if it was something eaten and not yet digested. The thought had implications, but she put it aside, as she did not feel the emotion and memory she had absorbed would harm her. Instead, she drew energy into herself, feeling the slight tinge of pain as it coursed through parts of her body that were already hurting from overuse.

Mimicking what she sensed Kas had done all those years ago when he was still alive, she let her own body direct itself. With the only conscious thought being the damaged arm, she felt the energy flowing into her limbs. Detached, she was mildly aware of blood flowing more forcefully through her forearm. She had the sensation of ants or other small insects crawling over and through her arm, but she resisted the urge to throw them off. However, after only a few moments, her head began to hurt and she realized she was drawing too much energy through her sore body. Cutting off the conscious flow of energy, she took a deep breath and realized the pain in her arm was much less than she had been enduring.

She tried to open her eyes and sit up, but she was unsteady and it took several moments and a lot of effort. Eventually she managed to get into an undignified sitting position. With her right hand and her teeth, she removed the bandage and looked down at her arm. Unable to believe what her eyes saw in the dim light, she grabbed her pack and quickly retrieved a light crystal. She giggled with relief when she looked down and the blackened hole in her arm was replaced with flesh. The charred skin was now just red as if she had suffered a severe burn, but at least it looked alive.

She moved her fingers and that still ached, but not with the agony that had previously accompanied her efforts. Grinning, she pulled down the neck of her shirt and pulled back the sweaty bindings she was wearing around her chest. She shook her head and frowned at Kas. "Well, looks like I'm keeping your mark." She softened the bite of her words with a smile. "I'd hug you if I could."

"You're welcome," he said, returning her smile. "Get some sleep and don't try to heal yourself any further until you have recovered more. Take it slow, but at this point, I do not think you will lose function."

She looked up and waved Henton and the others over. Holding up the light crystal, which the others had taken to with hesitation over the last couple of days, she showed them her forearm. "Kas showed me. I'm not sure how to heal others yet, but I know it can be done."

Henton knelt down to look closer, Will and Douglas remained standing, interested, but wary.

"It looks like a bad burn now. I'd expect a large scar from that alone, but with you, perhaps nothing to show it ever happened." He looked up to meet her eyes. "You've got a little blood on your nose."

She wiped the small trail away and nodded. "I'm exhausted, but I won't lose my arm."

Henton smiled at her. "You've been trying to be strong, but I've seen you keep looking at it. I'm happy for you. I wish I could have done something sooner to help."

She reached out and hugged Henton and then looked up at Will and Douglas. "I would never have made it this far without the three of you. I need all of you. Every one of you has saved me in one way or another, including Kas. Any success we have at this is thanks to all of you, and to Fish." She swallowed. "I will miss him and will not let that happen again. I won't lose any more of my friends. Not that way."

Douglas smiled at her. "Well, we're here to make sure you can do what needs to be done. Your dead friend has me a little uncomfortable, more so than what you are, but if he can teach you to heal and fight, then I can't see any harm there." He grabbed Will's arm, "come on guys, let her sleep. She needs the rest."

"We'll be right here if you need anything," Henton said as he stood. He smiled at her, glanced at Kas, then went the dozen feet to the blankets he was laying on.

Yes, sleep Stephenie. I will watch.

"Thank you, all of you," she mumbled, not quite in any distinct language before laying back and letting herself drift off to sleep.

Chapter 20

The next three days of marching went much better than the previous three. With Kas' help, they skirted around the northern end of the Grey Mountains and started heading southwest. There were many more soldiers and the remnants of towns. They passed more than one mass grave which looked to be a couple of weeks old. The stench and carrion eaters kept them from doing any more than a cursory inspection of the towns, which were as they expected, stripped of anything valuable, just like the vultures were doing with the bodies in the pits.

A day later and they had passed out of Selith into Ipith's small claim on the mountains. It was here that Kas started leading them more southeast into the range instead of through the foothills. The jagged peaks, always previously in the distance, were now approaching. The large granite boulders that had lay scattered about the foothills like discarded toys now filled the tree covered landscape of the river valley they were hiking.

Kas scouted ahead, spying on different groups of soldiers, learning that the main encampment was in a valley the Senzar had named The Mushroom due to the large, somewhat flat ledge near the top of the mountain ridge. It was not visible from their current vantage point. However, Kas had flown high and ahead, not being confined by concepts of gravity, and he estimated it would be at least two more days of strenuous marching before they arrived at the encampment.

The conversation he had listened to included confirmations of their expectations: the Senzar were using the captured soldiers and prisoners to excavate a rock slide on the southwest part of the ridge.

"And how are we supposed to rescue the prince?" Will asked, his tone a bit sharper today then the day before. "We'll have to escape once we get him. Otherwise, we'll just be joining him until they decide to throw us off the mountain."

Stephenie tried to keep any irritation from her voice; she understood his fear and concern. "Kas will scout for us and find him. Once we know what we are up against, we can better plan how to go about it. Worst comes to worse, we go over the ridge and head into the range."

"And what of everything you said before about fighting in mountains?"

"Will, I don't have all the answers, I've been upfront about that, but I suspect we'll need to do it at night so we have the cover of darkness to help protect us. I can see pretty good at night, so that won't be a problem. Depending on what Kas finds, perhaps I just go in with him and bring Josh out and the three of you won't need to get close."

Henton shook his head. "Let's not speculate too much, like you said, we don't know what we face yet."

"Well, we don't even know if Josh is alive. No offense Steph, but we don't know. It would be a lot of risk to find out he's not there. Send Kas in now and find out, then we can decide."

"Kas has been leading us around the soldiers and finding the best routes," Douglas injected. "We can't see much through this tree cover and scaling these rocky slopes is not easy as it is. With the valleys full of soldiers, it's not like we can take the easy route."

"Steph?" Henton asked.

She took a deep breath and conveyed the general conversation to Kas.

Kas sighed. "For now, finish going to the top of this ridge, then take the ridge toward the east. There are a few places the ridge is clear, so you may need to drop lower to stay in the treeline. Do that to the north. Once the ridge flattens out significantly, you will be heading up another peak. I'd skirt the southern slope about the same level as that ridge, then pick up the ridgeline again and continue east. The terrain is too rough here to station any significant force, so you should be safe. But you do not want to raise the alarm by being foolish."

"Would you even recognize him?"

"I have your memory of him. It was something I could not help but acquire the other night. I would be able to recognize him if I saw him." He smiled at her, "I can travel fast. I'll be back before morning. Since we need to see what they do with everyone at night, I will wait to observe." Without another word, he faded from sight.

"I take it he agreed," Henton said.

Scaling the slope to reach the ridge left their hands and knees cut and bruised. Closer to the top, they kept sliding on loose stone and if it had not been for the dense trees, they would have caused a large rock slide. As it was, they were surprised not to see a troop of soldiers waiting for them. The good news was that the last couple of nights of healing had left Stephenie's arm nearly as strong as it had been before she was hurt. The others had smiled at her with envious pride at her recovery, then for a reward, pushed her to the front to force a trail through the wind-bent trees and shrubs.

By late evening, they had moved off the ridge and were skirting the next large peak. The route was difficult and they had to actually climb several hundred feet up the peak to avoid a sheer rock face. Further cut and bruised, they continued onward, unable to stop on the side of the mountain due to lack of any level surfaces upon which to rest.

It was well after dark, and Stephenie had taken to having everyone lash themselves together with the rope they were carrying. While she could see reasonably well, the others were more limited and a slip here could mean death. The going eased up eventually and through a break in the trees, Stephenie noticed the shaded form of a ridge below them.

Changing direction, she led them carefully down the slope until they reached a reasonably flat surface. The others were exhausted and cold. However, Stephenie was feeling invigorated by being so close to their destination and the impending rescue of Joshua. She had the others lay down to sleep while she took the first watch. Despite the cool breeze blowing through the trees, she stayed warm from her body's subconscious regulation of her temperature.

She was not sure how much time had passed, but eventually Henton rose and came over to her. "Steph, can I talk with you for a moment?"

She turned to face him and noted he was wrapped in a blanket. "Sure."

"How are you doing?"

"I'm feeling pretty good. Worried a little about Kas and what we might have to deal with, but overall, good. Why?"

"The others asleep?"

She looked at him for a moment, sensing some apprehension, but nothing alarming. "Ya. For the moment."

He nodded his head. "We have not had a chance to really talk for a while and I don't want to disturb them." He shuffled around a bit, then sat down next to her on the fallen tree trunk. "Can you really not read minds?"

She forced a soft laugh. "No. Kas says I'm mentally deaf. I can see, or I guess more accurately sense, the energy around us to a level that I think surprises Kas, though he doesn't admit it. I mean, I can see it move and flow if I concentrate. I can see the potential just sitting in the stones and the air and in you and me. Stores of energy, just waiting. But thoughts are a bit different. Like ripples in a pond, Kas said. Little waves, sometimes coming faster or slower—changes in the frequency or larger or smaller in size, meaning different amplitude. I have trouble relating to them for some reason."

"But you've been able to sense people about and even get an idea of what they are thinking."

"People and objects cause ripples in the energy, I can sense that with ease. I can get an idea of what you are feeling, but believe me, it's little more than what someone who's observant can note by watching your face or the way you move. Just surface emotion. You're very guarded. I can hardly sense anything from you most days."

Henton was quiet for a while, then he took a deep breath. "You know, you are not like any princess I ever imagined."

"A bit too common."

He shook his head quickly, "not common. You're not walled off and stuck up. You're approachable. You do your fair share and don't complain about having to work." He smiled. "Not what I had expected. I really thought princesses would sneer at people like me and the guys."

Stephenie smiled back, but she doubted he could see much of her face. "You have not met my sisters. They are every bit the snobbish, petty, and pointless girls you would expect. Well, maybe Kara wasn't and Islet could be reasonable, sometimes."

"You are easy to talk to. At least when we are not marching through the whole day and into the night."

"I do my best." She patted his arm. "To be honest, I was worried about what you planned for me. You seemed a bit traditional in your beliefs. I'm just glad you didn't decide to end me without giving me a chance."

He took another deep breath. "Steph, you've challenged so much of my beliefs. I—well, I've always thought myself practical and perhaps there are a lot of people who need to change their opinions." He continued before she could say anything. "I need to tell you something that's been bothering me for a while." He turned to face her. "I can speak some of the Old Tongue as well. My close friend who was the priest, he taught me. I don't know it that well and much of the time what Kas says is hard to understand, but—"

Stephenie sat back. "You've been spying on me?"

"No—well, at first, yes, that was my intent. I didn't trust Kas and after a while, I wanted to admit that I could, but there never seemed to be a good time. I didn't—"

"I've been telling him some very personal things."

"I know. I, please don't be mad. I've been trying to get up the nerve to admit it for a couple of days now. I know why you've not wanted to tell us things. Admitting your fears about what's going to come would really hurt morale with Will. Douglas seems to be as pragmatic as normal, but, I just wanted to let you know that if you needed to talk with someone else, I am here. I accept your fears and am willing to continue on with you."

Stephenie took a deep breath. She was not sure if she was angry or flattered. *Perhaps a little of both,* she decided after a moment of thought. She took a moment more to decide how to respond. "Henton, I appreciate you telling me the truth. I have to think back about what I've been saying to Kas, but I think I understand."

"Steph. Please forgive me. I really meant no harm and then it just got out of control, too much time had passed. I don't know what's going to happen in the next couple of days and if I should die, I really don't want to die thinking you were angry with me."

She took a deep breath. "Henton, I'm going to do my damnedest to try and make sure no one dies. I don't want anything bad to happen to any of you." She put her hand on his arm again. "I forgive you. Just, if you know any other languages, let me know so I don't think I'm having a private conversation."

"Thank you. I've felt terrible these last several days. I really have."

"Hey, all's forgiven. Don't worry." She yawned. "However, if you don't mind, I might get a little sleep before morning."

"Sure. It's my turn anyway."

Stephenie jumped a little when Henton shook her shoulder to wake her. The sun was cresting the mountains to the east, which meant it was fairly late in the morning. She noted immediately that Kas was back and the other two were sitting nearby. "Why'd you let me sleep so late?"

"You? We all slept late. Well, you looked more tired and Kas seemed to indicate you should not be woken."

She slowly got to her feet and shook the dirt from her blankets. "You talked to Kas?"

"Well, he was primarily shaking his head and shooing us away from you. He can be rather imposing when he wants to be." Henton handed her a chunk of cheese and some dried fruit. "I'll take care of this, you find out what's up."

Reluctantly, she handed Henton the blanket to roll up and started eating as she approached her favorite dead man. "So, got a plan all figured out?"

Kas shook his head and looked back across the valley to the south.

"Well, at least tell me how bad it is."

Kas blinked back to face her, something she still had not quite grown used to. "They have a valley full of soldiers. The main camp is down there. I would guess several hundred mages, perhaps more. I could not spend much time for risk of them sensing me. I am not impervious to injury and would do little good for you if they destroyed me further." Kas appeared to sigh at Stephenie's raised eye brows. "Anyway, I would speculate that from the number of tents and buildings they have in the valley, there are between ten and twenty thousand troops there. Not all in this valley, but stretching back to the west."

"What about my brother? Oh, and Henton can understand some of what we say."

Kas performed a very living double take, mouth open, with a glance to Henton and then back to Stephenie. "When did this information become available?"

"Last night, we talked a bit. But more important, my brother."

"Well, I found him."

"He's alive!"

"Yes, but let me give you the bad news. They are digging where I would believe Gimtar's castle once stood. There is a peak that appears to have crumbled long ago into a large rock slide. The slide goes down into the valley, but they are concentrating near the edge of the semi flat area four fifths of the way up the ridge. It's just above the tree line and they have twenty five rough log houses near the edge of the ridge. The captives are brought out during the day to dig and haul rock. At night, they are locked into fifteen of the houses and there are guards. There are many more captives they keep in part of the valley, since there is only so much room at the top."

"Well, so far that sounds possible still. Is my brother at the top?"

"Yes. We'll need to move across the ridge, which is several miles long, quite rough, and follows a slight curve. It is also in the clear and visible the whole way to the valley, so we cannot do it during the day. The valley is unavailable to us and they could muster a lot of troops to come after you."

"What about going over the other side of the ridge?"

"Possible. The other side is a bit more treacherous, but with your practicing, you could probably lower everyone down some of the worst parts so that you can make it into the valley on the east side."

"Okay. Any places to hide along the way? Can we do it over a couple of days or do we have to do it all in one go? And what will we be facing?"

"There are places you can hide. There does not appear to be too many moving patrols, but there will be at least a dozen mages and a hundred soldiers. Four of the houses contain supplies so they don't have to bring up new things every day. The smallest building houses the mages, three for the soldiers, two for bureaucrats directing things. Fifteen for the four hundred prisoners, those are on the north of the slide, the others are on the south side. You free your brother and you will have thirty other men demanding to be freed as well. Which means you won't do it quietly."

Stephenie felt the strength drain from her limbs. "I don't want to leave the men, but I'm not sure I want to try lowering anyone with my power, let alone thirty other men."

"It is not just men, but women as well."

"You are not making this easier."

"I told you the news was bad." Kas drew her attention to his face. "There will be at least a dozen soldiers and a mage keeping watch around the houses. I could probably draw off the mage, make my presence known and see if he or she will come to investigate. I think you could probably sneak in past the soldiers, but getting your brother and escaping?"

"They have rope I'm sure. We can—damn, you said a dozen mages." Stephenie looked across the tree-filled valley. She could see the beginning of the crescent shaped ridge probably half a day's march away. "Know any great magic I can learn real quick to make this easy?"

"No." Kas moved in front of her, blocking her view by becoming mostly opaque. "It depends on how important your brother is to you. If we free thirty to sixty people, they would be a distraction. It would give you time to escape. Most likely the prisoners would simply be recaptured and harmed minimally. They are serving a purpose, at least until they find what these new Denarians are looking for. Then I would suspect they will all be executed."

"Kas you are not making my life easier."

"Stephenie. I am trying to give you options. The prisoners are likely to die, probably in the near term. If you free them, it's possible some might escape. Some might get killed, but most will likely be put back in their prison and made to work tomorrow."

She closed her eyes, wondering what had put the burden of this decision upon her. *My mother being a traitorous bitch and destroying father's and Josh's support.* Opening her eyes, she looked at Kas and could see the concern in his eyes. She could sense the concern he was feeling and she hoped it was concern for her well being. She nodded her head. "Practical. Damn, this will haunt me until I die. Perhaps I can get some free."

She turned back to Henton, Will, and Douglas and described the situation. When she was done, she retrieved her pack from Henton. "I don't like it, but unless I think of another option, we'll do the following: move to the start of the flat top during the day, avoiding being seen. Then after dark, make our way closer to where they are working, hiding out in a cave or outcropping of rocks. Tomorrow night, the three of you will start for the top of the ridge, taking our supplies. Kas will draw off the mage and hopefully some of the soldiers. I will sneak in and free Josh and one or two of the other log houses. The men will cause a distraction, Josh and I will join you at the top of the ridge, then we head over the other side and I lower you down the slope one at a time so we can get to a safe distance quickly. If anyone has a better idea, let me know now. I will definitely listen to it."

Henton shook his head. "We are not going to let you try that on your own. We will come with you. Or at least I will. At minimum we pair up. Will and Douglas can take our current supplies to the ridge, perhaps we can gather some additional supplies. At the very least, we don't want to be carrying too much extra weight when we are trying to run away quickly."

"Henton, I—"

"I am here to protect you. I can't do that if you are on your own."

"Fine." She took a deep breath and turned. "Okay, let's go," she looked back over her shoulder, "and if anyone comes up with something better on the way, I'll listen."

Chapter 21

They moved along the edge of the tree line through the morning and into the early afternoon, but stopped once they saw the full view of the valley before them. On their left, the ridge continued to the south, bending in a gentle curve to the west. The top one fifth of the ridge held a shelf, more flat then vertical, and was covered in a mix of snow and green tundra grass. There were only a few breaks where boulders and rock slides left nothing but rubble and gullies in the shelf. The most notable of these was the great wide scar that appeared to be the result of half of a mountain peak breaking away and crumbling over the shelf and into the valley below.

The next three fifths of the ridge were quite steep with many open rock faces that held only the most determined of trees. The lower valley was at least ten miles long and generally a carpet of green trees. However, swaths of forest were cut, revealing the gray stone underneath. Smoke rose up from the many fires, settling in the valley as a permanent fog. It was too far to see details, but the signs of human habitation were clear.

To the west, another ridge, far more jagged and irregular, was blanketed in green. Unlike the eastern ridge, side valleys broke that line of mountains, providing winding canyons into the western part of the range. The primary access to the valley before them was a side valley in the western ridge. It was a good six miles to the south. That side valley was delineated by another ridge line, leading off to the southwest toward several isolated mountains in the distance.

"This place would be hard to invade if you had troops stationed in the right places."

"Or filling the valley like maggots," Douglas added to Will's comment, pointedly looking into the distance.

Stephenie only nodded her head before seeking a comfortable place to sleep out the rest of the afternoon.

That night, they managed to carefully traverse four of the six miles toward where the mountain peak had broken in half and dumped tons of boulders, rock, and rubble across the shelf and into the valley below. They stopped in a boulder field created by a smaller slide from the ridge. The night was only half gone and they took turns keeping watch while the others caught a few hours of rest.

When the sun finally rose enough to illuminate the valley, they were careful to remain low and hidden, spying on the activity taking place a couple miles away. Stephenie watched as groups of people were led from the buildings on the near side of the large boulder field. While the distance was too far to see the details clearly, it was obvious that the prisoners were being forced to break large rocks and move the rubble to an area further south of the far buildings.

As the day wore on, Stephenie noted only two short breaks for food, and while water seemed available and plentiful, they were given little protection from the harsh sun and cold breeze. With everyone above the tree line, the only protection would have been back in the prison-like buildings.

She kept looking for Joshua, but from her vantage point, she could only tell the prisoners from the guards by their overall activities. The guards were more stationary and aggressive, while the prisoners were broken and hopeless in their movements.

As evening wore on and the sun was beginning to drop behind the western ridge, Stephenie turned toward the others. "I don't think we will have to use anyone as a distraction. They worked everyone so hard that I doubt anyone could do anything more than sleep through the night even if they wanted. I should be able to sneak in and find Josh without waking anyone else. Then we can slip away without putting anyone at risk."

Douglas nodded his head, "it's possible, but if others wake, then what?"

"Depends. If it is one or two, we can take them as well. If we get a lot, we'll have to go back to the current plan. I don't like it, but... well, let's hope it won't be necessary."

"We need to watch our supplies," Douglas held up a nearly empty pack. "We're going to have enough trouble with the five of us. Bring too many and we won't have any food."

Stephenie nodded. "Kas and I can hunt when we have the valley to our back and hopefully no longer pressed for time. I've not practiced much with heat and flame yet, but I can screw up a snake pretty easily."

Will leaned forward, "do what to a snake?"

"Don't ask, it ended up everywhere, but I think a rabbit or stag would be quite tasty." She smiled then turned serious, "Henton, you can still go with Will and Douglas."

"Don't waste your time. I am going with you."

Stephenie sighed, "I had to give you the option. We need to wait until halfway through the night, give everyone enough time to get to sleep." She slid back down between a couple of rocks and put her head against her pack. "Until then, I think I will get some sleep."

Stephenie awoke early in the night and concern for Henton, Will, and Douglas kept her from getting any further sleep. She talked briefly with Kas, but did not vent her fears since Henton was sitting a couple of feet away. Kas acknowledged her reserved demeanor with a scowl before fading into nearly complete transparency. Stephenie could sense him, visible or not, but was thankful he could hide in such a manner, as the soft glow his form emanated would give them away if someone was watching.

The others alternated between sleeping or resting. Eventually, Henton moved closer so he could talk quietly. "You know, whatever happens, I am very proud of you. It takes someone quite strong to do what you've done. You have more courage than anyone I have ever met. I know we face some significant odds, but I have faith in you."

She sighed and looked at Henton, his face was covered with many days worth of stubble. All the men had stopped shaving halfway through the journey when they had run out of soap. His odor was also fairly strong, but she knew she smelled fairly bad as well. "I appreciate your faith in me. I hope it's not misplaced. I don't want anything to happen to any of you. We just need a little luck."

"And you and Kas will give that to us."

She forced a smile, for once sensing a little emotion from Henton and it felt like jealousy. "I think it is late enough. Even I can feel the chill of the night." Slowly, she pushed herself to her feet, pulling up her pack with her.

The others followed her lead and gathered their goods. Once they extracted themselves from the outcropping of rocks, Stephenie pulled Will to her and gave him a strong hug. "We'll all see each other soon, so don't trip in the dark." Will smiled at her as she turned and gave Douglas a similar hug before handing him her pack. "Take care of this for me and I'll make sure we get a nice buck to eat."

"You have a deal."

She turned back to Henton and nodded her head. "Let's get going. Kas is already moving ahead to check the path."

Stephenie led Henton carefully across the three quarter mile wide shelf, which on her far left sloped steeply up to the peak of the ridge at the last moment. She remained closer to the drop off on her right, since that part was closer to being level and the tundra grasses beneath their feet were less slippery than the snow that was prevalent on the more vertical area closer to the ridge line.

They covered the nearly two miles in reasonably quick time, though Stephenie continually slowed herself down so Henton would not trip badly. As they grew closer to the scattering of buildings, she felt Kas return. She did not see his form, but she heard and felt his low voice.

"You are seeking the sixth building furthest up the slope and closest to the digging area. I have seen a man dressed as a mage. He is inside a small three sided building that keeps the guards out of the weather. It is close to the edge and near where the digging is taking place. There are five other guards moving about in two groups. If you go up slope now and then cross over to the buildings, you will remain out of their sight. The mage is likely too far to notice you, but I will keep watch and try to draw him off if needed."

Stephenie did not have time to respond, as Kas almost immediately started to move. She grabbed Henton's hand and pulled him along in the direction Kas had indicated. She kept low and moved quickly. Without the weight of her pack, she felt strong and light footed despite the thin air. After a short burst of speed, over worn and trampled ground, she came up along the side of the first building.

The building's logs were rough cut and the gaps had been filled with chinking made of tundra grasses and mud. The construction looked quick, but durable. There did not appear to be any windows. Coming to the corner of the first building, she noted the single door with a heavy beam of wood barring the door shut. Memories of her room in the tower came back to her, but she did not smile.

Taking a deep breath, she pulled Henton along behind her. She could feel a group of two men walking to the south between this row of buildings and the next row of somewhat randomly placed buildings. She slowed their pace, making sure the two guards continued along their course. At the corner, she moved more quickly, darting to the cover of the next building. They repeated the pattern of wait, check, move until they reached the sixth and last one.

Crouching down, she closed her eyes and opened her senses again. She could sense the multitude of people around her scattered about in each of the buildings. She did not bother to try and count them, the numbers were large enough and had the feel of about thirty each. The guards were out of her range.

She looked at Henton, nodded her head, and then lifted the heavy bar from the door. It rubbed against the steel bracket and the wood of the door frame, but did not make a great deal of noise. Subconsciously drawing in power, she hefted the hundred pound chunk of wood and quietly set it down next to the door.

She opened her senses once again, and while she was not certain, she believed that everyone was still sleeping. With a deep breath, she pulled open the door just wide enough to slide in, signaling Henton to remain with a quick hand gesture.

Inside the dark building she had trouble seeing. Outside, the moonlight coming through the thin layer of clouds made it easy to see. Inside, only the narrowly opened door provided any light and she was forced to rely on her senses to avoid stepping on the people who were sleeping on wooden planks laying on the ground. The stench of unwashed and sweaty people was staggering, but she pushed down the urge to gag and searched the room for the feel of her brother. While it had taken Kas to show her how to recognize the distinctions each person had in their mental energy, she knew that as soon as he had, she would not have trouble finding Joshua. And true to her expectation, it took only a moment for her to sort out her brother from the others.

Moving halfway into the building, she knelt in front of her brother, almost trembling from relief of finding him. Carefully, she put one hand over his mouth and shook his shoulder with the other.

He came awake almost immediately and struggled with her, fighting against the person covering his mouth. She had the advantage of regular meals and magic, so he was not able to shake her grip while she shushed him. "Josh, it's me, Steph."

Hearing her soft voice quieted him. He tried to open his eyes further, but even Stephenie was having trouble seeing his face clearly. She removed her hand from his mouth, "keep your blanket. I'm getting you out of here, but we have to go now." He nodded his head and she turned her grip on his shoulder to help him up.

"Steph? How?"

"Quiet. We can't afford to wake anyone." Taking his hand and the blanket from him, she led him quickly to the door. She could see Henton looking in through the narrow opening. She could also sense three guards on the back side of the building moving in their general direction along the work area. Moving a little faster, she pushed passed Henton, raising three fingers and pointing over her shoulder and through the building.

Feeling the men quickly reach the southwest corner of the building, she decided not to replace the bar, but pushed the others toward the northeast corner, hoping to hide between the buildings.

"Rush, no! Remain!" They heard in broken Cothish.

Stephenie felt a chill run down her spine as she realized there were subtle fluctuations in the energy around them that was not coming from her. She had not noticed them at first. Her mouth suddenly dry, she pushed Henton and Josh ahead of her again. "Go. Run. Now!" she whispered.

She turned around and saw the three men come around the corner of the building. They were dressed in leather armor and looked to be common soldiers. Each carried a sword on their hips, but none of them had drawn their blades.

"You stupid? Think we are? Think we not notice you? We wait, see you do."

Stephenie swung her hand behind her and hit Henton. "Get him out. I have this."

"No, Steph, I won't leave," Joshua demanded. However, she felt Henton pulling her brother away.

"Let us go and there won't be trouble. It's just one man," she said slowly, hoping to buy enough time that Kas would join her. However, she could not feel his presence.

The man in the center shook his head and Stephenie felt the wave of force strike her in the chest. She staggered back, barely keeping her feet, knowing that her mind reacted instinctively to block some of the blow.

The man in the center quickly said "wizard" in the Old Tongue to his two companions and then launched another attack.

Stephenie was more prepared for this blow, but it was also more powerful and more directed, taking the form of a candlestick like rod of force, designed to rip a hole through her. She stumbled to one knee. However, she did not start to retreat, she could still feel Henton dragging her brother away, which meant they were still too close. She stopped focusing on them, took a deep breath, and pulled energy into herself. The generation of a small rod of force was well beyond her control and she knew she would not be able to reproduce it. Instead she used one tool she was certain she could. Under the feet of all three men, she created a gravity well. The moment her force started to grow another rod of energy struck her, this time ripping into her shoulder and sending her onto her back.

She cried out once in pain, but kept her eyes closed and continued to focus on the energy around her. One of the other two men had started moving in her direction, the two that remained appeared to have many threads linking to her. Sucking in a wave of energy, she dropped the gravity well much more quickly and over a larger area.

The near soldier, sword now drawn, crumpled to the ground, his bones cracking and splintering as he screamed in pain. But the screams lasted only a brief moment as his rib cage crumbled and collapsed his lungs.

The other two mages resisted, directing their power to cancel out what Stephenie was doing. She felt another tendril reach out to her. Not wanting to deal with whatever that mage was going to unleash, she drew more energy directly through herself, focusing all of her effort into increasing the gravity under the mages. There was a sharp spike of pain that came from them as she felt energy flowing around the men in a last desperate attempt to save themselves. A moment later, the men crumbled to the ground like puppets that lost all of their strings.

She exhaled and forced herself to sit up. She sensed that several people in the nearby buildings had woken, but no one had come out of the partially open door.

Her right shoulder had a hole in it, but she knew it had not gone all the way through. The pain was intense and the warm blood running down her shirt was growing cool as it moved away from its source. With her left hand, she put pressure on her right shoulder and turned to follow Henton and Joshua.

She had only gone a few yards, stumbling over the rough ground, when she sensed a number of people coming up quickly across the work area. They appeared to be heading specifically in her direction.

Stephenie tried to move faster, just barely sensing Henton and Joshua ahead of her. She smiled briefly as she felt Kas appear behind her and between the dozen men pursuing her.

Stephenie ducked as she sensed something move quickly in her direction. At the last moment, she realized it was half a dozen arrows. Drawing in power, she stumbled as she deflected the deadly shafts just before they hit her.

She heard the commotion Kas' appearance was causing and turned back toward the dozen people nearing the edge of the boulder field. "Go!" she yelled again to Joshua and Henton, who now seemed to be moving in her direction and not toward safety.

Some of the soldiers had ignored Kas and were moving closer, pausing briefly to shoot again. Others seemed to be focused on Kas. "Damn it Josh, go!"

She took a step to steady herself and flung a wall of force toward the soldiers who were shooting their bows. The arrows bounced away, but one woman with a bow held out her hand and Stephenie felt resistance against her wall. Losing her focus, none of the men were knocked over as she had intended.

"There are six mages," she heard Kas' distant voice in her mind. Fear and panic bled over the link she had not expected. *No Kas!* she thought desperately, hoping she was able to send thoughts to him as he had sent them to her. But she doubted he would hear and knew he would not turn from engaging the mages even if he had.

She moved closer, wanting to get past the five who were now between her and Kas. Terror ran through her as people shot lightning through his form. Anger and frustration filled her as she noticed Joshua and Henton were still coming back for her. Pulling in the energy around her, she dug deep within herself and pushed with all of her strength against the mage who had blocked her wall of force. This time the resistance felt weak and failed immediately, sending the mage flying backwards, her bow broken from the impact.

An arrow struck her in the right leg and she stumbled, but others bounced away as her body reacted instinctively, throwing out a field to protect itself. Pain from the arrow had not yet registered, but the pain from drawing in the extra energy caused her to stumble.

She hesitated a moment, forcing herself to take a breath, tasting the blood in her mouth, as the archers were all drawing back to fire again. Sensing Kas cry out in terror, she reached for more energy, pulling it into her body from the air and the mountain below her. It resisted at first, then when it came, she unleashed a massive wall of energy and force, driving it into the near soldiers and continuing to push it toward the seven people engaging Kas. The four remaining archers flew backwards, like leaves blown by an autumn hurricane, bouncing and tumbling into the distance. The seven who were dumping energy into Kas staggered and several turned their focus on Stephenie.

She felt several threads of energy upon her and was dropped to the ground when a rod of force blew through her left leg and another into her abdomen. From the second blow she had instinctively deflected some of the force, but blood was now pouring from her wounds and she was feeling light headed and weak. Her insides felt as if they were on fire.

She noticed Kas pushing forward, trying to reach one of the mages. More lightning rolled over Kas and Stephenie could feel his presence fading away. "No!" she screamed. She felt another rod of energy penetrate her body, but was uncertain where the damage had occurred.

Holding her head and chest up with her hands, she pulled more energy from the ground. This time it was slow to come, difficult to release from where it was stored. She was so numb now that she barely noticed the pain. She tried to drop a gravity well under the group of mages, but it was countered immediately and she felt the ground below her sucking herself down.

Suddenly she could no longer sense or see Kas. She screamed and reached out for more energy. Distantly, she could sense the enormous reserve of trapped energy in the stone below her. For a moment, she felt as if she was a part of the whole mountain range. Drawing in the power, she gorged herself on it. She called out to it and grudgingly it responded, answering her call and flooding into her. She tried to focus, but her limbs felt afire. She could no longer see with her eyes, though her senses lit up, making her aware of all the threads and channels of energy around her and through the mountain, the air, and the people.

She sensed Joshua and Henton, still coming toward her. She sensed Will and Douglas and thousands upon thousands of people in the valley. The awareness was instant, but the clarity of the moment started to fade as her body was wracked with more assaults from the mages before her.

Kas, she sobbed mentally, unable to breath physically. As more energy surged into her, her body burned more acutely. Her bones seemed to break apart, fracturing and splintering as if they were in a blast furnace. The pain was unbearable.

Unable to hold the energy any longer, she gave one last tug at the mountain, directed the energy to flow up and overwhelm the men and woman who destroyed what was left of Kas. She could feel the power erupting from the ground beneath their feet. She barely sensed the shudder that rumbled throughout the mountain. A moment of silence followed, where even the energy seemed to pause. A heartbeat later, the mountain fractured, rock cracked, broke, and then exploded outward. She released a primal scream as her body crumpled into the ground, pain now a very distant concept.

Stephenie felt the energy fade away and with it, her awareness of the world.

Chapter 22

Stephenie tried to move, but found she was unable to do so. A brief moment of panic set in as she struggled to look around, but found she could not see. She paused, listening, but there was no sound, no vision. Just a sense of bleakness. *Kas, are you here?* She waited, but heard nothing. *Kas!* she cried out in desperation. Again, she heard nothing in response.

She tried to reach out with her mind, but sensed nothing, not even the energy that she had learned to feel. *Kas, please, I need you.* She remembered sensing Kas fade away from her awareness. She remembered the details of the face of the man who had last attacked Kas with a flood of raw energy and wanted to cry. She had not seen him clearly with her eyes, but she recalled the brief flash of immense mental awareness vividly. *I die, only to lose you. Damn you, damn whatever gods might exist. This is too cruel. Kas, please!* She tried to close her eyes, but realized they were not open.

Stephenie, I am here.

Hearing Kas' voice in her mind, Stephenie screamed with excitement. *Kas! You're not dead, or deader than you were. I was so scared I would be alone.*

It will take a little more than that to cause me to completely disassociate. It seems I have a fairly strong desire to continue to exist. Kas' sense of sarcasm and self projected strongly with the thoughts.

I was scared that even in death I still lost you.

Stephenie, you are not dead, he scolded, but with a reserved playfulness.

Stephenie paused, unsure if she believed Kas.

You have been badly hurt, but you are not dead. I am actually amazed at that. In fact, I am at a loss to explain why your body has not been completely burned away. I have no way to explain you living.

Kas, I felt my bones breaking, or at least it felt like that was happening. There was so much energy, so much pain.

Kas' dry voice continued, *I have only a bare awareness of what happened. I am unable to tell you what occurred beyond what I have heard the others saying. Though I can sense some of your memory of it, but hesitate to absorb much due to the obvious pain you were feeling.*

Then they lived?

Yes, but you need to wake up. It has been almost three days and I think you need to regain consciousness, otherwise you just might die from lack of food and water.

She sighed mentally, *would that be so bad? Kas, I just want to be with you.*

Stephenie, the chances of that happening are too few to count. You need to wake up. This is actually the most aware you have been since it happened. I imagine you are avoiding waking up due to the pain you will undoubtedly feel. But the time is past for you to lay about like a lazy princess, your brother will not leave the mountain and this is not a place for a large number of people to remain waiting on you to get out of bed.

Gee, thanks for the sympathy.

I'm dead, why should I have sympathy for someone, who if she wants to see me again, should focus on waking up and opening her eyes. Grow a set you lazy girl, or I'll let Henton and the others stare at your naked body.

While they had been talking, Stephenie realized her senses had opened somewhat and now she knew Kas was off to her right. She also had sensed an enormous exhaustion mixed with cold, like a distant echo in a cave. She suddenly became aware of Joshua's voice calling to her.

Taking a deep breath and realizing her body was breathing, she forced herself to awaken, willing her eyes to open. As soon as she sensed her body begin to respond, she felt the wave of agony for what she had done to it.

Crying out involuntary and hearing that wail with her own ears startled her. She tried to move, but her body was too weak to obey. "Kas, you bastard," she forced from her cracked lips in a mumble.

"I told you there would be pain."

"Steph! Open your eyes! Are you okay?"

Slowly she opened her eyes and looked up at Joshua who was kneeling beside her, holding her hand. She wanted to remove it from his grasp, the pain he was causing her was excruciating, but she lacked the strength. "Water," she mumbled, feeling the rawness of her throat and voice.

"Henton, bring me the water."

She winced as Joshua grabbed her shoulder and pulled her forward. The cot she was laying on shifted below her, but remained steady. The blanket that was covering her fell away, revealing her chest. Seeing a mug that she presumed had water, she did not care about being exposed.

The mug was put to her lips and she drank a mouthful before it was taken away. She strained her neck, reaching for more, but Joshua lowered her back down onto the cot.

"You need to take it slowly, too much water and you'll make yourself sick. Rest a bit and I'll give you more later. It makes me so happy to see you wake. I was afraid you might just waste away. Your ghost has barely let us care for you."

Stephenie felt her eyes growing heavy and she fell asleep as Joshua continued to talk.

Stephenie opened her eyes as her mind regained consciousness. She took a deep breath and rolled her head over toward Kas' direction. She sensed Joshua and Henton sleeping a few feet from her.

Kas' form illuminated as she moved her head. "It is good to see you wake more completely."

"Water you dead bastard."

He grinned and then faded slightly with just his upper body floating across the tent to where the mug of water sat. Forcing herself to sit up was excruciating, but once she managed, she felt a sense of pride. With an unsteady hand, she took the mug from Kas and drained all of the cold liquid. She drank slowly, refraining from gulping it down, but would no longer be prevented from drinking her fill.

"You've been healing faster than I would have thought possible. Someone who over-extends herself with that much energy has every right to never practice magic again. You are very lucky not to be burned up."

"Kas, I was not going to lose you. And then these idiots had to try and come back for me. Everything was falling apart and I didn't know what else to do. I felt the energy as I had never felt it before. There was just so much. The mountain, the air, the people. I pulled and pulled until I could pull no more, then I flung everything I could at those bastards. I take it that it must have worked."

"Stephenie?"

"Josh," she said with a smile as her big brother looked up at her with as much surprise as she had ever seen.

"You're alive," his grin grew, "and talking." Quickly he rose from the blankets that were laying on a pile of wilted vegetation. "Are you okay?"

"I'm starving and still thirsty," she said in the Old Tongue.

"I'm not sure—" he hesitated.

"Joshua, her body will need food," Kas said in the Denarian, guessing at Joshua's statement.

Stephenie turned her eyes back to Kas, who was standing beside her cot. "Decided to start talking to others besides me?" She moved and then uncovered her right shoulder. It hurt, but when she looked down, she saw her shoulder was whole, no mark left from where the mage had ripped it open. She slowly pulled aside the blanket from her legs, being modest enough to keep mostly covered. There were no marks on her legs. She checked her left breast and smiled when Kas' hand print was still there, if not even a little more vivid in coloration.

Joshua watched her self examination in silence.

She looked over to Kas who only shrugged as if he were alive.

Feeling exhausted from that little effort, she leaned back on the cot. "Are we safe here? If I've been out for almost three days or more, they're bound to send other mages after us."

"Steph, you brought the mountain down on their heads."

"What?"

"I don't know how, but the whole face of the mountain where we'd been digging exploded and slid down into the valley, then the rest of that mountain peak fell across the boulder field. There is still a deep gouge, but the valley was filled with boulders. Those who were attacking you exploded in a ball of fire and then were completely destroyed as the mountain exploded. The bulk of their troops in the valley, thousands and thousands, buried and crushed by the rock slide. Some of our people were as well; some of those that were in the valley. However, most of the prisoners were spared. They were being held in a less than pleasant part of a side valley. I think all of their witches and warlocks are dead. There are still a few thousand troops, but they are retreating. Their leadership is all but dead."

She turned to Kas, and spoke in the Old Tongue, "what happened? What did I do? Did I kill thousands?"

"I did not see it. I can say that once I was sure you were stable, I went to check on these new Denarians, to make sure we would not be overrun. Those that lived assumed that someone acquired or destroyed the focus that was being sought. They are retreating as fast as possible back to the coast."

Henton smiled at her. "You're a hero, all the soldiers and prisoners have been talking about how Princess Stephenie brought down a mountain to save them and her brother."

"I'm no hero. I didn't do it for them, I did it for you and Kas and Will and Douglas." She paused and shuddered. "I killed thousands?"

"Steph, you saved us. Will, Douglas, Me, your brother, and thousands of others. We'd have all been dead if you had not done that. You saved our lives and it seems ended a war. Your quick thinking won the night."

"That's not what happened. I was losing, I was being overwhelmed and Kas was dying and you two idiots were coming back."

Joshua stepped closer. "We could not leave you to fight everyone on your own," he said in Cothish, though she knew he spoke the Old Tongue. "I understand. The realization of what we do and the consequences are not easy to live with. I've ordered hundreds of men I respected to their deaths, knowing full well that when I told them that they could do it, that they would not be able to hold the line. Their lives I had to sacrifice for several thousand to have a chance to escape. It haunts me every night. Of course, no one escaped in the end."

She turned back to Kas. "Tell me, how many did I kill?"

"One day it will get easier Stephenie. You did not do it out of malice."

"I know that. I just didn't know that it happened and I would rather not be made a hero for it."

Joshua continued, finally switching to the Old Tongue, drawing her attention, "Steph, I didn't mean to upset you about it. However, considering what happened, it wasn't possible to hide your powers from others. Word is out that you are a witch. By making you a hero, saving thousands of our people, I am hoping we can spin this into something positive. I'd never allow anyone to hurt you, but I also don't want you to have to flee into exile to avoid a witch trial."

She had grown so use to Henton's and the others acceptance, that her mouth suddenly went dry. "Josh, you don't despise me?"

He smiled at her. "Father and I always knew you were a witch, we've known a long time."

"What?" she sat up despite her weakness. "Why didn't you let me know that you knew. I've been so scared and alone for so long. I was desperate for someone to talk to about this!"

Joshua glanced away and came over to kneel beside Stephenie. "Father and I discussed that a few times, but you were doing such a good job concealing your witchcraft, that we decided to not let on we knew. We feared you might get lax and say or do something that others would notice. We did it for your own good."

Stephenie closed her eyes, knowing that the look Henton was giving her was one of sympathy, but for some reason not wanting it from him. She sensed Kas' energy change to a state she associated with tension in him. Slowly, she let out a long breath and opened her eyes.

Glancing down at the blanket that she had managed to keep over her shoulders this time, she flexed her hand and felt the weakness of her limbs. She raised her head and looked from Joshua to Henton. "Either of you want to explain exactly why all my clothes are off and I'm naked under this blanket?"

Joshua had the decency to blush, but Henton got a satisfied look in his eyes as he took a step toward her. "Well, ma'am, you see, it is like this, you took your clothes off all on your own. Now, seeing as it was your doing and your body appeared quite abused, we decided to simply leave them off. Besides, it's made cleaning you up a bit easier. This is your third cot. You made a mess of the first two."

Stephenie paled, realizing just how exposed she'd been.

"Henton, I will not have you talk to my sister, a royal princess, in that fashion, regardless of what you've done for her."

"Josh, it's okay, he's my personal guard and I've told him to talk to me however he likes. Keeps my ego in check."

"But Steph, that is—"

"I just want to know why I would have taken off all my clothes?"

"Well," Joshua said, "it was more that you burned them off. I was sure you were dead. As we ran back to you, we heard this incredible roar. It was deep and very loud and filled with rage. At first we were not sure. It wasn't human, but then we knew it was coming from you. We could see you because you were covered in blue flames, they were billowing all around you and your hair was flying about, flames coming off it. It was bright enough that we even saw the group that was attacking you. Their triumph melted from their faces and they started to retreat. Before they could get more than a step away, flames and what Henton told me was raw energy leapt from the ground. A moment later the mountain exploded. Rocks shattered and flew into the air, shredding the witches, warlocks, and soldiers. The mountain trembled and we all fell to the ground.

"When I looked up and saw the mountain face sliding away, I was sure you'd go down with it, but you were just there laying on the ground, all your clothes burned away, but you were not burned up and the mountain where we were standing was solid. You looked bad, blood from your eyes, nose, mouth, and ears. Your arms and legs looked broken, so we wrapped you in a blanket and carried you as far as we dared." Joshua looked back to Henton.

"Ma'am, some of the prisoners after that decided to help us set up a small camp up here on the slope. We got one of the tents from the valley as well as supplies. Some of the enemy surrendered, others just started to run away. We started gathering as many of our soldiers as we could, getting the tents and supplies before they were stolen. His Majesty, King Joshua managed to establish some order."

Joshua smiled. "I've spent as much time here with you as I could, but for the first couple of days, we had to get the men together. Many are already on their way back to Antar, or some of the other cities. I've sent runners ahead to spread the word about what's happened. Henton told me what Mother did and I thought it best to reassure people as quickly as possible that we are still alive."

"That bitch planned to sacrifice me because she's convinced she can break the curse she thinks she's under. She's responsible for so many people dying, including Father. She's no longer my mother."

"That, little sis, is exactly what I have said publicly as well. I've declared her a traitor and no longer acknowledge her as my mother. I didn't want to speak for you."

"She's dead to me."

"Well, as soon as we can get you moving, we'll make our way back to Antar as fast as possible, salvage as much as we can, and rebuild. The countries to the west will have to deal with what is left of the Senzar for now. Once we get things secure, we can see what aid we can offer."

"Josh, thank you for not despising me because of what I am."

"Steph, you are my sister and I love you. I have always tried to protect you, even when it meant leaving you to fend for yourself so that you'd become strong on your own."

Stephenie looked up, sensing a couple of men approaching the tent. The others turned their head when someone called out for 'His Majesty'. Stephenie watched as Joshua rose and commanded the men to enter.

A tall and thin man with an unkempt beard entered the tent and bowed. "Your Majesty, you wanted us to let you know when the last of the supplies were organized and inventoried. We calculate for the three thousand soldiers we have, we've got at best enough for three more days before we won't have enough to make it back to a city large enough to supply us."

"Captain Crencaw, we might be able to break camp sooner than I was originally expecting."

The bearded man had obvious bags under his eyes from lack of sleep and finally noticed Stephenie lying on her side. "Your Highness, Sorceress Stephenie," the man said with obvious admiration as he bowed even lower to her, "I am so glad to see you are doing better."

Stephenie felt uncomfortable laying naked under the blanket with so many people standing around her, but the chill in her bones came from the ready and easy acknowledgment of her magic. Zac had sworn loyalty to her, then when he found out, betrayed her almost immediately. *How long before someone betrays Josh or me now?*

She glanced to where she sensed Kas, but he was not visible.

"Steph, how soon do you think you will be able to travel?"

She turned back to Joshua. "Anytime. I would like a chance to get dressed first though."

Joshua smiled. "Of course. Captain, we may need to go slowly, my sister is still recovering from the effort to blow up half the mountain. If needed, we can send a number of soldiers ahead of us."

Stephenie watched Henton carry over a small bundle of clothing and set it on the foot of the cot. "Don't push yourself too hard," he whispered.

"Okay, Henton, and Kas, if you're listening, let's leave my sister alone to dress in peace." He extended his left arm toward the tent flap. "Henton, keep your guards close, but outside the tent."

Henton nodded his head. "I'll also have someone let Will and Douglas know she's awake. They will want to see her."

Stephenie watched the others leave and when the flap fell back into place, she pushed the blanket aside as she reached for the clothing. Kas materialized in a sitting position at the foot of the cot and raised the shirt for her.

"You know I was not about to leave."

"If you had, I'd have been very displeased. I'd like to think that I did all this for Josh and Henton and the others, but it wasn't until I saw you in real danger that I was able to actually reach for the energy like I did. Something in me snapped. I don't want to live without the others, but when it came down to you, I found I could not bear to live without you."

"Stephenie, for the first time in a very long time, I truly regret no longer being alive. Since I met you, I have been happier than I can remember being, but at the same time more miserable than ever."

"I would have willingly died to be with you."

"Stephenie, what I am is just barely an existence. You do not want to be like this. I will look after you and protect you the best I can, but I cannot hold you like you want. You should find someone living to be with."

Stephenie took a deep breath, feeling some physical strength return to her exhausted body, but it was not much. She looked down at the blackened hand print on her left breast. She smiled. "Kas, you marked me, no one else can have me. Every other injury appears to have healed, but somehow this mark stayed. I like it. So you better just get resolved to that fact."

"Stephenie—"

"Kas, I'm too tired to argue right now, but if my dying won't bring us together, then we'll just have to deal with it." She looked up at him, her expression more serious. "I just brought down a mountain and I could swear I broke every bone in my body doing it. But what, three days later, I am alive and healing? I don't think I am normal. Not even for a mage. Who out there would be right for me?"

Kas' chest expanded as if he was taking a deep breath. "I—"

"That's right, you," she interrupted to prevent him from continuing. Then she smiled. "Kas, I don't want anyone else. I accept you as you are. I want you. I need you. Can you accept me? Whatever I might actually be?"

He grinned back. "You are Stephenie. That is what you are." He shook his head and sat down on the cot, but neither the blankets or the cot moved. "And yes, I accept you."

"Good." She lifted her arms a few inches and looked into his nearly opaque face and smiled in spite of her weariness. "Then can you help me get dressed so I can eat?"

37017189R00168

Made in the USA
Middletown, DE
21 February 2019